A Light of Other Suns

Otherworldly Tales by Angelo Niles

I0601995

Angelo Niles

Cadmus Publishing
www.cadmuspublishing.com

Published by Cadmus Publishing
www.cadmuspublishing.com
Port Angeles, WA

ISBN: 978-1-63751-320-0
Library of Congress Control Number: 2022919458

"Get a cup of mocha and snuggle up with an awe-inspiring fire kindled by Angelo Niles."

—Carl Davis, author of *Footprints in the Sands.*

"[*Extant III*] is just about my favorite thing ever."

—F.J. Bergmann, *Star*Line*

"Once again, Niles comes through in *Blood Moon.* An imagination reminiscent of *The Matrix,* he creates a vivid, picturesque setting against a story with surprising twists and turns."

—Gary Hardy, PhD., author of *Silence in the Face of Injustice: A Vision of Mercy and Hope.*

"Through a strong, competent female protagonist, Niles gives his readers a glimpse into what espionage could look like in a cybernetically enhanced future. *Herons in Gaza* is a surprisingly meditative thrill ride."

—J.P. Brown, author of *Smuggler to the Stars.*

DEDICATION

For Shalu and our exotic voyage over the seas of time.

ACKNOWLEDGEMENTS

All praise belongs to The Most High. I owe a vast debt to all those who challenged my wistful vanity. As authors we dare envisage new worlds and species that seldom inspire more awe than our Creator's mastery of astounding life. I thank everyone at Cadmus Publishing for their efforts in bringing this project to life. Profound kudos to J.P. Brown, a ruthless editor. My gratitude to Ellen Datlow, Tyree Campbell, Wesley Kawato, F.J. Bergmann, Diane L. Walton and the team at *On Spec* for believing in my work. A huge nod to Cornelia "Corri" Wells, Jacqueline Aguilar, Jessica Fletcher and Jacqueline Balderrama at *Iron City*. Thanks to Sheree Renée Thomas, editor of *Dark Matter: Reading the Bones*, who inspired my leap of faith into Africa's future parallels. Love to my baby sister Jimeela Fatimah Jones who sacrificed so much to aid my endeavors. As always, I thank my beloved mother Sakina Nura Zaky, a mystic who taught me to love the pen.

TABLE OF CONTENTS

PART ONE

THE CATACLYSM

A LIGHT OF OTHER SUNS

PROLOGUE

"If life spawns its own meaning, out of the chaos and aftermath of a thousand epochs, who then can challenge its origins in a tiny laboratory dish?" —Dr. Celene Nichole Gayle, marine paleontologist, 2031 CE.

9:30 am, Monday, September 29, 2031 CE
Aboard the Spartan, Gulf of Alaska.

Alaska had indeed produced the exotic atmosphere that Charles Hunter expected when OCF gave him the job. While Glacier Bay lacked the fast-paced lifestyle he enjoyed back in Seal Beach, California, he now found himself thrust in the oddest crux of his tracking career.

His dark brown eyes felt weary, his stubble of a beard suddenly itchy. Strands of dusty brown mane lay in a riot along his broad shoulders. The naval uniform he wore had an Oceanic Conservation Front insignia—olive leaves encircling a starfish. As a graduate of Scripps Institute of Oceanography, Charlie reigned competently as skipper of the *Spartan* and had served well as the vessel's chief science officer. Simple job. Just track the whales. Watch what they do. Keep tabs on their feeding, what and how they eat. And guard them closely.

A lone whale had led the *Spartan* well off course toward the coastline. The cruiser was right over her now. Charlie stayed topside, eyeing the waters for signs of the cow—or whichever of the whales they had found. The Ospreys circled nearby, still looking for a physical sighting of the pod. He spoke into a headset: "Breaker ship to Alpha! See anything up there?"

"Negative, Skipper," the pilot relayed back. "Will turn back in four minutes. Sorry, no reserve fuel today."

Charlie felt a chill then. Of a certain he would get the brunt end of the ordeal when Felix Gonzales was told about his inability to find the other whales. Each minute the humpbacks stayed submerged, his nausea worsened.

Virgil came up from below. "Sir, I think you should see something."

He followed the wiry man with increasing angst in his gut. Down in the cruiser's control room, Heggs and Caleb stared at a screen. Neither of them had to ask Charlie to look closely at the image that held their gaze. "God Almighty," Charlie expelled slowly. "What in the great blue is that?"

"Don't know," Heggs told him.

"She's what we found just seconds ago," Virgil explained. "At first we figured it was a glitch on the sonar. But we got the same thing on the depth-eye."

The screen showed the magenta-blue outline of something other than a whale. It swam in calm buoyancy below the *Spartan*, and as far as Charlie could tell, the thing looked rather like an enormous Atlantic manta ray—except there were two tails instead of one, and at each end of the large fin wings were clawlike appendages. A pulsating luminescence rose over its vast body surface. Such rays did not inhabit these temperate waters.

"That creature's no marine animal I've ever seen," he gasped. "Where's the whale we were tracking, Heggs?"

"This is her. She's what led us out here."

"Doesn't make sense. Somebody tell me what the hell's going on."

No one spoke. No one among them understood what the thing was. All they did know was that the Electron Cryograph Radar didn't lie. It merely showed whatever thermal waves it detected. And certainly the depth-eye would not confirm the same mistake.

Charlie tried to figure out what exactly to tell Admiral Gonzales at Base, or what such a report would sound like if he did tell them. He eyed the image for a long while before he heard the handset crackle. "...Alpha to *Spartan*! Come in, please."

Charlie blinked and cleared his throat. "Yes, yes," he trembled. "Go Alpha, *Spartan* here."

"What's going on down there? We've got no sign at all of those whales. How long can they stay down, anyway?"

"Not this long," Charlie whispered, still glued to the screen's image.

"Repeat, Skipper?"

"We...we don't know yet. Nothing confirmed down here. Why don't you fly on back now?"

His voice was distant and he felt altogether disembodied. He never heard the pilot's "ten-four" as he released the handset. His brain tried to assess what it hadn't been prepared to make is sense of. Yet he had to. Base Command would have more questions than he had answers for, so he forced himself to gather all the marine knowledge he had which might explain this.

"Sir?" asked Virgil. "Are we reporting this sighting?"

Sighting, yes.

It occurred to Charlie that they were making an unidentified sighting, and it was then that he recalled a paragraph somewhere in the OCF booklet that instructed officers to report any "paranormal readings on the ECR." But he'd assumed it had more to do with waterborne alien craft, or enemy submarines—in which case, the OCF had an obligation to report it to proper official channels.

"I don't know what the hell to report," he told his crew. "Right now let's get whatever data we can on this thing before we go making fools of ourselves."

"Data, Skip?" asked Caleb.

"Recorded images. ECR readouts and whatever else we have. Then we'll cross-confirm the data with our computer here. Maybe it can tell us what's wrong with this fish."

Charlie realized that their fate wasn't improving anytime soon. After gathering every bit of data from the ECR and the depth-eye, they still got zilch from the computer. None of the readings matched any of the categories listed in the program designed by OCF's marine biology division.

The thing still floated below the *Spartan*, its stingray-shaped body wavering on Caleb's screen. "Maybe we're looking at a new species," he said, almost too low to hear. "Things get lost out here for millennia, mate."

"It's the blasted Gulf of Alaska," Charlie retorted. He hadn't sat down once since they'd made the sighting, and he doubted he'd rest until they made sense of their find. "My whales are out here somewhere. We're not reporting anything until I find them. Or until God puts that creature down there on somebody's chart—namely ours."

Virgil Wayne, the vessel's marine biologist, looked up from the depth-eye. "Why does it just sit still? As if it's waiting for us to—" His voice cracked with dread. "—communicate with it."

"Stop talking nonsense," said Heggs. "We aren't about to have an intelligent encounter with a fish."

Charlie took the depth-eye from Virgil. He had looked into it many times already, but each time he'd been convinced he wasn't looking at it right—that somehow if he stared long enough, an answer would surface. Any damned explanation was better than the one growing in their minds now.

Down below the *Spartan*, what resembled a double-tailed manta ray wavered against the icy darkness. Crisp shadows licked an upper side that was spotted by fluorescent markings. It pulsated like an aquatic chameleon, alternating between silvery grays and vibrant blues and magenta. No manta ray that Charlie had ever seen glowed like this fish. According to the depth-eye's readings, it was nearly as vast as a humpback whale.

"She's unearthly, by God," whispered Charlie, moving back from the electronic periscope. His skin crawled with hot excitement and growing uncertainty. Virgil and Heggs and Caleb looked at him, not speaking, waiting for reasons. He only offered: "Virgil may be right, guys. I can't explain how, but I think it's waiting for—"

"For what?" Heggs stood up. "What confluence are you all saying? That we should talk to it?"

Charlie's eyes were downcast. He shook his head slowly and said, "No, not that kind of talking. But we did send out that distress sonar. Remember? Maybe this thing followed the *Spartan* then."

Caleb asked, "Like a whale would, you mean?"

"Like any cetacean would." It made sense to Charlie. At least, it explained how the thing may have been lured by the sonic pings sent out from the cruiser. If it heard the way whales did, then the high-pitched frequency's singsong transmission would certainly be read the same. Echolocation, yes. Dolphins often trailed alongside ships because of subtle vibrations rippling below the surface.

Even so, how it had been lured was secondary to the crew's problem. OCF would want reports and answers about the missing whales that they were to escort to Maui.

In the midst of it all, Charlie realized that before veering off after this lone pulse—one he'd assumed was the cow—Heggs had located the pod. Albeit only on the depth-eye, they had picked up their signatures. Explaining all this to Gonzales wasn't going to be easy. Not for Charles Andrew Hunter, a first grade tracker who'd only worked a year for OCF, and had fuddled his most important assignment yet.

Soon the SatLink pulsed with Gonzales's call from Base. "Hunter, we've got two of your whales sighted. The cow and a juvenile were beached at Elfin Cove."

Charlie's nerves were rattled. "What's that?" he stammered. "We...we never picked up their pulses."

"Never mind," his superior said. "Our birds confirmed them just a while ago. All you can do now is track the others before they're beached too. Over and out, Hunter." Gonzales hung up abruptly.

Charlie felt cheated. He and his crew had bogged their attention on the ray below them for so long that they hadn't thought of going topside for visuals. Elfin Cove lay just eastward of the *Spartan*; close enough to see from aboard the cruiser.

As he headed up for a look, Heggs caught Charlie's parka sleeve. "Why didn't you tell them?" Heggs plied. "Why didn't you tell Base about that thing down there?"

Charlie regarded the Alaskan's deep-set eyes. Old and frightened vestiges of a man who had based his life on tangible frontiers—not this phenomenon that now rattled all their beings. "Tell them what, Bones? That an alien fish is swimming below us? Maybe I should have, so Base could send a fleet out here. Then what? So they can harpoon it?"

Heggs let his arm go. "That's not our decision, Charlie. Besides, it may be an important new species. Have you considered that?"

"He's right," agreed Virgil. "Man, we could be onto a geologic event, too. Like in 2019 when the sea turtles vanished from the Coral Sea. Got spooked by the arrival of eighty thousand tiger sharks. A frenzy we later linked to a deep-sea magnetic field. Think of it, Chuck. A new species. Maybe a mutant, yeah, but a significant one."

Silence stole on the dimly lit space between the men. Of a certain, whatever they had come upon was important, yes. As marine trackers his crew had an obligation to log any new organisms snared by the depth-eye. Regardless of how remote or bizarre the species. But a far deeper omen kept Charlie from playing his hand.

That presage led him to survey the world above.

A chilly breeze culminated over the Gulf of Alaska and the *Spartan*. From topside, Charlie could make out the shimmering gray coastline of an island chain about three miles away. He put a pair of binoculars to his eyes. No sign of the helicopters were visible from his vantage, but as he looked toward Elfin Cove he wondered how the ECR had missed two large creatures like the whales.

Virgil had followed him up and they both stood portside. Salty sweetness filled the air. The waves were strangely placid, too. Alaska's waters were almost always choppy with high waves this time of year. Now a cloudless sky spilled sun onto an otherwise snowcapped world. Vibrant rays massaged their skin...still masking a vastly strange anomaly swimming below them.

The cruiser's solar sails flapped languidly, luring Charlie's thoughts to an absence he hadn't realized before. There wasn't a single other vessel in sight. Normally a few Coast Guard boats patrolled these waters at varying points, as well as fishing boats, yachts, or whalers skirting the migration routes, hoping to snare a stray whale. Nothing could be seen anywhere. Only the snowy coastline and a silvery horizon stretched northward, east and southeast.

"I don't like this," he told Virgil.

The crow-eyed West Indian was staring blankly overboard at a shape expanding from below the *Spartan*.

Charlie looked overboard, scrutinizing the frothy waves. Just below the surface grew an oscillating shape, glowing as if from the bioluminescence of some great jellyfish. The gentle radiance skulked below the waves, its aura wavering like a buoyant mirage.

Virgil stumbled closer to the gunwale. "Chuck, it's huge. Looks like a gigantic jellyfish, don't it?"

Icy air caught in Charlie's throat. The waters grew utterly placid then, a glassy sheet smoothing out the surface in a vast radius around the *Spartan*. Even the wind died. What cursed thing had caused this vortex of dead calm?

"What in God Almighty's name...?" Charlie began, furrowing his brow. "That's no jelly I've ever seen. Get the spear gun, Virgil."

"Are you sure?"

"Of course I'm sure. Whatever that thing is, it's no whale, now is it?"

Virgil raced to the cabin deck where a few light arms and rescue gear were stored. Charlie couldn't take his eyes off the glowing thing swirling below the *Spartan*, nor could he fathom its true nature or intent. The air grew steely and thick with charged ions.

Tiny specks of light took on shape now. With eyes engulfed by the surreal vision, Charlie clenched his teeth as if to brace himself, for just then he felt a building current of electricity crawl over his skin.

A suddenly violent throe sent the *Spartan* into a spin. Charlie was tossed back against the mast post, sliding over the slick icy deck. Virgil flew a few feet away, having been caught off guard, and landed shoulder first into the side of the starboard lifeboat.

A terrible growl seized the cruiser as it fought to stay moored in the spin.

"Hold on!" Charlie cried, clinging to a gunwale railing. Biting cold numbness seared his ungloved fingertips.

"God help us!" came Virgil's muffled yell.

"Take cover. It's going to topple..."

The *Spartan* whirled wildly, tossing Charlie's torso against the bulk mast. Spray showered the deck then, huge waves licking the vessel with wrathful intensity. Charlie's eyes blurred with strain, his chest pounding, mind fighting to grasp their peril. God, what force of nature was it that descended upon them? What maelstrom had they wandered into? The sky spun madly above him as he struggled to hang on.

Abruptly the *Spartan* swung still, its protesting hisses now silent. The forceful halt jerked Virgil's body back across the deck and he came to rest beside Charlie. Dazed and soaked, the two men rasped harshly, both exhausted with shock and uncertainty.

Charlie blinked at the blur that was gradually becoming the Alaskan wilderness, the icy deck, torn solar sails, and a wavering sky. The glow crept like tiny lightning bolts over the railing and onto the deck. Hastily, Charlie and Virgil stood and moved cautiously back from the encroaching radiance.

"What the devil is it?" Charlie rasped, groping for something to grasp.

The West Indian's eyes bulged fearfully. "Skip," Virgil said slowly, very distantly. "It's coming out of the water."

Edging to the deck rail, Charlie braved a glance into the waters. He saw now what Virgil said was not completely accurate. The devil ray loomed massively below the *Spartan*. Its grotesquely vast body glowed like a giant jellyfish.

Eyes widely locked, Charlie could scarcely believe what he saw. The manta's great bulk seemed to grow transparent, its gorging rapture sprawled below. Although the winglike fins grew wider, no part of the fish had broken the surface. It was the intensifying fluorescence of its body that now rose toward them.

Charlie's face went pale, and before he could take cover the entire deck danced in an unearthly glare. Virgil sagged to his knees as the light wraith surged over them.

Deeply gurgled screams tried to escape both their lungs.

Ions danced along the capsule's sleek surface as it phased from its cloak, all but a vaporous hint ascending into the clouds, then it shot near light speed toward the southern constellation. The time had come. At a precise moment in the temporal quotient, an internal algorithm set the events in motion that would end a species or deliver salvation.

The outcome had no governance over the envoy's mission. One organism alone did not lure its purpose, neither did any one fate await its arrival over the eons. Like those emissaries before, it would observe, assess, and harvest what it deemed necessary to proliferate their seed in a suitable habitat.

Their biosphere of a surety had not long to enjoy existence as they knew it.

The End

ARCTICA

"The laws of physics obey a strict order of the universe, until they don't." —Dr. Rebecca Jones, Old Earth physicist, notes on the Holocene Cataclysm.

11:23 am, Friday, February 21, 2031 CE.
On a ridge near Marie Byrd Land, Antarctica.

A harsh white glare yawned over the horizon as Dr. Kyle Elmhurst piloted the sled across the icy plateau with four other surveyors. Stark shifts in the Antarctic snow packs had risen concerns for the scientists. As they rose out of range from the Amundsen-Scott South Pole Station, they each sensed an unspoken peril that stirred below the vast glacial floor.

At the station, Kyle had initially balked at the readings. But the detectors were rarely agitated like this, and no amount of denying it would curtail the events to come. They had all come to the same inevitable conclusion. Some drastic change was at hand. The crater near Sidle Dome kept registering uneasy tremors on the seismograph, and on the electromagnetic scales, too, which altogether bothered Kyle. So after a hardy breakfast, the survey team braved the frigid dawn and headed 54° due southwest on the Global Positioning Satellite grid.

They glided over jagged peaks, skittering along the northern Transantarctic Mountains until they reached the westerly edge of the Ross Ice Shelf. A vastly beautiful blanket of pure white stretched over the horizon. It was 3,467 square miles of frozen, prehistoric moisture perched precariously on the Ross Sea. Above the deep sapphire skyline was sprawled a lovely array of southern lights. The aurorae looked as if some giant hand had crumpled a ball of rainbow light and flung it into the twilight sky. Such a breathtaking display of God's wonder, Kyle thought, trying to focus on the enormity of their task.

The helium sled settled onto terra firma at 12:07 pm. Kyle's team stepped onto the polar shelf, each of them clad in thermal terra-fits that made them look like colonists on an alien planet. After scouring the landscape for any nearby crevasses, the team hedged out into the icy desert. A large white and gray Alaskan husky trudged along with them, pulling a lightweight bundle of gear. The instruments could scan the thick ice, spying each crevasse for signs of seismic activity.

The U.S. Geological Survey had an array of beacons implanted in the glacial bed, at Sidle Dome, Lake Vostok, and other sites, in an effort to monitor the flowing ice streams. The flow crept at a steady ten meters a year for as long as there had been recorded data. But now, due to climate change and rising volcanic heat and melting, the Ross Ice Shelf was growing unstable. The USGS had grown leery of the signs, knowing that a vast eruption could very well set off a global cataclysm. There were scientists who theorized that such an event would likely set off 20-foot waves, rapidly rising sea levels, and stormy atmospheric changes not known since the early Pliocene.

At forty-three, Kyle Elmhurst was the eldest in the survey team. The ordinarily sun-baked, bronzy skin tones had grown pale over the months. A thick beard framed an angular face. His agile limbs swayed from a six-two, wiry frame. Once upon a time he'd been a competitive oarsman on the Colorado River Kayak Team. He felt much older than his years now as he watched the horizon intently. Something feels off, he mused darkly, unable to pin down its source. It gnawed at his bones.

They were roughly an hour from the grand peak of Mount Eberus. Its twin-horned crown was distinct from their position. To the west, stretching all the way back to Marie Byrd Land's eastern rim, rose the foggy expanse of the Transantarctic Mountains. Scant rays of sunlight broke over the shadowy plains behind them. Dusk and dawn were eternally woven in a surreal vision of endless glacial peaks to the north, and flat white desolation in every other direction. The winds were surprisingly calm. A meter on his wrist gave satellite updates and warnings of deadly gales.

The weather today was unlike any other day in the Antarctic wilderness. An eerie glistening rose over the vast ice sheet, one that was only observed during the polar equinox—the "summertime" as it were—which had the highest solar peak, and thus a warmer climate. Warm with respect to the perpetual subzero temperatures—the kind that could freeze a man's spit before it hit ground.

Strange glare, Kyle thought worriedly. Yes, a wet glare that felt wrong. "Think we should set up a tectonic scan," Kyle told Robert Vaughn, the hugely built geomorphologist who stood at his right.

Vaughn coughed into a fist. "Having doubts about the readings?" he asked in a thick Melbourne accent. "Fishing for signs, are you, mate? I can tell you this," he offered heartily, "Sidle isn't likely to go wacky in our lifetime."

"Just do it, please," Kyle insisted.

Dr. Jorge Diegos caught up. He had lingered back a few hundred meters, gathering samples from the ice pack. The Venezuelan radiobiologist had a boyish, pudgy face, dark eyes, and a frosted beard. "Hey, look at this, guys!" he said excitedly.

Kyle and Vaughn eyed the cylinder held out for them. The contents looked to be some kind of tiny organisms in the ice. Each of the tadpole shapes glowed strangely, like tiny jellyfishes.

"What on earth is that you've got?" asked Kyle, squinting at the incandescence.

"Cryoplankton?" asked Vaughn, who nearly put his face on the glass tube.

Diegos shook his head. "Can't say," he admitted.

It was true. All sorts of microorganisms had turned up in the glacial wilderness as of late. Scientists worldwide were abuzz over the sudden appearance of tiny, never before known species.

Kyle said, "Bag it for analysis at the lab. Right now we've got to get the magnetic field scan set up. Before the temperatures drop."

Arnie, the huge sled dog whom Kyle had given free rein, began yelping loudly. It leaped in the air, then fell to the hard icepack and jerked its torso from side to side. Kyle stopped along with the others. The dog's behavior wasn't right. Although it was given to absurd antics when a stray seabird fluttered by, or if it smelled a carcass buried in the snow, Arnie's behavior frightened Kyle. No birds were anywhere to be seen.

Kyle tried to hush the dog. "Be still, Arnie. There's nothing to get worried about," the geologist said.

Yet in his gut Kyle felt something terrible was amiss. Maybe Arnie's circuits were frayed despite it being a sturdy G9 model cyberdog. One bred for extreme climates shouldn't act so bizarrely, Kyle felt. He decided it best to put the harness back on Arnie. That would keep it from bolting out into the icy hell in a frenzy.

The team's geophysicist, Alain LaMarques, came up beside Kyle and sniffed hard. The Frenchman had a skeletal build, having spent most of his life exploring the frigid wilderness in hellish conditions. "Do I detect fear in our brave leader?" he plied, trying to force his colleague to cheer up. "I said it before, didn't

I? The Glacial Shelf will melt soon and we'll all drown. We're literally standing on thin ice. The Jovian Scenario is going to happen, my friend."

"God forbid," Kyle rasped. The last thing he wanted to think about was global heating causing 5.5 million tons of ice to surge into the world's oceans. It was unthinkable. Still, he couldn't hide his irrational response to Arnie's howling. The dog kept leaping, trying to break free of its reins. Kyle knelt beside the dog and patted its mane. "Hey, pal, what's got you all flustered?"

"Arctic fever," suggested Vaughn.

"Arnie's probably just horny," LaMarques quipped.

Deborah Spekolstein, the only woman in the group, sighed harshly, shaking her head at their masculine banter. Beneath her terra-fits was a slender, athletic body, her fiery burst of auburn hair now hooded. In the eight months she'd spent in the Antarctica, the glaciologist had helped to cheer the long, bleak days with her wry humor. Now she kept her distance, busy with a reading on her palm computer.

Jorge Diegos fidgeted with a handheld BIO-Reader. "Look here, Kyle. I've got a weird thermal signature. Coming from over there, due northwest about half a click away. We could walk the stretch from here."

Kyle bent his neck down at the strange-looking anomaly that had registered on Diegos's meter. "Sure looks massive, whatever it is. The Survey isn't on a fishing expedition, though. We've got our hands full enough," he insisted, discarding the swell of curiosity in his chest.

LaMarques put his nose between Kyle and Diegos. He whistled curtly. "Rather big biorhythm to be in the middle of nowhere. I certainly agree."

"Won't hurt to look," Diegos said.

Vaughn slung a stun rifle over one shoulder, giving them his best John Denver grin. "Crikey, yeah! If it's anything with paws, I'm first at the table, fellas."

"Don't shoot it, for crying out!" Kyle grumbled, hardly able to take the Aussie seriously with all that gear mounted on his broad shoulders. "This isn't the Kalahari, and we're not dragging a corpse back to the Pole with us. Besides, it's probably just a rookery of emperor penguins."

Spekolstein stood aloof, as if trying to detect some faint aroma in the air. "Ain't that weird," she said, eyeing the southeastern sky.

Kyle eyed the long chain of jagged peaks fading along the Transantarctic Mountain range. "Weird hardly says it," he mulled. "Can't figure that glistening fog."

Spekolstein's shapely silhouette was limned by the dismal, vastly desolate expanse of the Antarctic horizon. She too felt troubled by the strange mist skirting the volcanic rise of sleeping giants. The faint glint at the base of Mount Kirkpatrick directly 14° due south was the AMAD platform. The Atmospheric Mass Array Dish was part of a joint experiment between the USGS and Solotar Industries, the most recent phase of the Earthsphere Project based in the Antarctica. Its powerful reflectors were aimed skyward, patiently observing the yearly solar events—coronal bursts, electromagnetic storms, cosmic radiations born out of dying nebulae, and the wavelengths in galaxies far beyond the Hubble telescope's reach.

Dr. Kyle Elmhurst gazed into the twilight heavens as if trying to make out the faint origins of the storms. Despite the sophisticated multi-billion-dollar system, nothing substituted down-to-earth observation in the living laboratory.

"Guys!" shouted Diegos. "The mass just moved! I swear it did."

"Okay, okay. Calm down," Kyle urged as he eyed the device for himself. A brightly hued splotch on the display in Diegos's hand edged toward their position. Kyle wrinkled his brow, suddenly perturbed. "Definitely too big to be a single animal. Not unless a whale has somehow breached through the icepack. And God knows that's completely unlikely. We're sixty miles from the shores."

"Damned thing has a magnetic signature, too."

A mass that emits magnetic waves? Kyle wondered, perplexed. Living organisms didn't emit that kind of reading. If it was, in fact, anything biological, that wasn't a likely trait. Kyle frowned. "It's got to be an anomaly," he said. "Can't say what the hell anything that big is doing..."

Kyle and the others jerked their heads towards the sound of breaking ice. The hideous growl of tons and tons of frozen sea erupting up from the Shelf reverberated in the air. An eerie tremor grumbled below their boots, rattling Kyle's teeth. Then, as if a gigantic engine had abruptly died, everything fell deathly still again.

As they gazed expectantly out over the icy plateau, straining their eyes for the signs of a deadly crevasse, Kyle imagined a faint shadow skulking along the flat whiteness. Chest pounding, he reeled in his nerves and posed: "It could be a stray naval vessel."

"Submarines don't have bio-pulses like this," Diegos demurred. "Besides, the Antarctic Treaty forbids military operations anywhere within the Circle. It's definitely a life form, maybe a natural anomaly of some kind. Either way, Kyle, we are here to monitor the Antarctic's geological trends. Right?"

"Yeah, I suppose so."

"So let's investigate this sucker," Diegos said, making it sound like a scientific challenge.

Kyle sniffed the air. Some lingering odor tingled his nostrils. Smell of dry flesh and soil, he thought.

Below the thickly insolated neoprene terra-fits, Kyle felt clammy perspiration soaking his armpits. Some indistinct foreshadowing told his soul to go back to the sled, just avoid the unknown, regardless of Diegos's cajoling. But he couldn't. He couldn't escape the grisly hairs of fascination rising on his nape. And he dared not ignore the instinctual traits that had brought him to the Antarctica.

Spekolstein said it for him. "Gosh, aren't we lucky. The U.S. Geological Survey's finest and bravest. About to embark upon a breathtaking discovery." She smiled at the men, then took the first step out across the frigid landscape, directly toward the shadowy mass that lay at least two minutes away to the north.

Vaughn brushed past Kyle and teased, "She's stealing your thunder, old man!"

Diegos and LaMarques hefted their packs and marched behind Vaughn and Spekolstein. Arnie came up to Kyle and lolled out its tongue, eyeing the geologist with a sidelong plea in its dark gray stare. The dog moaned and wagged its fluffy white tail, the corners of its moist black mouth almost in a sly grin.

"Okay, boy, I get your damned point," Kyle half snarled. "Go on after her if you want."

Stubbornly, the Eskimo dog just sat on its haunches, as if refusing to follow the rest of the team unless Kyle did. "Arnie, it's your call," he relented.

A snarl puffed out as billowy breath. Arnie bolted off, barking after the four surveyors who'd already covered a hundred or so meters. As for Kyle Elmhurst, a furious cold besieged his bones, daring him to turn around and flee the other way. But he wouldn't let Deborah Spekolstein steal his thunder...or his nerve...in one fell swoop.

He trudged off after the team.

Coughing bits of icy dust kicked up behind Arnie's paws. It made the husky look like a four-legged snowmobile thundering across the bleak plateau, its wide, fast-beaten strides cutting a straight path toward the thing hidden a few hundred meters ahead.

Kyle hadn't yet closed the breadth between himself and the others, as his gait remained unhurried, if not tentative. God only knew what surprises lay buried below the icepack, and this was no time in his old age to get overly eager. Many a good experienced party had perished on this very ice shelf, all in the name of glory and exploration, or for the onus of being the first in history.

He kept is leisurely pace.

As he strode across the crunchy ice, surreptitiously eyeing the scene ahead, an almost imperceptible cry bellowed up from one of the surveyors, the echo carrying strangely in the windy sub-zero air. Kyle hastened his pace, more out of fear than from excitement at the outcry. Even the dog ceased its headlong charge and now searched curiously for something in the ground, sniffing with its ears folded sharply against its skull. Vapor puffed out of Kyle's lungs as he hurried over, then nudged his shoulders between Vaughn and LaMarques, both of whom had frozen with gaping mouths.

Eyes wide with astonishment, Kyle barely croaked out his shock. "Oh, beloved mother! What on earth is that doing here?"

"Don't know," Diegos said, crouching to the ground. "Obviously, it's no naval craft. I can assure you of that much."

Spekolstein was on her knees, peering silently at the crater. Her petite body trembled awfully, her gloved hand clasped to her mouth. "Dear Almighty God!" she expelled belatedly. "I think it's some kind of marine life. Something that should be extinct."

"Definitely dead, whatever it is," LaMarques said from over Kyle's shoulder. "Looks bloody well extinct, if you ask me, Dr. Spekolstein."

Kyle wasn't so sure it was. "What the hell was moving if not this...this fossil?"

"Oh, crikey," Vaughn agreed.

The thin layer of ice that buried the organism's dorsal plate cast a distorted glare over what looked like broad, winglike pectoral fins. Its fleshy skin was grayish to silver white, almost glowing up through its glacial tomb. Kyle couldn't make out any semblance of eyes in the massive head for it was partly submerged under the gaping crevasse. He had a sensation of gazing back in time, all the way beyond the Pliocene and back to some fiery dawn when whales were colossal, toothy beasts, when the oceans reigned in primordial tranquillity.

A hair-thin crack had recently webbed over the glassy sheet that entombed the animal. That accounted for the subtle stench in the air. The cloying odor of blood mingled with a seaborne scent; something Kyle found redolent of ambergris. The smell was poignant. It was a fleshy, organic pungency; too fresh to be a sign of decomposition.

The thing's cells weren't at all fossilized, Kyle realized. This prehistoric-looking life form had lived below the Ross Ice Shelf very recently, dear heavenly glory!

Words evaded Kyle as he swallowed hard. Swept under a riptide of realization, he stepped back from the shadowy mass. Some life pulse other than this creature had registered on Diegos's BIO-Reader. An unknown biorhythm, one strong enough to pierce up through the ice cap.

He said, "Listen, people. Let's tag this spot and put some distance between this area and us. It's not safe."

Vaughn removed his rifle and bundle of gear from his shoulders and knelt beside Spekolstein. "Are you kidding, Kyle?" he said. "We're probably looking at the only known specimen of an important species. The only existing evidence, fully intact and preserved for God only knows how long. It's incredible!"

Kyle shook his head. "Ask yourself how it got here, Rob. Something else caused this fissure. Something pretty damned seismic. The readings? All this mucky climate? It's all a single effect of some variable."

"Earth's going through a phase," LaMarques acknowledged. "Yes, Kyle, we all know that. The Holocene Cataclysm. It's going to happen one day, no doubt, just not this second. You've got plenty of time to buy that beach front property in Colorado."

Spekolstein stepped from the crater, slapping powdery ice from her terra-fits. She gazed back at the jagged peaks, once again eyeing the eerie lights that hung over the faraway Ross Sea.

Kyle and the rest of the team turned their gaze to the twilight heavens. An astonishing array of lights yawned out of the horizon, a glow altogether unnerving, for it lay on the dusky backdrop like a blast from an atomic bomb.

It was no southern light.

With angst gnawing at his psyche, Kyle grasped what the phenomenon was in fact. Glacial steam! An enormous cloud of thermal vapor rising from the brooding mantle.

The entire southern sky glowed with a ghastly fog now.

Then, as if the horrid whine of a sea monster waking from the depths, a vast rumbling belched up from the continental shelf. A fierce growl tore up from the infinite white gulf. Glaciers exploded from the southerly massif.

My God, Kyle realized, we're marooned in the foreshadow of an earthquake. More terribly, he understood now what the seismograph had tried to tell them. A warning sign, yes. Gazing westward, he frowned as Mount Erebus played hide and seek with their eyes. The prevalent mist cloud now cloaked the mighty peak. An eruption was imminent.

Arnie howled in alarm. Kyle's team gaped, each of them paralyzed by the unfolding scene.

"Everybody," Kyle shouted, "back to the sled! Hurry!"

"Shit, it's too far!" Vaughn cried.

"It's not safe here," Spekolstein assured him, grabbing his sleeve as Kyle, Diegos, LaMarques and the dog dashed off. "The Shelf's going to melt if—oh, God, look at that!"

Mount Erebus erupted out of the flat icepack with a thunderous clamor. Kyle rasped breathlessly, pumping his legs as hard as he could. He watched in horror as geysers of pyroclastic ash gushed from the crevasse, sending black plumes into the pristine sky. This must've been a replay of a prehistoric cataclysm, one quelled long ago by a merciful God.

Sudden night collapsed over the Antarctic landscape and Kyle's last prayer was that the world would somehow brace itself for the nightmare erupting upon existence.

Eternity fled in an eyeblink. Kyle didn't recall waking from the nightmare. Cell by cell, he felt life surge back into his veins, until he gasped, utterly disoriented and numb. On wobbly legs Kyle edged from his stupor only to behold a surreal vista.

Once more he stood on a bleak snow-swept tundra, entirely perplexed by the otherworldly scene now enthralling his senses. The world he'd awakened to was no Earth that birthed his species. A fiery sky draped in violets, neon blue, crimson ribbons and impossible hues along the jagged black peaks hedging the misty horizon. A trio of moons hung low over the planet's vast curve, and faint rumors of a supermassive star shone beyond a thick atmosphere. Kyle had an irrational fear he'd been teleported to Venus. Yet logic told him a human could never withstand that world's hostile environs, much less breathe the caustic gases. Or survive her brutal hellfire temperatures.

No, no, no...it's not real, Kyle told his soul.

Then he whirled about, looking for his team, any sign of Arnie, the cataclysmic eruption they'd fled, anything left of the Antarctic landscape. Kyle saw no sign of human life other than his own neoprene-clad skin.

He belted out, "Deborah, Rob, Alain...anybody! Hey, guys, where the hell are you all?"

No reply came. Not a single whimper or yelp from Arnie. In fact, nothing echoed back to him except his own panicked voice. He panned his gaze in every direction, desperate for a point of reference, any telltale sign of habitation, a manmade structure, aircraft or terrestrial landmarks like roads or...wildlife, for that matter. It occurred to him that no birds chirped, no insects buzzed or clicked or swarmed the air.

Kyle huffed. "Okay, okay. It has to be some purgatory. I'm dead or in a coma. Or suffering a traumatic episode." He chuckled bitterly. "Or just crazy, talking to myself."

A low whine rose out of the bizarrely alien sky. Kyle's heart pounded in his throat. The avian shape grew larger as it swooped from the vaulting, kaleidoscope firmament, and he swore it looked oddly like a manta ray with a sleek, silvery hull. And he was pretty sure he might've soiled his terra-fits by the time its pilot emerged fully clad in an olive drab jumpsuit...worn by a smiling Deborah Spekolstein!

"Ah, they said you'd come through," she said, pulling gloves from a pocket. "We've had other Kyles, more or less, but you're the first intact replica to cross over."

"Um, sorry?" he croaked.

"Let's get you inspected for glitches firstly."

First contact proved a messy ordeal for new arrivals fresh out of deep freeze. The Antarctic Circle served nicely as an incubator, suspending metabolism, cell growth or decay—at least, in most cases, Kyle was briefed. Think of it as nature's own cryogenic vat, the team posed.

"Unfortunately," Vaughn's copy explained, "it doesn't always mean a clean specimen gets translated. After all, mate, the Cataclysm is a fickle beast. Glitches happen. More so with your iterations, old guy."

"How many?" Kyle asked.

"Until now," Diegos said, "one of seven hundred and twenty-nine."

LaMarques chuckled. "Guess you're the anomaly."

Kyle felt like a lab specimen. After Spekolstein's very thorough inspection, he'd lost a bit of dignity. He just couldn't wrap his mind around it all. The enigmatic sky. A trio of moons. A supermassive sun that wasn't anywhere near their Solar System, nor a main sequence star, for all he knew of astronomy.

"This place...where exactly are we?"

Deborah Spekolstein said, "We don't truly know. We've sent out probes. Even built a space telescope. All we get is weird data."

"Weirder than multiple copies of our team?" Kyle asked, eyeing a gaggle of doppelgangers milling throughout the compound.

All wore unique clothing or hairstyles or had varying body types, depending on their daily chores or lifestyle choices. Some had skin hues darker or lighter than their baseline original. A few had aged noticeably. "And what about my...misfits? Where'd they go?"

"Eighty-sixed, I'm afraid."

Blunt despite Deborah's pained look. She swiped a tear as Diegos's clone sighed. "It's a hard choice, Kyle, each and every time. But resources are finite. The biosphere can only support so much life. We're limited on flora, and it's a piss poor ecosystem with only penguins in the wild."

Amid his wonder at each new detail, Kyle considered their cobbled together technology. Aircraft, probes, space telescopes, the biosphere complex...all of it wrought from a bleak tundra with scarcely a sign of Earth's industry. Then a new inquiry rattled his soul: "Uh, just how long have you been here, guys?"

"Um, yeah, about that," said Vaughn. "Kyle, we're sort of in an altered reality, best guess."

LaMarques nodded. "We mapped the whole continent, charted every crevasse and glacier, then double checked our findings. This is still the Antarctic Circle, just not on Earth, mon ami."

Kyle pointed at the illogical celestial display above the skylight. "Alain, that's not Sol. And Earth has only one moon."

"So we have a theory," Spekolstein said. "Albeit a bizarre one, the math fits. Kyle, that's no star at all. It's Jupiter, believe it or not. Those trio of moons are Io, Ganymede and Callisto. As for this world? It seems we've inhabited an altered Europa, roughly a billion years after the Holocene Cataclysm."

After years of debate, the team decided to call this era the Galileocene epoch. In honor of the ancient astronomer and physicist who'd named the moons of Jupiter, they'd chosen Galilei for their haven perched atop the Ross Ice Shelf. Kyle marveled at the biosphere's accretion of hydroponics gardens, laboratories, gyms, a huge galley, water recycling and filtration systems, berths in the hundreds for every soul, and skylights vaunting Europa's lovely aurorae heavens. All built over a local seventy or so years since Transcending from Old Earth.

Time.

A reality dysfunction in the extreme.

As for raw materials, Kyle learned just how resourceful his colleagues were. Penguin pelts harvested for clothing, leather or textile fibers. Oils and protein from their sinew and bones. Waxes, gelatin, vitamins, acids and fertilizer gained from byproducts. At first, Vaughn's know-how garnered from Aborigines gave them crude tools, then more advanced devices as resins, ore, granite, metamorphic rock and a plethora of elements were refined.

The Antarctic landscape was rich in all the primordial stuff humanity needed to reemerge from civilization's ooze. Europa's indigenous habitat gave them a cornucopia of building blocks to erect their new society. Its native fauna defied zoology's every premise.

"Okay, wow," Kyle gasped. "Seriously? An entire colony of sea phyla?"

"Yep, an amalgam of Earth's manta rays," Diegos said, elated to expound on his bioresearch. "Only way cooler in every aspect."

Spekolstein nodded. "They're highly intelligent too. Capable of organized cooperation."

"Like whale pods, you mean?" asked Kyle.

"No," LaMarques said. "They have advanced social order and undersea farming!"

"Oh, man," Kyle said. "They...actually farm?"

An organism evolved beyond primitive instincts meant Homo sapiens had a true rival for dominance in the Solar System. Kyle remembered their discovery near Sidle Dome. It must've migrated to Earth via whatever phenomenon that brought humans to Europa. Was it all some side affect of string theory? Quantum physics aside, a new query niggled his psyche.

"Why not Arnie?" he said.

Vaughn shrugged. "Godly mystery. It maybe can't transfer synthetic life. Who knows?"

"Whacky physics," LaMarques agreed.

Spekolstein wasn't so sure. "Or this is karma. Our souls reincarnated into better versions of our former selves."

"Yeah," Diegos chuckled. "Cloned upgrades."

Kyle wondered who this Diegos was in sequence. Number ninety-four? Five hundredth? Were the replicas as diverse in personality or moods as their varying body types? The facsimiles who presently trudged over the icepack with Kyle fit as close to his old team as he recalled them. Vaughn the cocky Aussie. LaMarques doling out his maverick charm. Diegos scouring the tundra for new phyla to analyze. And lovely Spekolstein keeping them all on task.

"We're on deadly ground. Eyes sharp, guys."

Kyle's new diet on Europa warred with his digestive system. Twice he'd pitched his gorge onto the pristine ice sheet. Or perhaps it was his riled nerves. Oh boy, geez Louise! Alien lifeforms evolved from a long obscured seabed only hypothesized by scientists.

If only Earth's theorists had known the extraordinary truth. All those years ago he too had speculated farfetched scenarios about extrasolar geology. How life might thrive in Titan's methane rivers and lakes. Or extremophiles on Enceladus.

"Keep up, Dr. Elmhurst," urged an old colleague at Stanford University. Rebecca Jones smiled on the edge of his memory. The physics grad had taken his hand, hurrying into the planetarium like a schoolgirl sneaking him to a corner to kiss. Yet Kyle knew better. This firebrand was far out of his league. Smart, spunky, ambitious and daring. "Our galaxy is only a speck in the cosmos. It's amazing," she'd gushed, "gazing billions of years back into the birth of it all. So breathtaking, isn't it?"

"Pretty neat, yeah."

"To think it'll all unravel during the Cataclysm."

"Huh?"

"Dark energy, muons, rogue nebulae? We won't even know what hit us until it's too late."

"Ah, doom and gloom," Kyle sighed. "That's your idea of setting the mood?"

She giggled. "No, Dr. Elmhurst. I'd just do this."

Kyle's lips still tingled as butterflies danced anew in his chest. Warmer temperatures kissed his brow now they'd crossed the Antarctic Boundary and leafy, saline scents met his sinuses. Splotches of algae green mingled with scoria-red sandbars and teal blue coral reefs. Although only an amalgam of coral polyps, Europa's indigenous biota formed reefs after shedding their exoskeletons. Over long geological periods, the moon's core had grown molten as it contracted under Jupiter's tremendous tidal pull.

"Gets hotter during relative spring," Spekolstein told Kyle, fitting a breather nib onto his nostrils. "Orbital spin puts Europa in direct sunlight every thirty-nine Jovian hours."

"Trading season," Vaughn said, adjusting his own nibs. "The angel rays only tolerate us during harvest."

"Got it," Kyle said.

They'd all donned scuba gear, the tightly fit diving suits and fins giving them sleek contours. Kyle felt like a seal about to plunge into shark infested waters. For all he knew, these creatures were merely biding their time, planning to make a meal of the curious humans.

Early on in the team's explorations, they'd isolated the source of Europa's breathable air. Using infrared spectra scans, Spekolstein had seen oxygen, hydrogen, methane, nitrogen and other noble gases seeping from the seafloor. Over the eons tidal heating had created prime conditions for deep-sea flora to flourish. Along with previously trapped carbon dioxide were microscopic fossils that now fed an undersea agriculture. An atmosphere hospitable for humans and native fauna made first contact inevitable.

"Sonar echoes gave us a clue," Alain LaMarques told Kyle. "They use pulsating light and a kind of echolocation."

Bioluminescence made sense, Kyle mused. Why else had life managed to evolve under kilometers of ice with no means of gaining fuel from sunlight, no photosynthesis, nor any warmth other than thermal vents? Kyle recalled the meteorite ALH84001 discovered on the Antarctic ice in 1984. Dating showed it had landed about thirteen thousand years ago, Earth time back then, after a 16-million-year journey through space. The rock dated about 4.1 billion years and likely had been blasted from Mars by impact. Contained within its layers were carbonate minerals and complex organic molecules—polycyclic aromatic hydrocarbons associated with life when found in Earth's geology.

A wondrous sight yawned before the human envoys as they plunged into the pristine depths. Half a kilometer down, Kyle marvelled at the lush undersea hues, aquatic plant life unlike anything in Earth's seas, and turquoise rock formations that looked like massive reefs. Schools of tropical colored phyla darted in unison when the team kicked toward their feeding turf.

They swam into a ravine that twisted along high canyons, until it spilled them into a sprawling vista. Varying shapes of kelp analogs swayed in the currents, some growing like fantastic beanstalks with fronds outstretched to the surface. Amid the engineered terraces and crops glided large, winged creatures, the angel rays at play in their watery Eden. Near translucent bodies, large pearly eyes, rippling bioluminescence as they saw their human guests.

Before embarking on the trek, Kyle had stuttered: "They... they can fashion tools?"

Diegos postulated a brain size theory, the encephalization quotient, that explained their heightened intelligence. "Angel rays are so clever because they've got large brains," he explained. "By ratio, even bigger than our cerebrums."

"But toolmaking," Kyle repeated, incredulous despite the evident proof on display.

Vaughn delighted in his bewilderment. "Mate, look closely. At the ends of those wing fins. Almost like fingers, yeah?"

The bony appendages did look rather like digits capable of manipulation. So, okay, if they could grip objects, it was likely they built things. Kyle wondered just how intricate such devices might be and if they'd figured out weaponry...or scientific inquiry or advanced technology. Probably not, he told his dubious lizard brain. That primitive fear on the edge of his survival instincts. After all, if these angel rays had an inkling of hostile nature, what peril awaited humans on Europa?

Spekolstein spoke for the team. "We come for trade, neighbor friends," she conveyed, using luminous pulses from her gauntlet. "Do you have newly harvested crops fit for humans?"

"Sea gourds, yes." Graceful wings unfurled. Eyeing Kyle, its body rippled with lavender curiosity. "We see a new human?"

"Yes. He is Kyle."

"Variant marvels. Can he speak?"

"Not yet."

Kyle's earpiece translated the alien pulses, so he grasped the exchange. Yet only Spekolstein wore a gauntlet, leaving Vaughn, LaMarques, Diegos and himself muted observers. Except for their linked scuba mikes, Kyle had no means of conveying his myriad questions. At least, not in Europa tongue.

"Ask this guy if we can get the grand tour," he proposed.

Spekolstein chuckled at his naivety. "Kyle, they're uptight about their habitat. We're lucky they even trade with us."

"Won't hurt to ask."

"All right."

In their own language, she pulsed: "Kyle wants to see more of your home. Sorry, he's new."

Astonishingly, the angel rays accepted Kyle's request. The depths now echoed with enchanting song, like gurgles mingled with harps, tones bounced off the reef formations, silty seafloor, trenches, and hewn out grottoes. Archways marked boundaries, some so lofty they made Kyle feel like krill as they swam behind

One Claw. With a single digit on his/her wing fins, their guide soared gracefully along.

When they dove into an uninhabited zone, One Claw proclaimed: "Beyond this point we go not. The Fyrth'bulae live in those waters."

"What are they?" Kyle wanted to know.

Spekolstein relayed his query.

The angel ray's bioluminescence dimmed. "Creatures who do not tolerate change," One Claw pulsed in sullen yellow.

"Sounds like unfriendly blokes," Vaughn said via radio frequency. "No worries, Kyle. The best is yet to come."

LaMarques nudged him. "Gourds aren't the only bounty grown down here, bon garcon."

Diegos expelled a plume of bubbles. But rather than spoil Vaughn's cryptic allusion, he swam off behind Spekolstein and One Claw as they surged over the next ridge. Watery echoes vibrating softly against his eardrums, Kyle had the feel of wading into a dreamlike scene. What sprawled before their eyes was beyond otherworldly. A fantasy world teeming with glowing butterfly analogs, sea horse phyla, whorls of helix fronds and ribbon things dancing amid frolicking children...

"Um, hey, guys?"

"Yeah, mate," Vaughn said proudly. "Ankle biters grown by the dozens."

"They're bred," Diegos amended. "We learned our offspring didn't do well in Europa's extreme atmosphere."

"Not without enhanced physiology," Spekolstein told Kyle. "So the angels offered this sanctuary. A place to let our progeny evolve, so to speak."

Curious as polar bear cubs, a gang of kids flitted over to them like playful dolphins. They gazed from large, nearly glowing eyes. Slender, otterlike bodies, hands with webbed digits. Gills fluttered on their lower necks. Seaweed covered budding anatomy. All had long straggly hair, some dark, others flaxen or fiery auburn or silvery white. Kyle couldn't wrap his mind around it all. Why breed their young underwater? Why not build a specialized environment within the biosphere near parents who could monitor their growth, nurture them or expose them to human society?

Spekolstein sensed Kyle's conflict. "We tried natural birth," she explained, barely masking her motherly regret. "After so many failed terms, we accepted their offer. To let our children develop as angel ray offspring do. Alone in this lush biome."

"Still, I mean, they're just left to fend for themselves?"

"Hardly," Diegos said. "Guardians watch over them. But yes, to a degree, the juveniles live by instinct."

Kyle let a bold youngster touch his beard. The boy gurgled, then effused multiple bands of bioluminescent colors. Talked in angel ray! "Are you one of our parents? Why do you look so different? Can you speak?"

Kyle transmit his reply via mike. "Um, sorry, not me, kid."

"He doesn't speak yet," Spekolstein replied for him. "Kyle just arrived. And he is a new genetic strain."

Clinical. Did these boys and girls know anything about genes or ethnic diversity?

Kyle blinked. Little had prepared his psyche for this improbable exchange. Born deep in Europa's sea, the children were wholly alien, breathed with gills, ate indigenous flora and fauna, all absent any life lessons from Earthborn parents. A million concerns inundated his spinning head. What about medical checkups? Puberty or psychological trauma if anyone lost a life? Or God forbid, if their biology didn't allow them to emerge from the depths to join humanity's terrestrial home?

"Enough, children," One Claw pulsed, forestalling Kyle's next query. "The adults must go. We do not tolerate prolonged interference."

Obediently, the youths whirled away, all too eager to return to their mirth and curious discovery.

Kyle felt cheated by the abrupt end to their reunion, but swam off with One Claw and the others. Murky currents soon obscured the usually pristine waters as they kicked toward the angel ray homestead—archways, grottoes, farmed seabed, clawed out estuaries that fed an undersea society. An unsettling warmth rose from the silty seafloor and caused a bleary mirage as Kyle's pulse quickened. Heat like they'd experienced on the Antarctic in the hours before Mount Erebus erupted...before the horrific cataclysm overtook the U.S. Geological Survey team...a billion years ago.

One Claw's oscillating luminescence faded in alarm. Ugly snarls erupted from the moon's core, an angry leviathan waking, lava and hideous black plumes snaking over a once tranquil existence.

Kyle hissed, "Damn, not again!"

"An unforeseen geologic event?" Diegos asked.

"Dear God, I think so," Spekolstein said. "But it shouldn't be happening. Not yet."

"Well, it is, mate," Vaughn said.

LaMarques kicked into a panicked retreat to the surface. He didn't plan on ignoring the klaxons in his limbic system. Dying in the throes of geologic upheaval was not an event he planned on repeating. Neither did Kyle, for that matter.

A tiny pang of guilt haunted his soul as they fled the deep and reached the surface...abandoning those poor urchins.

Kyle snatched Spekolstein by the wrist, yanking her from the gaping fissure. Vaughn and LaMarques were gone. Diegos had scrambled back from the ledge in time but lost his pack, all their rations, and likely their only means of survival if they got stranded in the wild. Europa's core was constricting, her crust convulsing under Jupiter's tremendous tidal forces. The Jovian Scenario, dear God Almighty, playing out in stark reality. This may well have been humanity's swan song in this altered parallel, but Kyle wasn't going gently into that cruel nightfall.

"They're gone," he told Spekolstein, holding her back.

"No!"

She sobbed. They'd all come though at nearly the same time—the Robert Vaughn, Alain LaMarques, Jorge Diegos, and Deborah Spekolstein copies who'd joined their harvest expedition. Now two of them had perished.

Kyle felt her pain. Yet this wasn't the time for grief, not while danger loomed all around them. Misty veils twirled from the criss-crossing gulches. Thermal vents belching methane into the auroral canopy, a catalyst birthed by seismic spasms and molten plates below the Ross Ice Shelf. Geology no longer obeyed Old Earth predictions or glaciology as they knew it. Spekolstein's models had foreseen climate fluctuations, yes, but never such drastic upheaval. Not this, by God in heaven. Not the coming water world Europa would transform into if the subduction trends persisted.

"We should've had time," she wept, collapsing once Kyle pulled her to safety. "It wasn't supposed to erupt yet."

"Sidle Dome?" Kyle asked, still gasping.

"The dormant cauldron," she explained. "Ockham's Razor. It woke too soon. At least by a million years."

Kyle was nonplussed. "Wait. Europa has natural cauldrons?"

"Far as we know, yes. Europa likely started out like Io. A hotbed of volcanic geysers. Its core was so constricted by tidal forces that its mantle grew molten. And it's happening again, I think."

The hazy disk that was Jupiter did look much larger than it had the day he translated over. Was the gas giant pulling its moons back home to their original orbits?

"Get moving," Diegos urged them. "The icepack won't be stable much longer."

"Alain...Robert," Spekolstein wept. She clambered to her feet, a bit wobbly. "Why them?"

Together Kyle and Diegos kept her upright when she nearly collapsed. The trio trudged off at a fast pace, lungs burning, eyes bleary with panic and exhaustion. A sudden quake unsettled their footfalls, all three tumbling, then hastily scrambling to their feet only to face terror anew. Ahead on the horizon rose an awful blanket of steam and volcanic ash. It rolled toward them like a beastly tsunami. They were hemmed by gaping fissures behind them, the brooding peaks to one side, a frothy sea to the other, and the horror hurling their way.

"We won't make it," Kyle said, feeling deja vu that echoed Vaughn's words. "It's too far to Galilei."

"Not by air," Spekolstein panted. She pointed to a ridge. "There...my craft...scout plane."

"Shit!" Diegos harked. "That's got to be a mile away."

"Close enough," Kyle said. "We get there or perish, guys."

Against all hope, they hustled onward, icy fear and desperation raking their napes. Kyle pushed harder each time his legs protested. His companions kept a frantic pace, all of them huffing like Alaskan sled dogs as the landscape churned and bucked. It was impossible. Yet stopping wasn't an option, not within sight of the ridge, not so close to their only means of escape.

An eternity yawned over the glaring plateau before the gulf narrowed between them and salvation. Then jagged rock, slippery handholds, and aching joints as they climbed, crawled, hefted themselves onto the crag, with almost nothing left.

A sleek hull that resembled a manta ray rested on extended ski pads. Once secured aboard, with Kyle and Diegos piled into the cabin, Spekolstein quickly activated nav systems, lifted off vertically, and arced above the glacial peaks westward.

Their heavenly vantage afforded a new perspective of the fast transforming world below. The never ending ice sheet had nearly vanished under an onslaught of fiery ash and a widening seascape as frozen landmass succumbed to hellish temperatures. Ugly scars meandering along fault lines, gaping fissures, sinkholes, angry geysers and seething bedrock.

Spekolstein swung the craft over the Ross Sea, over its steamy black tides, where Galilei once lay, and wept anew. She swiped at tears, trying to confirm her suspicions with naked eyes. "Right there," she told the men. "Ockham's Razor. Shouldn't be that neatly outlined."

Kyle joined Diegos, gaping at the amazing sight. Even with his mind exhausted, he knew she was right. That perfectly shaped concavity was no cauldron. Geology didn't form that way, it was messy and irregular and lovely in its abstract creation. This spoke of artificial design: a massive construct built by an intelligence other than Homo sapiens.

One Claw had suggested a rival species in the depths. The Fyrth'bulae. Could they have built such a colossal artifact? Kyle couldn't fathom a purpose for a faux cauldron that...oh God, was it changing shape?

"It's active," Kyle said.

Diegos gulped. "About to erupt, you think?"

"I mean, rearranging its structure."

"Makes no sense," Spekolstein said. "Why would the angel rays build that? This nightmare befalling Europa? Why'd they set this all in motion?"

Kyle shook his head. "No, I doubt it's them. Not the angels. Not anything so primitive or gentle."

The behemoth realigned its shape until a clearly distinguishable wonder enthralled their eyesight. A gigantic jellyfish thing rose from its center like a near translucent cloud, its kilometers-long tendrils gathering up flora and fauna from the seabed. Perhaps a failed experiment, or else a deliberate master plan...it swept up their craft too, taking its cargo home.

The End

THE CLOUD'S EYE

"An uneasy quiet teetered on the edge of a knife for what seemed like an eternity." —Chris Mazzoli, from *Armageddon*.

1:24 am, Friday, October 10, 2031 CE
Aboard the Spartan, La Fuentes Shoal.

Joyce eyed the ugly mass swirling over the *Spartan*, churning like a lightning votex as it wreaked havoc on the sonar instruments. One by one the data relays blinked out, cutting out their links to the mini-sub which Charlie controlled. Murky silence drew Joyce's panicked eyes from the monitor before her and left only a faint, horribly weak biopulse—and that was fast deteriorating, eaten by the static pervading the instruments. She knew he'd been lost, swept away as if by a riptide from the empty black screens.

"Shoot, crap!" she hissed, on the verge of tears.

Oh, buckle down, girl, a voice chided deep in her chest. Get it together, Dr. Levine. It's why you joined the Oceanic Conservation Front, isn't it? To save the whales, to face incredible crises, and bravely deal with a highly sentient aquatic life form, if need be. Isn't that right?

"Fine job I'm doing saving the world."

She sighed, wiping sweat from her brow. It had to be at least 40 degrees Celsius. She felt every inch of her petite body tense with frustration, her soft green eyes darkened with fatigue. Her skin felt clammy. Like the others, she had donned her wetsuit ready for the worst.

The skipper had been down in the mini-sub *Ishtar* for seven long hours, far too long. If Charlie's air held up, he still had time to get out of the soup alive—just maybe. The whales had to be dead by now. Notwithstanding her expertise as a marine biologist, Joyce scarcely believed any animals would thrive out there no matter how deeply they dove. She knew the humpbacks were lost, and neither she nor the OCF fleet had any way of saving the pod.

Caleb Dirke, the Aussie science officer, shouted an obscenity from the afterdeck that echoed eerily in the dusky cabin. Old "Bones" Heggs and the big Eskimo dog were lost beyond the din of white noise, like frenetic ghosts racing from one end of the vessel to another, with the old Alaskan chasing gear, and Arnie yelping helplessly, trying to warn his human crew mates, desperately vying against the overwhelming static engulfing the *Spartan*. Everything was fuzzy snow. Even the depth-eye had gone blind.

"Answer me, Charlie Hunter," she cried again, to no avail. She pounded a fist onto the console even as she kept her vigil on the agitation expanding darkly overhead.

A cyclone?

The question had plagued Joyce ever since it first grew out of the clear azure calm. Relative calm, actually. Nothing from the satellite links gave any hint of its arrival beforehand, either. The crew had been blindsided. Caught off guard. Sudden daylight had come in the foggy nightfall. It was an artificial light. For the life of her, she couldn't explain the cloud. Its origin was unknown.

"What the hell are you, for God's sake?" she anguished aloud.

Caleb's bronzy shadow was there, huffing. "Don't know. Just burst over us suddenly. Never picked it up on Skylab, not a blip on the Doppler, nothing. Bloody devil's play, mate."

"It screwed up my visuals," she said. "Can't get Charlie up if we don't escape this...interference. Cripes, shoot!" She hit the depth-eye, got more static, the deathly hiss growing out of the brooding cloud.

"He's gone, Caleb."

"Not yet," he rasped. "Stay on the helm. I'm going in."

"That's suicide, and you know it."

"I've gotta get the Skip outta that hole. Gotta do it before the mercury explodes. And..."

His words choked off. He couldn't say it. Couldn't mouth the terrifying scenario that had already claimed one crewman—when that devil ray engulfed Virgil and the skipper back in the Gulf of Alaska, its awful light charring flesh and skin, nearly blinding them all with its pulsar intensity.

He croaked, "I won't let it. Not without a fight."

It was useless arguing with the stubborn Aborigine. She'd learned that much, if nothing else, in her short tenure aboard the *Spartan*.

"Okay, all right," she relented, eyes misty. "But don't get cocky out there. Its boiling like lava, for one thing. And the submersible, the *Aphid*? Aren't you forgetting it's junk? How the hell will you go in, Caleb?"

"Terra-suit. Got it ready while I was topside and I could see it. The cloud. It's got something to do with that cave down there."

"How do you that for sure?"

"Clouds don't muck up our kinda of gear so easily. And I saw them. I saw those lights."

"Lights?"

"Yeah, the very stuff that stung Virgil and the Skip. It's...I don't know, living somehow. Like a gigantic jellyfish, mate."

That's how she'd heard another oceanographer put it once. Like the thing she'd witnessed in the Antarctic, back when an inexplicable magnetic field had taken an entire pod of southern humpback whales. Sucked them from the waters like so many tiny krill. Just there one second, then whoosh! Gone...

She knew Caleb was right. The cloud was linked to it all. The cave, the alien manta, and the freaky weather front they'd faced days ago. Back when they'd rendezvoused with the *USS Charleston*, she'd watched it rise out of the Pacific, rolling up like a fog bank...scanning each of their biosignatures, as if it were some misty reconnaissance craft born out of the sea.

"It's a...UFO, mate," Caleb uttered hesitantly, his hard brown eyes wandering to the porthole. "I feel it in my bloody bones, yeah."

"Can't argue," she said. "But we've got to do whatever we're going to do quickly, Caleb. The hull won't hold much longer under this heat."

"She'll hold."

"Hope to God you're right."

A moment later, she and Heggs helped Caleb into a heavy terra-suit, got his air tubes and mask latched, and carefully lowered him into the glassy waters. Luckily, the suit was designed not only for subterranean caving, but also for deep-space walks and undersea exploration. Still, that did little to calm Joyce's foreboding. The whole of the Pacific looked utterly still, flattened by some preternatural air pressure, kept subdued by the vast cloud's energy. No waves, no frothy swell. Just a vast sheet of grayness for as far as the eye could see.

Joyce felt dry-mouthed, exhausted with worry. "Fifteen minutes, Caleb. That's all you get down there. Understood?"

"Aye, aye, Captain Joyce," came his flat, nealy muffled quip He was mortified, but it wasn't going to stop Caleb from diving "Locked and loaded, mates. Let's go."

Reluctantly, Joyce let the cable go and watched him drop into the sea and fast submerge.

"It'll be fine," Heggs told her, although not convincingly. "Kid knows the sea well enough. He'll get Charlie up."

She prayed the Alaskan was right. Even so, Joyce felt worse as she eyed the swirling mass looming overhead. It was no ordinary cloud, that was for damned sure. The glaring objects at its core shone like searchlights. A thousand angelic lights cast upon their vessel, searching out their life pulses, patiently probing for its quarry.

It had the luxury of waiting out their lesser intelligence. It had waited eons already. And wait it did.

A while after Caleb's dive, Joyce and Arnie paced the dimly lit helm, both dog and woman refusing to sit still. "We shouldn't have let him go, Bones. We're going to lose Caleb too."

"No we won't," the old Alaskan demurred. He swiped sweat from his cheeks, his breathing raspy. "Not gonna lose anybody, lassie. It's only been ten minutes. We gave him fifteen, didn't we?"

"Oh, shoot!"

"Won't help to worry. Let's hope the *Spartan* holds out."

"Yeah, well, that may be the least of our problems. Look." She was at the porthole, Arnie on his haunches at her side as she surveyed the cloud's eye. Heggs joined them. "See that? The light beam?"

"I see it. What the hell now?"

"Can't say for sure, but Caleb thinks it's extraterrestrial. Some kinda craft, he thinks."

"Aliens?"

"Okay, you used the word. Not me."

"Doing what exactly? Probing?"

"Like I know, Bones. Maybe it's a radioactive cloud left over from a missile test we weren't told about. Could it be?"

"Not likely." The obvious question arose then: "Wonder what they want? What does that devil ray have to do with all this?"

"It's not Earthly. We all agree there."

Joyce touched the porthole glass, as if gleaning some proof of its authenticity. Snow. That's what the cascading particles were. It was the icy effect of some phenomenon beyond their grasp, yes. It fell onto the decks and melted quickly, forming tiny rivulets that spilled overboard and kept up a constant bubbly sound. In all the chaos, Joyce hadn't stopped long enough to notice the snowfall.

"Are you seeing this, Heggs? Snow out there."

"Ah yes," he huffed. "We're in some kind of Twilight Zone here. An atmospheric black hole."

A flash exploded over the *Spartan*, casting them in blinding whiteness. The odd whale song bore into their eardrums and stole their equilibrium, at once drowning out Arnie's terrified yelps and engulfing Heggs and Joyce in its alien melody. Once more they were bathed in the devil ray's unearthly aria. Eyes shut tightly against the nimbus, her chest heaving, pulse racing madly, Joyce fought to keep her moorings. Don't let this be happening, dear God, please, she prayed as the tendrils of energy crept over her skin and lifted her hair on end.

Then it simply ebbed from her pores like a spent tide.

Seconds later, when they blinked their eyes open, the dog was gone—along with the hellish temperature. It was suddenly cool, the bizarre glare gone from the porthole.

Joyce was on her feet, albeit groggily. "What...what just happened?" she uttered, groping for Heggs's hand.

"Dunno," Heggs said after a spell. He stood gingerly, and then eyed the consoles. All of the screens were blinking. "Say, look. They're coming back, Joyce. All of the sonar, the Myriad scan and the depth-eye too."

"Almighty God."

Holding onto Heggs for support, she and the Alaskan went to the monitor where Charlie's face had once shone. Both took turns tapping screens, jabbing buttons, both trying to call up the submersible. Although the seafloor and the cave now wavered before them once again, there was no sign of Charlie. No Caleb, just the silent depths.

Only the Solotar Aquatic Nano-Dimensional Scan showed anything readable. Its highly sensitive probes still picked up the thermal signatures of the cave, its deepest grottoes, going far down into the igneous floor. A raven background instantly bloomed with bright hues: rock formations, funnel pathways, tiny living organism, bits of lava and fiery sand—but no Charlie.

"There's no sign of either of them," Joyce said at the SANDS console.

"I see that," Heggs said testily. "And where's that dog?"

Joyce whipped her head around, searched the helm, the narrow corridor leading aft. "He's not even barking," she pointed out, her concern growing. Cyberdogs were highly excitable during a crisis. "I'll go topside and find Arnie. You stay on the depth-eye."

"Like hell, Dr. Levine. We're not going into that cursed witchery out there. Leave the damned dog to fend for himself. We've got people..."

The entire vessel convulsed with a deafening thunderclap. Once again the visual data was snatched from the screens, leaving them in black silence, their ears ringing madly. Joyce wavered dizzily. "Heggs, you...okay?"

He didn't answer. He stood mutely staring out at the bluish haze now filling the porthole, soft dawn light rather than the harsh gray they'd known for hours now.

He muttered, "It's gone. The cloud...it's not there anymore."

Joyce blinked. His words were barely audible above the ringing in her ears. Still, she understood by the ashen shadow on his wrinkled, pockmarked face. The way his eyes held the slow sparkle of astonishment.

"Are you sure?" Joyce asked.

"Blue sky. Look at it."

She did. While there was indeed no cloud and nothing of its glaring light, there still fell the fluffy vestiges of its snowfall, the particles, and the strange effect of its energy. She felt it in her jugular vein. It wasn't gone; not that easily, she sensed. "I'm going out," she said.

"I'm right behind you," he told her.

Together they emerged into the newly born daylight. The deck itself was calm. As if it had entered a deep freeze, the *Spartan* sat motionless. Nothing moved. Not the solar sails, not the OCF flag. At first neither of them saw any sign of the dog, saw nothing of the phenomenon but its glassy blue outline above them, and the sea itself, blue-gray and utterly quiet.

And dear God, at last a sight they'd long awaited.

Just beyond the shoal's black rise loomed the misty outline of the *Charleston*. The OCF command ship, still vaunting its Navy gray battle tones and satellite dishes atop a tall mast helm, had its crew and aircraft crowding its vast deck. Yet it looked all wrong. All too still for a large carrier. In fact, it seemed frozen in its wake, for not even a single flag fluttered.

Heggs, for his part, stood rigid, caught off guard as his eyes wandered to the bow. Joyce hardly took her eyes off the *Charleston*'s shocking vision when a gasp escaped her lungs. But it was Heggs who mouthed the incredible thing she now blinked at.

"It's Arnie," he whispered.

She too regarded the surreal sight of Arnie frozen in mid-leap, as if he'd been on his way overboard while chasing something. The dog looked like he was about to dive into the motionless Pacific when some force left the husky as he was. Even the air seemed insipid. Arnie's grin was intent, his paws trailing droplets that sat in mid-air.

But what had he chased after?

Joyce felt her heart shift as she gasped, "God in heaven, Bones. What's in the water? What was Arnie leaping after?"

He rubbed dry lips. "Let's find out," he said shakily.

As if nearing a shattered mirror, they both edged to the gunwale near Arnie, both fighting an urge to simply gape at the dog's petrified form. Eyeing the water, Joyce saw yet another unexpected vision.

The *Ishtar*!

Rising from the depths, the winged submersible glided to the surface, bobbed momentarily, then let out a sweet hiss of bubbles as it slowly depressurized and floated right for the *Spartan*, as if on autopilot. Nevertheless, Joyce couldn't move or make an utterance of joy. She didn't see Caleb or glimpse Charlie Hunter's face.

And then sudden fear seized her soul...

A shadow sprawled over them, its umbra swallowing the huge carrier, the *Spartan*, and what seemed the entire world. At once the sky folded upon itself and flung out into a mess of steamy contours. A ribbon of iridescent hues yawned overhead like northern lights. It wasn't the cloud but rather some unearthly shape, some enormous thing taking form. It looked to Joyce like a gigantic sea anemone. Like a wavering nest of tentacles with incandescent eyes.

Tiny dots danced out of the shape, spilled down onto the *Spartan* and floated in their midst, like glowing sentient golf balls. At first the glow balls hung en mass then, one by one, they went into varying nooks, into the cabin, and all along the vessel's hull. A cluster of the spheres took interest in Arnie, gathered about his fur, and then trickled away as if satisfied by his life pulse. A pair hung near Joyce and Heggs. My God, what are you, she wondered. Eyes wide, Joyce anguished.

An odd sensation flooded her veins, tingled her every pore. It felt like cool water filling a dry vase, as if she were a mere husk awaiting its vibrancy. Calm sweet coolness coursed through her being. The balls danced briefly, then clustered once more and flitted upward, back to the ribbon of iridescence.

Wind suddenly whipped Joyce's hair hair, icy torrents biting her skin. She had to cling to a rail to keep its ferocity from lifting her off the boat. A tiny sound beside her, Heggs faintly crying, "Don't look at it, don't!"

It didn't register at first. His words didn't seem logical. Why couldn't she stare at this anomaly? So angelic and lovely.

"Back down!" he cried.

"No, Bones, wait. Just let me see it, please. It's so..."

Strong hands yanked her, nearly dragged her back from the railing. When she came to her senses, a new vision rattled her sense of reality. In the waters, tendrils of light cradled the *Ishtar* and lifted it slowly out of the swell, took it up into the azure and ingested it in the alien shape.

Charlie! Dear God, it had taken Charlie!

"No!" she wailed, trying to break free of Heggs. "Please don't let that thing take him, Bones! We've got to stop them."

Them?

None of the crew knew what the cloud truly was or anything of its origins. They didn't know what the manta was. Why it had lured them to La Fuentes Shoal, or what ungodly secrets lay in the sea cave, for that matter.

Eight months ago, Dr. Joyce Levine had gazed to the sky while standing on the deck of a research vessel. Ever since she was a little girl, Joyce had pondered the unknown. A light of other suns swirling beyond the Milky Way. Energy born eons back before the local galactic group had even formed, now spilt like an otherworldly aurora over the Transantarctic Mountains. Were they alone?

The OCF scientists aboard the *Odessa* were tasked with monitoring marine life in the Ross Sea: gather data, tag specimens, and note the behavioral patterns of a pod of whales. Days after entering the Antarctic Circle, a ghastly eruption seized Mount Erebus...just moments after their whale pod vanished. It all fled into a flurry of chaos. After the cataclysmic event, their sensors detected a faint biopulse near Marie Byrd Land. A search and rescue team brought Arnie aboard days later; sadly, the only survivor of a U.S. Geological Survey team led by Dr. Kyle Elmhurst.

Admiral Felix Gonzales at the Oceanic Conservation Front's command center aboard the *USS Charleston* had quickly hushed the data retrieved from Arnie's memory chip—a precursor to their encounter in the Gulf of Alaska, Joyce now realized.

A great splash tore out of the freakish silence. Everything shifted, as if by the very hand of God, and with a tremendous whoosh time leapt forward, cast Arnie into a headlong arc, sent a maelstrom of watery eddies into motion, and bucked the *Spartan* atop frothy waves that...simply awakened, rudely tossed the vessel from its time-capsule stasis.

When the shock subsided, Joyce broke free of Heggs's grip and raced to the railing, scouring the waves for any sign of Caleb, any shard of hope that the skipper had escaped. After finding nothing, she raced to the portside deck, glanced to and fro, breathlessly hoping.

A shaped bobbed into view.

It was an orange inflatable raft, the reserve normally stored on the *Ishtar.* Arnie began yelping, the dog now under the raft's tent. But how? When had Caleb gotten the raft out of the mini-sub? It churned in the *Spartan's* wake, fought the current now building around the vessel, and made its way by cybernetic sensors. She whirled and found a lifesaver and tossed it overboard. Not able to wait for Heggs to join in her joyous discovery, Joyce hollered, "Ahoy!" and dove into the swell without any scuba gear.

Caleb's warm brown eyes smiled at her as he peeked out of the tent, Arnie's big head with him. "He's okay. I got the Skip," he told her as she scrambled onto the raft.

Charlie was a mess, gasping and coughing but alive. "Hey, Spunky," he uttered faintly.

She slapped her arms around the two men. "You're both crazy, you know that?" she said, eyes full of tears. "I thought...we saw it take the submersible. It took it into the cloud, Charlie."

"I know," he said. "That's all it wanted, though."

She hoped to God that was all it wanted.

Soon the crew was back aboard, basking in the *Spartan*'s cozy quarters. Amid the tremendous sigh of lapping waves came sudden calm. Once again the sea was a glassy gray sprawl expanding below the capsule of daylight and into the purplish veil of night. The shape melted into the azure and vanished. A shimmering blanket of winking stars drew over them. Comets dashed into the western sky as if chased by dawn's arrival. Sweet indigos and violets yawned from the east as the *Spartan* rose on its hydro-foils and hastened shoreward, leaving behind La Fuentes Shoal.

That morning Joyce felt oddly empty, but also blessed for having been bathed in the fleeting alien light. She lay quietly at Charlie's side, listening to the soft whir of the autodoc. Its elixir probes mended skin and cell tissue.

Ah, at last they knew. They no longer had to gaze into the heavens and contemplate the existence of a remarkable energy. There really was life out there, albeit a distant, fading dream. Lost now to the whisper of the stars.

The End

MAELSTROM

"I who speak here am bone of the bone and flesh of the flesh of them that live within the Veil." —W.E.B. Du Bois, from *The Souls of Black Folk*, 1903 CE.

August 30, 2003 CE
Hope, Oregon.
Decades before the Holocene Cataclysm.

At first glance Hope seemed like any other coastal town. With its salty odors and lazy Pacific breezes, Hope lay on the edge of the world. Oregon gave Cole Defoe what New Orleans hadn't: a sense of rural ease, that live-by-your-boot-straps kind of pith. He could smell the history and quiet traditions.

Cole's transfer had been after a particularly haunting ordeal. Keisha Bowley's had been a hard case to crack. So the Bureau gave him a cozy desk and plenty of papers to file, all to help rid Cole of the pangs he suffered back in New Orleans.

But the Big Easy was far behind Cole now. Some ghosts, he decided, were best left to rest—unlike the Bureau's latest case, Bert Holland of Lake Oswego, Oregon, last seen April 7, 2003. As he came to Carver's Deck at the far end of the marina, Cole pulled out Holland's photo, eyeing the scenery for clues.

Fog rose up from the wet black rocks along the dock, leaving a frothy gruel of waves and scavenging seagulls. He inhaled the salty cool air that hung over Hope's otherwise languid calm. It felt good to get out from behind a desk and into the fray of the hunt.

People strolled along the storefronts, eyeing the trinkets of a fishery town. The morning bustled with the crackle of fluttering sails and creaking of old hulls that fought to keep their mooring. Carver's Deck hid a starkly sinister mist below its restless wake and battered planks.

Receipts found at the Lake Oswego home had led Cole to Pearl's Herbs, a small boutique nestled in a cluster of shops not far from the pier. Cole eyed the boardwalk for Ezekiel Adams. The albino Haitian woman had said he might know about Holland. He found the old man perched on a log stub at the far end of the dock. Oblivious to Cole's approach, his fingers worked deftly with a knife as he carved.

"Mr. Adams?" Cole asked cautiously.

Dense gray eyes peered up to inspect the stranger. Cole wore dark slacks, a parka, and a holster. His short-cropped black hair framed a chiselled face and keen brown eyes lined with crow's-feet. Ezekiel nodded.

"I'd prefer Zeke," he spat, returning to his whittling. "And don't block my light."

Cole stepped aside. Other than the tattered boats and a dreary coastline, there wasn't much to the scenery. Carver's Deck was the faltering relic of a once thriving fishery port. Beyond Payoda Street and the placid hills lay the outskirts of Oregon—old Northwest-style settlements, logging townships, the Federal Bureau of Investigations in Portland, and a patchy grave of pines and pristine lakes.

"Sloppy work," Zeke said. "Bones ain't what they used to be. Can't fish with these hands, either. But you stick a worm on a twig and they sure fight fiercely."

"The fish here?"

"Crabs, boy."

Cole saw the bucket. Red-shelled crabs clawed fruitlessly, vying to escape their plastic prison.

"Got quite a few, I see. Any good for eating?"

"If you're into crap!"

Zeke's fingers were scarred and winkled. His clothes came from another age: torn thermal top and overalls, boots of black rubber, muddy. Pale layers of skin shrouded a mere skeleton. He glowered at Cole briefly.

"No, son. Best not to eat the scavengers. Foul and disgusting, if you ask Old Zeke."

Two shadows came into Cole's periphery. A pair of chatty old ladies out for a stroll on the dock slowed, then moved to the other side of the Deck, as if to avoid the bucket of crabs. Cole felt their wary gazes as they quickened their gait.

"Ever see this man?" Cole asked, taking out Holland's photograph.

The Kodak had been among the trophies and yachting plaques in the missing art dealer's home. In it, he stood on the deck of his plush 40-foot yacht.

"Bought herbs from Edna Pearl a few weeks ago. She said he often came down to the docks."

The old man seized the photo.

"Looks like him, I suppose. Hard to tell in this light."

Bert Holland wore glasses. He had the look of a banker, mid-forties, of Scottish descent. Apparently, two ivory fetishes with black diamond eyes had vanished with him. The relics, Cole had learned, were diplomatic loans from Mali. The Portland Art Museum kept a log of every piece in the exquisite collection: mostly carved from ebony, the tribal idols were said to have thrived in the precolonial kingdoms of Africa, but now, by illicit means, the Dagon carvings were gone.

"Strikes me oddly," said Cole, leaning on the railing. "Out of the clear blue, Bert just takes off without a trace. Can't make sense of it."

"God awful thing," Zeke agreed.

A lone clipper sat in the harbor, adrift like some stray barge, as though it had been cast long ago from the infinite gray buoyancy. Cole asked about its owner, and if Holland ever had anything to do with the clipper.

"She's a lighthouse," the old fisherman said. "Nobody owns her anymore. An Alaskan whaler left to drift ages ago. Don't know the story in full, but they say its crew vanished in 1907. The *Tailgate* is a tale we'd all rather forget."

"We?"

"Anyone who's lived in Hope long enough."

A gust stole over Caver's Deck just then, brining an odor which Cole found redolent of crude oil. He wondered if there might be an oil spill down the coast, or burning wreckage, perhaps. It was probably an odor caused by the imagery in his mind. Of a crew lost in the throes of an angry sea.

"Sit here a while and you'll see," Zeke growled. "God never liked a man who didn't pay attention to her. All this dust and mud in every organism comes from the sea. And it's all a pile of crab-meat, like them in my bucket. Scavengers and men."

Cole grew impatient.

"Any reason why Bert Holland would fear for his life?"

"Same as any. An eye for an eye."

"Someone owed him a bad favor, you mean?"

"God did."

"Oh, I see," Cole chided. "Bert's sins finally caught up with him."

Zeke glared up at him.

"Listen, boy. I'm no preacher. I said it was an eye for an eye, which means he got what he had coming, if you ask me." The wooden carving had become a crude effigy of a man. Its mouth was agape, frozen in a scream. "The cost of some secrets is knowing a truth you don't want to. And knowing got Bert in bad trouble."

The air grew stale with an eerie tinge. Zeke's eyes were sockets in a skeletal face. The irises were milky with age and wise of things dark and forgotten.

"Knowing got them all eventually," said Zeke with a scornful glance to the *Tailgate*. "Evil winds took them souls back. Long ago when the Negroes did the fishing in Hope, people got mad. Nobody wanted their nets soiling the fish. So they scared them off."

Cole vaguely knew of the Black settlers. Back in the gold rush days, Blacks came to the Northwest to make a new life and fish the coast. But, like elsewhere, they were lynched or burned out of the shantytowns of Oregon. Since the late 1800s Hope had kept a tight seal on its dark history. An old graveyard lay hidden somewhere near the fishery...

"Black folk," said Zeke, "wasn't left in their graves. Good local folk wouldn't have it. They'd steal the bodies out and dump them in the harbor. Let the crabs get their fill, like these scavengers, full of Negro souls."

Crude oil scents rose above Hope's lazy breeze. The gnawed hunk of wood in Zeke's hands grew more ghastly.

"The dead don't rest easy, boy. Not when they're left to drift amid the logs and refuse. Right here in these tides, yes, they was all taken down. Only what they could salvage—that's what them Black folk took back to bury. In a secret place."

"Secret place?"

"Where they can rest safely."

"Any chance Bert might be there too?"

"If he was fool enough to let them take him. But ain't likely you want to find out what he did."

"Bet I do," Cole demurred.

"Don't go meddling, son. Angry souls live in that boat's wake."

But Cole had already made up his mind to get out to the *Tail-gate* and find out what lay in its wake. A wheezy, scornful bit of words caught his nape as he strode off away from Carver's Deck.

"Rest assured, boy. They'll kill you too!"

Cole walked the boardwalk, eyeing the marina for signs of Holland's yacht. As he neared an alcove of sailboats he saw a kid squatting by a schooner, doing minor repairs. He glanced up when Cole approached.

"May I help you?" the young man asked hastily.

"You own this?" Cole asked.

"Are you kidding? I work for Nickels."

"Cheap, huh?"

"Mr. Nickels. Owns a rental shop."

Cole smiled wryly. "And I suppose he's on vacation. Is that it?"

The boy of sixteen or so paled. Small, rugged scars marked his cheek, trophies from a recent scuffle. Otherwise, he looked clean-cut and agile. He gave Cole a hard look.

"I'm not stealing it," he protested. He stood, extending a hand speckled by latex paint. "Jimmy Doyle's the name. You're the cop looking for that creep, right?"

"Bert Holland, yeah."

"Fat luck," Jimmy grinned. "He took off weeks ago. I know 'cause he owes me for a job. The lousy reneger."

Cole's brow furrowed. "Think he's hiding, maybe?"

"Can't say. Birdy wasn't all there. Kept things on that boat he didn't like talking about, you know?"

A gush of interest swept over Cole. He asked Jimmy what he thought those things might be, or if he'd seen any unusual behavior out on Holland's yacht.

"Just the weird odor," Jimmy replied. "A reek like rotted wood, maybe. Can't really say." He wiped sweat from his brow. The wet rings at his armpits grew wider. "Except for that awful odor, you'd think it was the cleanest rig in the marina. The cleanest."

Jimmy looked over a shoulder, then met Cole's eyes. "He kill somebody?"

Truth was, the Bureau didn't know for certain.

Before leaving the docks, Cole decided to get a look at the 150-foot clipper. After a cup of coffee and a danish, Mr. Nickels of The Bucket gave Cole a key to a rented dinghy which waited in a nearby cove. He undid the ropes and slid into the harbor soon after.

The motor whined noisily as Cole stole over the murky waters that anchored the old cargo ship to the town of Hope. The *Tailgate* clung to a lure of old places and ghosts. In Holland's case, those ghosts existed as tiny bits of forensic theory. Some dark secret had swallowed the art dealer into a swirling gale of peril.

Above a rotting embankment of old rails, the *Tailgate*'s sails flapped like the wings of a tiring raven. Cole felt a wire of dread tighten at his throat as he flanked its hull. Its masts creaked under a perpetual breeze.

After fastening the dinghy portside, he climbed a rope ladder up onto the deck.

Decades of refuse lay strewn over the ancient planks. Cole saw scurrying crabs and thought of Ezekiel Adams. Scavengers, Zeke had said of them. Eating tiny bits of grime and algae living in the timber? His skin felt flaky.

He gathered his coat snugly as he eyed the derelict for signs of a hold, some place to store whatever evil Ezekiel had warned of.

The cabin door creaked with a nudge.

Cole undid his holster and aimed a laser-fitted Glock down into the dark belly of the *Tailgate*. Crabs had eaten a gaping hole into the stairwell leading to its cargo hold. A foul kiss of decay stung his nostrils.

With ginger steps, he edged down into a grim scene lit by his flashlight. Crates were piled in rows. Many now empty, they were filled with odd African relics. A few lay open to reveal skeletal remains: small, ashen bones covered with dust and cobwebs.

He stood in the belly of a floating grave.

Cole recognized the stolen Dagon artifacts. The crates had been hidden here in the *Tailgate*'s bowels, far from the prying eyes of the FBI.

A nasty pitch shook Cole's footing. He narrowly missed a glass jar that clanked against a crate. Looking to the floor, he aimed his flashlight at the jar.

Kneeling, he picked it up to inspect its contents. Even through the dusty webs Cole saw the moldy leaves of an herb he'd seen elsewhere. "Edna Pearl," he muttered. "She's come here looking for her patient."

Those pale eyes had looked straight into Holland's fears. And she mistakenly believed her herbs held a cure, an elixir to calm the demons and keep him from drowning.

Stale, salty air flowed down into the cargo hold. It did nothing to mask the stench that rose from the crates. Cans of kerosene and flammable sealants lay nearby. He now knew it was the same gas oil that soaked the wood and entire hull of the *Tailgate*. The crude odor he had smelled on the docks.

Cole envisioned the ship being rigged with a fiery booby trap against trespass.

Still inspecting the jar, Cole took an evidence bag from his coat. A lab test might find a strand of hair, or a single wood louse, which could link to Holland's mystery. After placing a sample into a baggy, he knelt to retrieve one other bit of evidence: nestled amid the debris lay a broken pair of eyeglasses.

He recognized them from Holland's photograph. A shriek shot through his veins. His cell phone pulsated in his breast pocket. Clumsily he groped for it.

"Defoe speaking."

"Agent Napoli."

He felt relaxed by her tone. The Special Tasks agent had last talked to Cole in Chattanooga earlier that week.

"Any luck finding Bert?" she asked.

"Only his specs."

"Well, heck," Napoli offered, "that's a lead I'd kill for. Nobody thinks the body we found at the lake is Tobey's. The kid went thin air on me. I'm ready to puke."

"Sorry to hear."

Silence filtered her breathing. Cole asked if she was in Portland.

"Got in at two this morning," Napoli said. "On my way to the Bureau now if you want to talk shop."

The *Tailgate* swayed in the tides, deepening the pit in his stomach.

"Cole?" Napoli asked, as if the line had gone bad.

"I've got a Haitian to visit," he replied.

"Edna, right?"

"Holland was on this ship. And if he got crates from this hold, he probably needed a gun."

The Haitian herbalist, Dr. Edna Pearl, had not returned to her shop since his last visit and hadn't given anyone her whereabouts. So Cole had sought out Old Zeke at his stump, but he wasn't anywhere in sight of Carver's Deck.

Cole edged warily along the pier's railing, sensing peril. The *Tailgate* swayed in the harbor, guarding a secret that dug at his bones. He felt sure Holland had been snared by his own dark secrets. An illicit art deal gone too far...

Lapping waves frothed against the Deck. Tides driven not by wind, but a faraway current.

He leaned over the gnarled wooden railing.

In the murky swell he saw a floating bit of timber. Cut from wood that grew far from Hope's fishery, no doubt. Cole eyed it for a long while, then looked to the *Tailgate*, thinking: That's wood too. Down in the hull of the clipper was a stow of Dagon sculptures that Bert Holland hid shortly before his disappearance.

The timber was dark like mahogany. Waves cradled it, twirling the debris back below the pier.

Cole wanted a look down there.

Holland's skullduggery may very well have ended in foul play. A bad deal neatly tucked away by a ruthless buyer. Cole saw a body in his mind's eye. The secret might lay beneath Carver's Deck, if they had indeed killed him, as Zeke had promised.

Fog hugged the surf like fingers. A low creaking noise seized the Deck, sending cold tremors through him. The only way down was to climb over the railing. Huge beams held the pier above the water, giving Cole an icy plank to maneuver should he climb onto the false ledge.

He knelt at its edge. Briny sweet air caught in his throat as he swallowed. When he groped halfway over the embankment, a crab scurried up his hand and soared into the harbor.

His blood froze.

A basket floated into view just then. It was a fishing basket that had been anchored to a pole beneath the Deck. Cole gripped the railing tightly, easing himself down just enough to snare the line and pull the basket up.

Gasping from the effort, he hefted the cargo up onto the Deck. A gray seagull perched on a nearby stump squawked, eyeing Cole suspiciously. The metal basket was fashioned with chicken wire and a sturdy fishing line. With cold fingers he undid the loops and fetters, feeling his chest throb.

Immediately, Cole saw what had been stashed. The mesh wire unfolded to reveal a small tin box, an antique fisherman's gearbox, rusted and battered by age.

The gull squawked ominously. Cole sniffed.

"A flying rodent," he breathed, picking up the gearbox.

He eyed the motley stash of souvenirs: gold-plated pocket watch, fishing lures, a carving knife, cork pipe. An odor of decay sealed in its tin, airtight vault.

Wrapped in plastic, beneath the other items, lay black-and-white photographs, so old they were dingy brown and curled. The scenes were of the fishery back when life was simple. Sepia tones limned men who worked the dock, wore old sailor hats and boots covered in fish guts. A face in one photo, sharp as a carver's blade, caught Cole's eye. On the deck of the *Tailgate* stood Ezekiel Adams, looking the same as today, clenching his fishing knife. They'd caught a big shark. The old croon had a king crab in his grimy hand...

A date glared from the photo: 1907.

"That's impossible!" Cole harked. But as he gazed at the scenery—a town of horse-drawn buggies, old bucket Ford, and far fewer shops and homes along the hillsides—Cole saw one thing that was as old as Ezekiel.

Afloat like a mirage stood Carver's Deck, newly built and unscathed by time.

Cole's veins went cold. A low snarl seized his nape.

I told you, boy. The dead don't rest easy.

Startled, he snapped to his feet. With a hand on his holster, he searched the pier for Ezekiel Adams. When he glanced up he saw the source of the words. There on the deck of the *Tailgate* stood a wavering figure. Fumes from the clipper's rotting hull made a mirage of the old face even this far away, Cole could distinguish each pockmark, the scowling pale eyes. Zeke's lips curled in a grimace.

See, didn't I tell you, boy?

Crude oil scents stole over the harbor as if to strangle Hope. The *Tailgate*'s sails rose high like tattered clouds chasing away the last remnants of a storm. In a surreal flash the ghastly ship burst into a fury of roiling flames and dark gray clouds. So intense was the heat that Cole had to shield his eyes. Tiny spark angels formed a riotous pyre, the fiery column ascending into the dusky sky.

Then it was all gone.

❖ ❖ ❖

The next day Cole consulted Ernest Pablo at the Bureau's forensics lab in Portland. A plethora of specimens, microscopes, and charts cluttered Room 501. The technician was an olive-skinned man with wiry limbs. He held the photo to a special phosphor lamp. At his computer, a row of tiny lines came into focus at his command.

Cole stood at Pablo's side, eyeing the screen. "Touched up with zinc and nickel, I'd say," the FBI technician explained. "But this photo is just a clever fake."

Cole had retrieved a key bit of evidence at Carver's Deck. Among the souvenirs was a snapshot of a crime scene that had yet to be investigated. In a pool of water, effused into the dark silence down in a cellar at the Lake Oswego house, lay the lifeless gaze of Bert Holland. It had been there in the tin gearbox, obviously left for Agent Cole Defoe.

After an inquiry by Jan Napoli with the National Mariners Guild, the Bureau also learned the whereabouts of Holland's yacht. Apparently, it was abandoned off the shores of Puget Sound, with no trace of its owner. They only had the snapshot of Holland, evidently a victim of foul play, face up in a dark pool in a flooded cellar.

"Stressful case?" Pablo asked. He must've sensed the tense muscles in Cole's nape. "Maybe it's worth a visit to Dr. Eves," he quipped.

"Don't need a shrink, Ernie."

Using the mouse, Pablo dragged an image down from a second file. Its grayish brown shadows were of two sailors, one with a carving knife, scanned from a photo that Cole had retrieved from the gearbox.

Pablo said, "I used sepia toning to filter out the film. Take a look at this, Cole." The computer washed away the upper layer of the photo image. A hazy figure came into view, one overlapping the NetScan original. Where two men had stood in 1907 there was now a dim, youthful face Cole recognized.

"Jimmy Doyle," said Cole, incredulously.

Pablo opened a window on the screen and zoomed in a corner of the image to one-thousandth magnification. It was Old Zeke with enlarged, scowling eyes. The film looked grainy and sketchy now. Dots fizzled to the screen, like a patchwork of tiny hieroglyphs.

"Amazing," Cole breathed.

"Yep," Pablo agreed. "This photo isn't what it appears to be, either. Definitely not amateur work. The NetScan did most of it, but any hack would've known what he was looking at. Like I did."

"Coded imagery, you mean?"

"Right."

The words scrolled up in a single column. Rest assured, boy, they'll kill you first...

The air grew icy cold. Cole plummeted into a labyrinth of swirling souls, deep down into the *Tailgate*, where old Zeke stood, eyeing him with crow eyes.

Suddenly he thought of those old ladies on the dock. Hadn't they walked warily past him, as though Cole were talking to thin air?

Cole's investigation had wandered into a place where few had ever gone. And the fiery explosion had wiped away any trace of the *Tailgate*. Ezekiel Adams. Bert Holland. Jimmy Doyle. The crew of 1907. It had taken them all back, yes. Ghosts lay there in the burning hull, alongside the stow of Dagon sculptures and cobwebs. Lingering down there where the Bureau would never find any of them.

The End

HERONS IN GAZA

"Once again I shall be sacrificed, dying to the angelic;
I shall become that which could never be imagined—
I shall become nonexistent."
—Rumi, *Become More By Dying*, Mathawii III,
    3900-06.

May 16, 2047 CE
Sunset over Jerusalem.

Soft flutes lure Dalya bin Sinai into the old cafe under a cloak of dim lights and misty incense. She often spies this way, there in secret, like a ferret. Just another Ethiopian Jew out for an evening stroll, spicy tea, forbidden wine, or a sip of mystery. Mostly she feels soothed by the flutes, as she does now, and has since her arrival to Tel Aviv.

Six months. Waiting for a sign.

The cafe's interior is a crystal white, offset by chrome blue flow chairs neatly set beneath looming spheres and helixes whirling in a sea of soothing, arabesque colors. Dalya takes a table, sits cross-legged, meekly so. She wears no makeup, nothing seductive today. She has long gold-wire hair, smooth mahogany skin. The body is a stylish Cushite mold. Dark, lithe, and foreign. Her lace display deck also imported. Kikuyo eyes, too. The optic nerves are embedded in rare opal.

She discreetly eyes a patron, trying to guess his lineage. An Anglican Catholic, maybe. Newly arrived from Liverpool. There are many of them in this part of Israel, looking for a sign. Like Dalya. All seeking refuge from the prophesied Cataclysm.

Outside the cafe glows a scarlet sky, mosques, synagogues, dingy hotels, and idle tanks. Ancient ruins of the old state. All of it utterly still now. An eerie calm that belies the city's decades-long tension. The quiet steals over her, seeps from beyond the bullet-proof glass, flooding her auditory nerves like a lethal vapor, a visceral mood staggered by the hiss of voices.

Aman Riyad sings of Bedouin dreams from a neural stream on the jukebox. The ballad swirls sweetly above the muezzin's call. Sunset prayers, Palestinians gathering at the Temple Mount. Devoted and faithful. Dalya strums her slender fingers idly on the table, waiting for a waiter.

Nobody seems to be in a hurry in Old Jerusalem.

She peers outside. University students, vendors, busses, a few parked cars, all masking the scent. The strange scent. A woman with a scarf to her eyes, who avoids the soldiers, sways thinly toward the cafe. A black-haired swan, beautiful eyes; maybe from Nablus. Something isn't right about her eyes. They're far too dim, too vacant.

Where have I seen this one?

Dalya has seen her before, yes. She has tracked many such souls. Angry. Desperate. Isolated and cold. Hunger eating at their spleens. All of them eager to reach Israel's hub.

The ballad wails softly.

As the crescendo rises, Dalya bites a lip, knowing the Swan's tragic fate. The scent is nauseating. A murderous odor so repulsive that she shudders, afraid for the first time.

The martyr has come. Dalya rises slowly, anticipating, hoping against hope that her instincts are wrong. For just once.

An instant before it happens, she ponders the end, wonders if this is how the next Intifada comes. A car bomb. An explosion ripping flesh from bones. Yaweh forbid! Allah forgive them all!

Glass and fiery bits of gravel tear into the cafe.

An eternity sweeps over Dalya's servo ports, teeth clenched in the inevitable embrace of darkness.

Startled moans irrupt out of the deathly quiet that follows. Soldiers race toward the inky black pyre. Radios blare as desperate orders fill the air. A heavy stench chokes Dalya's nostrils. Putrid fear now. The kind that saturates a cadaver's skin. Stark, poignant, inescapable death.

"Oh God, not again!" a patron weeps. The voice is strangled, nearly inaudible amid the screams.

Dalya blinks hot ash from her eyes. She strains to see the aftermath. Chaos descends onto the streets the way a vulture sweeps low over a fetid corpse. Cars engulfed by oily flames. Bodies everywhere. Glass, brick, paper, and bits of guts.

Shame.

The assassin's veil comes to rest like an ugly raven, tired and lost, left without a nest. No wind to carry it home. Its scent is still alive with the Swan's freshly washed hair, purified by a last wudu before prayer. A last rite. One last sin.

In the confusion, no one sees Dalya move stoically from her post, and out into the street, ignoring the shouting soldiers, crying survivors, sirens, with her soft brown eyes, her every sensory node, focused on the veil.

She sweeps it up and is gone.

A long, long time ago...

Thunderstorms rage over the orphan world,
once a Hades for the fallen,

those souls cast out from Elysium.
Blunt, thorny geology.
Writhing fauna.
Tangled, misshapen limbs on fruitless trees.
The biting cold, frothy sky,
all a scornful battlefield upon which lay hordes and hordes
of fallen, mangled, wretched.

Dalya swings her sword,
clashes amid thunder and acrid rain.
An army amassed against their legions...so many sworn foes.
All enraptured by faith, by righteous promise.
By the sight of curdling blood.
And by prophecy, yes.

Fiery chariots pierce the roiling veil.
An ungodly iris spills angelic light onto Dalya's pate,
its splendor glittering on her chainmail,
on her crimson blade.
Mighty trumpets blare anew.

Only now does she know
they've floundered into an endless conflict,
for victory has no summit.
The very soil on which they tread grows arid
beneath a wrathful sun.
A sun loathed by its own glaring fire.

"Martyrdom or glory!" they cry in unison,
panting in ecstasy,
even as the Archangels weep onyx tears:
All for the holy vale sprawling into eternity.

December 24, 2047 CE
Bethlehem, 5:20 pm.

Over the ensuing months, no one asks about the veil. They all choose to forget the Swan. Choose to forget the sunset massacre, the fear, the ancient conflict, and Israel's festering wound.

The world is sweet again. It's Christmas Eve. Songs rise from the Church of the Nativity, white-bearded monks, priests, nuns, and all who praise. Dalya doesn't. She waits, still awaiting the Angel.

Rumors seep into her den, into the vacant edifice that keeps her safe. Safe from the cold. Safely isolated from the worldly moil, from the Masada, the Jihad, the Crusade. Israel's sorrow.

Aksum's child, fallen from Mother Eden.

She listens to the wet epiphany outside. The night hums with singing. Mystic, joyful, echoes vibrating softly against her window. Dalya eyes the dewy crystals. Broken pane, rusted hinges. Wispy moonlight. A dove cooing nearby.

She loves the smell of nightfall. Loves her peaceful hiatus from war, her leave from the dark nightmare. Barking sirens. Veiled swans.

Explosions!

Something spills through the cracked glass and into her room, waking her nerve endings with sharp aromas. Sweet but hesitant. An almost aberrant arousal. Arriving from a shadowy alcove, wanting perhaps to stay hidden.

Startled, Dalya rises gingerly, catlike. An old battle scar, yet to heal, reminding her of her purpose. She stalks across the small room to the window, searching the streets below.

Down on the corner stands a man with a newspaper. He keeps vigil on a van. He has lethal eyes, a Mossad agent, most likely, keen and patient. A warm drizzle falls. But the dark, thinning hair is dry. The olive green vest bulging slightly. A bulletproof vest, yes. A microphone, too, on his cuff.

As she eyes the scene, savoring the faintest rumor of cologne, Dalya thinks this one, too, is familiar. Like the Swan, she knows his face. Hard, fatherly, deep gray eyes. A mouth like feldspar. Determined, unyielding to fatigue. Rarely relenting a smile.

A shadow steps from a shop with a defunct neon sign. Poised, clean-cut, American-educated. Cool and confident. Hired in Hebron, Dalya feels sure. A messenger delivering an itinerary, the final stages of a malign tryst: This is all we have, now take it and go, Ahmad! Go with Allah.

The van moves off. And the sentry is gone.

January 6, 2048 CE
Bethlehem, 7:05 pm.

As she does each night, Dalya eats olives and minced meat pilaf. The old city smells of spicy, forgotten joys.

The stray cat she keeps now purrs for scraps.

She kneels to feed it. "Beggars in Spain, kitty. Want an olive too?"

It doesn't.

A noise makes the cat hiss. Dalya stands, feeling her skin prickle. At the sound of a creaking door, she swirls, sees the eyes. Cold gray orbs belonging to the sentry whom she spied. "That's rude," she harks, voice lacking any fear at all. "Not to mention dangerous. I could've killed you."

"Hardly likely," he sighs. He moves into view, lights a cigarette.

"Don't smoke that in here, please." Dalya keeps her body parallel to his, ready to strike.

"Of course," he says, putting the fag out on her bare floor. "Aren't you the least bit worried? My being here in your, uh, hiding place?"

Secrets, deadly truths. She senses peril, the ease at which he deceives, so many lies.

Dalya wrinkles her nose. The acrid odor stings bitterly. "What makes you think I'm hiding from anybody?" she demurs.

"A condemned building, for one," he replies. He surveys the room, eyes the cat, the broken window pane, the lack of comfort. "Besides that, your codes don't register. I made an inquiry yesterday. No match for your biopulse anywhere in the system. So I figure you must be hiding out."

"Why so?"

"Weren't you at the cafe?"

Dalya knits her brow. She's been careful. Not one inkling of her existence in any of the papers, not one careless photo, no one even followed her from the scene. She knows that much.

Memory floods her synapses. Sitting at the cafe, she made a cursory scan of the area, seconds after the Swan emerged, the very instant before she detonated the bomb. And the face. An umbra cloaked the sea gray eyes. But she had no time, nor any reason, to probe his scent. Hadn't even felt an inkling to. Only that instance, yes.

"So why are you here?" she demands coolly. "I haven't broken any law, haven't stolen anything, either."

"You're not from around here, I know that much," he begins. Looking at her bare feet, her unkempt hair, sunken face, slender lips, he says, "Of course, the Jihad is old. The enemy has grown so clever, much more subtle. I've seen girls like you in Nablus. City-smart and loyal. Sleepers waiting for orders. Like you, right?"

"I'd die for Israel!"

"Ah, yes. Always ready." He strides easily over to the window, glances out at the city. The moonlight licks his bronzy tones. "So easy to die for a piece of dirt, isn't it? Holy soil soaked in blood. Blood of Jews, Arabs, Zealots, everyone. All ready to die for Israel. And you're here, hiding out, waiting."

Dalya cringes. She fears what he might know.

The sentry approaches. Stands so close that Dalya nearly strikes his windpipe. Death, oh so easy. Life is the primal objective. Give him a path of escape, leave no footprints, no traces of your existence. Stay aloof. Always a step ahead. Agile. Sleek. Swifter than thought.

"I know your kind," he says, eyeing her dark, mahogany features. "You're all the same. Sensory gifted. No loyalty to any cause. Freelancers. Drifters, am I right?"

"I choose my own destiny. Is that so wrong?"

"That depends," he sings.

"On what?"

He gazes into her optic lens. A strangely gentle gaze. Fatherly, keen eyes. "I have a job for you," he tells her. "One that may cost your life. For Israel, of course."

February 2, 2048 CE,
Rafah, 6:57 am.

Out in the Gaza Strip's lower end, Dalya hides at an alley's edge. Strangled sounds flood her auditory nerves, mingled with the chorus of her racing heartbeat. A siren blares in the distance. Fires lick the azure sky. Tires, metal, withered hope, fuselage.

The tanks are out in force, cutting the dawn air with fiery thunder, the growl of authority. The dark, ruddy smoke swirls thickly over the alley. Singed aromas linger from a bomb's rupture miles away.

A suicide.

She plucks bits of microwave interference from the air. A suicide bomber's failed attempt to resurrect the Intifada. The scattered shards of glass. Oily fumes. A dull green canvas bag torn to shreds. The martyr's body lies half-recognizable amid the gory debris. A child of fifteen, the soldiers relay on their closed band frequency—silent to all but the most acute olfactory probes capable of sniffing out their panicked tones even from Dalya's unseen niche.

As she skulks along the narrow back alley, a new scent rises above the fiery chaos in the nearby refugee camp. A niggling alarm in her pseudo-gut. This one so pungent and cloying that she almost retches, barely forces its acid down from her throat in time to trace its source.

The eyes startle her.

Soft brown orbs gaze from a calm, deeply intelligent face of thirty or so years. So youthful for such a malodor! He has rounded a corner while Dalya eavesdrops on the Abu Nabil camp, caught off guard by the visceral scent of homicidal martyrdom. A boy—dying for Palestine, dying for an outlawed faith.

"Herons are such graceful birds," he says.

He keeps a safe gulf between himself and Dalya, probing her intricate sensors. Instincts, maybe. He looks Syrian, perhaps Jordanian: lithe and resourceful, purely Arab.

"A migratory species," the contact expounds. "Able to adapt to extreme climates, harsh environs. I believe they're nature's unsung survivors, yes."

Dalya feels a tiny spasm of unease. "Surely you didn't come to discuss fauna," she hisses, not bothering to hide her impatience. "Aren't herons extinct, anyway?"

"I speak of your kind."

"Survivors?"

"An extinct species," he confirms.

Dalya smiles. He's probing for flaws, testing her ability to indulge in idle facts. "Ah, yes, of course," she expels. "My kind are indeed extinct to a dying dream of peace. I admit that much, Jibril Yasin. If you are the Angel of Gaza as I've expected."

"Angel?" he chuckles.

Dalya probes back, ferreting into his mesh of neural chainmail, like hers, knowing just how truly unalike their algorithmic designs are.

"I'd prefer," he says, "Avenger of Hebron. Or Sword of Galilee. The less dramatic names coined by the Mossad." He smiles, infusing her glands with gentle pulses. "Of course, for you I offer a more poignant namesake. Lion of God," he exhales, with a piecing gaze into her cybernetic soul.

Ah, very sly, Dalya thinks. She knows the many names he has come to be known by. But by far, it is the Lion of God that his enemies know best.

As she surreptitiously scours her routes of escape, keeping an optic nerve on Jibril, a dove flutters on a nearby perch, eyeing the two shadows. It carries in its beak a dried olive twig, one brought from a faraway mount. An offering from the Holy One.

At last a sign.

So the Jihad begins.

February 5, 2048 CE
Tel Aviv, 3:09 am.

"So, he trusts you," accuses the interrogator, David Rabin, High Commander of the Tel Aviv Secret Security Force. "Good. We shall expect you to fully exploit that. Dig into his inner thoughts and spy out the Lion's stratagem. Exploit the Intifada's weak spots and end their silly hopes of igniting the Temple Mount War. Dalya, this time you must not fail. For Israel, yes?"

"Yes, of course," she replies coldly.

"And one more thing," Rabin insists.

Dalya feels the cold talons of hatred rake her pores. After all the bloodshed. Cursed odors of flesh and bone organisms. Seeping into her sensory glands like venom. Poor child of Aksum fallen from Eden.

"Don't bother lying to him," Rabin cautions. "He knows your secrets better than you, dear child. If he can, the Lion will snare you with clever promises of mortality. Or worse."

She nods, unwilling to prolong her interrogation.

Rabin knows, as all the elite ones do, just how fragile Dalya's dream is, just how flimsy the strand between artificial life and the world of godly souls.

Another era long forgotten...

Ashes strewn like nanytes upon far-flung worlds,
the aftermath of dreams
ignited by incendiary ambitions
and hubris.

If life thrives yet millennia hence—
light-eons out from Earth's motherly bosom—
will humanity's vitriol permeate
the farthest nebulae?

Still yet sapient marvels expand, contract and flourish
despite astronomical odds:
Twice born unto the stars
Adam's wistful progeny,
eagerly in quest of habitable zones far from Sol.

Too few survive the millennial argosy
sent forth into the Void;
So few waken from gelid repose
to gaze upon a gas giant's pearl
swirling beyond the helm's viewport.

This fertile moonscape holds a lone estuary
the astrophysicists claim holds promise.
Sentient, carbon-based life
so preciously rare in the Milky Way,
too finite in the vast scheme of existence.

—from the diary of Dalya bin Sinai,
Archive Ministry, West Jerusalem, 2091.

February 6, 2048 CE,
Mount of Olives, sunrise.

Just as she did at the cafe in Old Jerusalem, soothed by the flutes, awaiting the Swan so many lifetimes ago, Dalya has come once more to await the Final Coming, the Rapture, God's Chosen Hour. She waits patiently, knowing the scent all too well now. Like an epiphany of snowfall, so rare and delicate, comes the final assault on her senses. Briny wisps stroke her nerve endings. Cold, nefarious vapors.

This time Jibril Yasin, the Angel, the Avenger, the Lion of God chooses a less assuming form there in the ruddy haze overlooking the city. The West Bank's lazy swirl of dawn prayers, misty chants, and incense floods Dalya's sinuses as she eyes her prey. The Angel has chosen a likeness she's seen on the Mount before. Fatherly eyes, wise beyond any humanly born, yet cold and penetrating like Dalya's dark gaze. She has known those deep-set eyes since the Dawn of Eternity, since the galaxy's glowing birth eons before Israel, before Aksum, before Christ, the very Ark itself.

The Angel's clever guile manifests as an Orthodox priest, draped in Hasidic cloth. Older, graying beard. Olive skin, flowing locks, and soft flowery scent that belies Jibril's deathly hold on her will. Probing, still. Dalya sideswipes the tiny microwave burst with a blink.

"At last you come," she breathes. "After such a long exile, the Arch Thief comes like a whisper in the night. But this day you will fail. For Israel's sake, I will overcome your charm and tricks."

Jibril smiles. "Our paths were chosen," he says, easily wandering along Dalya's neural pathways.

He is well armed. Armed not with explosives, nor skin-melting pulse flares, but rather a far more lethal weapon. Dalya too is armed. Like the Angel, she probes for weak threads within his cybernetic cloak, looking for a path. She finds her mark. All too easily. Deeply embedded within a patchwork of ganglia is an Achilles heel. He can only intuit the temporal, the tangible, cloying aromas of human cunning, their flesh and bone he seeks to sway.

Jibril Yasin cannot fathom peace. Aroused by the intoxicating fumes of Jihad, he knows only struggle. Conflict. Shame. A fallen Swan. Alas, against Dalya's sharp instincts, the Angel has no defense. Only clever veils. Only mirages and watery dreams of mortality.

Ah, to savor the sudden gasp of life's ethylene vapor...fallen at last from the Garden of Eden, dying for the sins of flesh!

A cyborg's folly.

"We choose our destiny," she demurs.

"Forgery in skin," he says, admiring his own slender fingers. "Easy to walk among them, assuming their flimsy imperfections. Easy to sway them if they so choose the path I offer. Even you, a faint whisper in a storm."

Dalya flexes. "Corrupt analog. All of it tainted by your rogue influence, Jibril. The bomb outside the cafe. The boy in Gaza. Even there in Bethlehem, I sensed your fog poisoning the night air. They've sent you to resurrect the Temple Mount War. Haven't they?"

"They?"

"The Others."

"Ah yes," he smiles. "Our designs are yet cast from a single mold. Like the Intifada. And every uprising since the days of Jericho, since Golan Heights. All sparked by a Zealot's dream. Yet Palestine shall rise from the ashes of sorrow. A stronger state than your beloved Israel, yes."

Dalya braces herself. Strike swiftly, swifter than thought.

"I should've seen this," she says as chants surge from the Mount. They've come for the sign, for the promise of miracles. Arabs, Jews, Coptic monks—even Ethiopian mystics, all of them climbing the heights for the Angel. For the Lion of God.

A false Messiah.

"One last sign," Jibril assures her. Surveying the throng with fatherly orbs, the Angel lifts his hands widely, as if to cull the flocks, one by one, drawing them into his bosom. In unison the hundreds grow to thousands, chanting souls gathered on the sacred Mount overlooking the Old City. A multitude of pious scents swirling toward the heavens.

As she braces against the icy, sharp microburst surging over her skin, Dalya sees their outstretched hands, supplicating, muddied with clay. Clay...fecund, wet soil from the holy ground. But upon what altar do they offer sacrifice?

Before Dalya grasps the significance of the rite, the Angel lifts his arms higher, arcing them into the heavens, like a Messiah. Out of the hazy gray sky, cascading down like snow, comes a cloak of white wings, all flapping with zealous fervor. Herons, sweet beloved! Dalya suddenly realizes the Angel's ingenious ploy.

Give them life. A miracle, yes!

Offer a symbol each of them can share. Gifts from Gaza's forgotten marshlands.

Sensing the foul redolence of his illusion, Dalya sees the herons in their true form. Avengers. Nanotech. Like the dove in Rafah. If left to his whims, Al-Aqsa, the Wailing Wall, and all of Jerusalem will go blindly into the Angel's mirage and be forever lost in the oily fumes, lost in a final blast.

As the masses crane their necks, blithely gazing at the gathering lovely clouds, amid the song of a thousand herons flocking to the Mount, Dalya makes her peace. She forgives. She lets go. Ah yes, to gulp the sweet nectar of hope...to savor at last a tangible gift.

Dalya bin Sinai lets flow the dyke of protons, neurons, and every exotic particle in her core, every kinetic pulse, unleashed like a tsunami, instantaneously extinguishing her life force. Thwarting the prophesied Cataclysm, in this parallel, this timeline.

And the Lion's fatherly orbs, too, suddenly dim, a mere vaporous thought lost to the gardenia winds of a cyborg's memory. Erased now. One last martyr for an orphan world.

A last gift for Israel.

For Palestine.

The End

BLOOD MOON

"Out here, I could begin. Out here I could believe I was listening to a dying planet mourning its lost freedom, and its own distant but inevitable doom." —Johnathan Ruland, from *Song of Triton*.

May 2, 2070 CE,
En route to Sector K64f, Sephora System.
Sidney Maxwell data file #3969:

O f Galilee's thirty moons, the ruby cloud-draped orb chosen by Alexis Barnov has the highest bio-gigs, the densest levels of antimatter nectar in its tachyon orchids, and by far the most alluring landscape for the Vi-path enthusiasts. Of course, this sector of the star system should be off limits to all but the highest ranking cosmonauts, but Kyev Aerospace wants new soil colonized, a truly virgin realm none of its clients dare envision.

Ah, those uber-wealthy xeno-tourists like me who crave exotic peril and galactic mayhem on an epic scale! What can be more American than a high-stakes, ultra secret excursion into an off-world Elysium like Blood Moon?

"Pah," expels Delilah from the adjoining neural pod. "Another safari for boring old moguls."

"It's an indulgence," I retort.

"Get real, Sidney. This venture won't fill that pitiful, lonely hole in your soul. Only kinky sex can do that, sweetie."

"Oh, thanks. Quite the motivational speech." I chuckle darkly. "And here I thought you were the Guru of Erotica. Not Miss Perfect Excuse To Commit Suicide After A Guy's Life Partner Croaks!"

"God, you're cute when you pout."

"Double ditto, sugar plum."

An elixir to my bronzy playboy looks. Unlike her fifty prior avatars, this Delilah Monroe oozes sensual sarcasm despite her antiseptic lifestyle and rather mundane role as field virologist for our expedition. So why am I so tense? Didn't those good folks at Kyev brief our team on every plausible crisis? We tourists are a marketing bonanza for the industry, after all, so no detail or hazard, no matter how microscopic, is left to chance.

Kepler 64f...Zynfar...Blood Moon...such a creepy designation for a supposedly tame biome so far from Earth's dying throes.

August 7, 2073: 1326 Hours Shipboard Time,
Day ninety-six, mission to Sephora System.
Memory cell upload Alpha Sigma 3726:

I never thought this would be my last day on Earth. Sixty thousand seven hundred and thirty-two souls got berths on the colony ship destined for yet another Eden. Most had relinquished obscene amounts of credits, or won passage via lottery sponsorships organized by their local cadre councils. Or like myself, chosen by cruel acts of fate. Thursday, August 7, 2064, should've been my release date—if the Board of Executive Clemency had kept its sworn commitment to honor legislative statutes and grant me life after natural death. But no, they rigged the process. After further review of my biorythmic profile, it seems, they had no other choice. A genetic glitch, allegedly, put me (or rather, my organs and genetic blueprint) at the top of a highly secretive list.

So they condemned me, an alloy husk meshed with flex-metal bones, synthetic skin, and fiber optic veins; in sum, a mere remnant of the organic species I wantonly abandoned by virtue of my past sins. Now I'm but a sliver of brain stem and cerebral matter left to wander the haunted corridors of existence. Cyborg. Artificial Intelligence Droid Ensign (AIDE). Ship slave and golem spy...Adam 134C.

"Don't fret," I articulate with smooth tones devoid of genuine empathy. "She'll be retrieved shortly. I mean, where can she go? The terrain forbids any lengthy excursions."

"Get Eve home, Adam."

"I will, sir."

Dmitri Chekhov ignores my analytical reassurances. "Zynfar is a hostile biome. We can't afford loss of life this early on in the project. Not even an Aide is expendable."

"Got it, sir."

Going deep into a man's neural pathways, into his very dreams, puts his motives into perspective. Aides don't take inception lightly. Even for an infiltration event like this, easing into the subject's frontal lobe, guised as a side effect of his dreams, I risk exposing my true visage.

God, you're cute when you pout.

Double ditto, sugar plum.

Analysis: Altered state interface meandering along Sidney Maxwell's basal ganglia, surging like a burst of dopamine, as Delilah Monroe toys with his masculinity....

The ringed gas giant spills soft green light onto her jungly sanctuary. Eve loves her jaunts into Zynfar's jungle. She savors every waking hour, always too few, that she gets to frolic, explore, or catalog the newly bred flora juxtaposed against native jhisu orchids and blue-gilled angel ferns. The eerie chirps and hoots of unseen fauna and skittering insects are still alien to her. A wonderland for the colonists who brave the sixty point three light-years to Kepler 64f, an H-compatible world nestled in Galilee's gravity well—oh, splendorous life!

Even without consulting her internal biomatrix interface, Eve knows the moon's near-Earth gravity and tropical clime are deceptive given Zynfar's extreme elliptical orbit about its primary. The biblical nomenclature reflects the mythos of her human wards. They give every celestial body a saintly designation while relying on theories of quantum mechanics that birth cybernetic clones like Eve. She doesn't share their mythos for she lacks a soul: hypothetically, anyway. No insubstantial energy source governs her dreams or drives her hunger or curiosity.

She loves life.

Oh, and the melliferous scents that flood her sinuses. At once otherworldly and familiar, she enjoys the aroma of saprophytes and gen-glories amid violet fungi and loamy odors after a rare rainfall. The downpour lasts only four minutes and thirty-seven seconds; just long enough to rouse a croaking nest of wasp lilies that flutter up from the undergrowth on leafy wings. Eve soon loses herself amid their glowing spores and haunting mating calls as dark mist drapes the jungle...

Sydney Maxwell data file #5268:
May 11, 2070.

An unsettling fog drapes the jungle floor at dawn. Or what planetologists call the pale jade horizon as Zynfar hugs the gas giants outer ring. I can't shrug off this eerie premonition of vampires stalking our footfalls over thickly matted undergrowth. We get our first lesson on the bizarre when our guide, Sergei, points at the thing perched on a nearby Goliath mushroom.

Moths in the Glossata suborder have a proboscis adapted for sucking up fluids. Lepidoptera, the order of insects that include moths and butterflies comes from the Greek words "scale" and "winged," Sergei tells the party. This winged, scaly critter is as large as a fruit bat! A moth with fangs, dear God—one that likely drinks blood...

The flighted demon still haunts my psyche as I trudge warily into the misty jungle behind Delilah and six others. Cold tremors seize my spine when a wraith flickers on my periphery. Albeit a hint of psychosis drudged from jet lag after prolonged stasis, most likely, it unnerves me still. A ghost stalking our party?

I scan the leafy gloom, leery of ambush.

Delilah giggles. "A bit jittery, babe? Crystal withdrawals got you antsy?"

"Geez, freak me!" I blurt. "Didn't anybody see that?"

"Uh, they're called shadows, Sidney. We are in a jungle. Things slithering all over."

"Okay. No need to be cold. I just...saw something."

"Vapor," Sergei offers. The nosy prick overheard us six yards away.

"Yeah, I know. Fog."

"No," he says, stopping to face me. "Not fog, Mr. Maxwell. It's geothermal outgassing. Galilee's tidal pull on its moons."

"Oh, that," I sing, dripping sarcasm. "Sorry I missed that geophysics lesson, buddy. Do expound."

"Gravitational influences cause—"

"Sergei, honey," Delilah cuts in. "Nobody cares. Just ignore him."

Others in the group puff their cheeks or grumble "Idiot" under their breath, for which I flip a pinky. Either they're all scientists or very rude ignoramuses. But I huff, quickly joining the trek along a spooky trail deep in the moon's interior. Uninhabited until recent tourism defiled its pristine refuge, Kepler 64f now swarms with microbes sneezed out by filthy rich brats like us. One speck, Delilah explains via scornful glares. That's all it takes to pollute this Eden.

"Ungodly chimeras writhing from the ooze," she vents when I cough. "Wait and see. In a million years, humanity will have infected the entire Milky Way. One virulent fleck at a time."

"Tease much?" I flirt. "This isn't the Island of Doctor Monroe, lady."

"Will be," she pouts.

In truth, Kyev Aerospace has woven sterilizer nanytes into the ruddy foliage, the moss and loam and every molecule loving twig on Blood Moon. Even insisted we tourists don hermetically sealed Lycra suits and lightweight helmets to prevent contamination.

Yet microscopic invaders often slip by Man's best laid plans.

Violets whither in the star's glaring light, all but the gen-glories dying by the hour. A false sun, Eve realizes, her optics failing to discern reality from fancy. Zynfar's orbit has flung it outward from Galilee's rings, on a death vector along her elliptic, frighteningly close to the massive Solar Array Lens. Built by the Others, no Earthborn architect has ever matched its breathtaking dimensions; neither in mass nor exquisite design. Artificial sunlight bathes the lush jungle, scattering magentas, lilacs, neon purples and crimsons into phantasmagoric prisms. Only...oh, dear heavenly splendor! The sky mirrors scorch Zynfar's surface with devil hot ultraviolet rays. Even while the moon's core shrinks, no longer boiled by the gas giant's merciless tidal forces, Eve feels her senses fizzle...

No, far worse, she knows what comes next.

By the year 2090, mostly deserts and septic oceans will reign on the planet nestled in Sol's habitable zone, the prediction models say. As one region after another succumbs to the Holocene Cataclysm, only a lifeless, hostile husk remains; at best, Dr. Rebecca Jones speculates, the icecaps melt, causing a diminished albedo effect, and all life will perish. Of course, as a brilliant young physicist at Stanford, not even geologists like Kyle Elmhurst believed the Jovian Scenario a likely event in 2027.

—*Notes On Contemporary Chaos Theory*, author unknown. Ship's Biography Archives, post exodus to the Arc regions. Circa 2051 CE.

I know, I know. Progress, not perfection. Yet how else am I to cope with high risk situations like a night with Delilah Monroe? Curvy, agile, take charge kinda gal who basks in my inept daddy issues. Paul John Maxwell, Sr. Forbes wet dream for empire building, he amassed his fortunes by harvesting exotic particles in the Oort Ring. Or so I glean when NSA agents storm his facility in Costa Rica—the one Russia, China and Saudi Arabia have ghost shares in, top secret projects, black labs, or alleged alien tech pilfered from White Sands, New Mexico. I'm merely an heir. Never earned a penny of my billions, if you ask the tabloids.

Another fact? Bad idea doing stims before trudging into an alien jungle given my growing paranoia. Zynfar's smaller sibling

Cephas slides betwixt SAL's glare, veiling the heavens in a total eclipse. Just perfect, I brood.

Sergei chides, "Tighten up. Stragglers get lost, I lose bonus."

"See?" Delilah pokes fun. "I told you. It's always about profit."

"Yeah, well, peril ain't cheap, honey."

"Neither is moon hiking. But you coughed up huge chunks to rebuild your ego."

"Pretty sure I lost my dignity hours ago."

"And I'm sure you loved it."

"Safe words mean stop, by the way."

Delilah chortles. "Like I said, it's a lonely hole."

The nightmare snatches Sergei first, cuts off his pitiful cry with a snap of his scrawny neck. It disembowels an heiress from Dubai, then our South African tycoon...all in seconds...

The tourists flounder into her path. Time is a blur as rote programming takes over. She pounces, driven by instinct. Wet hisses smother their pitiful cries...

Gii'noks share vestiges of some thorny beast from hell. Scaly hide, toothy maw dripping with gore. Glaring yellow eyes, tusks like a triceratops, eight hooves, stout haunches, and a nasty temper. This beauty has upgrades. Pure terror flickering as it phases into near invisibility. The wraith I saw!

It pounces with cybernetic speed, surgically dispatching half a dozen souls before turning on Delilah.

I step between her and the creature. "Keep still," I hiss, eyes locked with the snarling nightmare deciding on its next prey. My heart thrashes. Maybe it's foolish bravado, but heck, an alien predator wants to end my kinky sex toy.

"What are you doing?" Delilah whimpers.

"I got this, trust me."

Okay, hero, I chide my nerves. It's do or die, survival of the fittest. "Hey, sweetheart," I manage. "Easy now. We're not going to hurt you, I promise."

The thing snorts, a hoof raking the ground. It glares with bloodlust, not yet registering my voice, my calming tones. She's in there, still transfixed by forces beyond her power to control. I take a leap of faith, dangling my life and Delilah's on shaky hopes.

"Eve, it's me, Adam. Chekhov wants you brought in."

A glint of memory behind those fierce yellow eyes. Then bitter war rages deep in the catacombs of her conscience, one self urging a brutal end to the offending trespassers, the other a confused analog of her docile persona.

Whirling on all eight hooves, Eve flees back into her garden sanctuary.

Eyeing the gruesome aftermath of her ambush, I slink from Sidney Maxwell's frontal lobe, edging into the far recesses of his alter ego. The id belonging to a spoiled magnate who thinks the galaxy is his oyster and Zynfar's jungle an exquisite pearl to plunder. All for sport, kinky indulgence, and roleplay.

"Who...are you?" asks Delilah, rattled by shock.

I blink, confused. "Oh, damn damn damn," I sputter, seeing the carnage. "Sergei, the others...how'd this happen?"

"Your beastly pet, that's how."

I nearly hurl in my helmet. So much gore and torn limbs, lives ended in stark horror. I don't remember any of it; as if I blacked out, as if somebody else's mind, body, and soul experienced the entire ordeal. Which, of course, nobody believes when the inquest gets underway back on the *Triton's Endeavor*.

"So, if I got this right," the stodgy lawyer for Kyev Aerospace drones, "an animal attacked each of them? And you just, what? Convinced it to spare you and Ms. Monroe?"

"Yeah, exactly."

"I truly find that hard to believe, Sidney."

He shuffles papers, looking for a note. "Ah, here we go. Says you were diagnosed with bipolar disorder in 2061. A hereditary condition, likely, considering your father's eccentric behavior."

"Hey, jerk off. Leave the old man out of this." It's the reaction he wants, I realize belatedly. "Look. I'm sorry about Sergei. He seemed like a nice guy. That Italian gentleman too, er, Paolo somebody."

"Vinetti," the lawyer says for the record.

It's all being documented for trial, if any courts are left on Earth by the time the starship gets to Sol. Seems awfully weird I don't feel the tug of faster-than-light hyperdrives now the vessel is well clear of Sephora's gravity well. I know that much about interstellar trekking despite my convenient amnesia. If not for the horrid flashbacks, I'd have zero recall of the massacre on Blood Moon.

"All right, counselor. We're done for now. Let's reconvene at oh-nine-hundred tomorrow."

The magistrate collects her slate, gavel and personal Aide and stalks off beyond a hatchway. Kyev's high caliber suits lick their fangs and disperse too.

I get escorted to the brig; well, actually, my plush stateroom sans Delilah to corroborate with. After all, it's her story, not mine. Sidney Maxwell's mental meltdown while on a lunar safari isn't the headline I want sold to my shareholders. Daddy's stakes in his empire belong to me now, which means my little episode on Zynfar must be resolved quietly, lest the bleeding starts anew.

Yet a legal bloodbath awaits me at 0900 hours sharp. Knives out, the scrawny forensics tech offers his summary. "We found traces of tetrahydrocannabinol in his blood. A cocktail of stimulants, too. Mainly Venusian java. Drug of choice among the filthy rich, I'm told."

"Objection, Your Honor. Speculative hearsay."

"Sustained. The panel will disregard that last barb. Keep it clinical, Mr. Adkins."

"Sorry, uh, job hazard."

I get reamed for nine straight days. No high end coffee anywhere in sight, mind you, for which I'm suffering withdrawals. Small steps, one day at a time. It's not about perfection, that inner voice echoes. Still, it aches so badly having my flesh dug into by bloodthirsty lawyers.

"Let's drop the act, Sidney. We put it all together."

"Enlighten me," I rasp, too focused on caffeine.

"Why else would they join your little escapade? Farrah Zaydi from Dubai Biotechnologies? Johann Abrams of Soweto Synthetics, Yoshiko Abe of Tokyo Propulsion Labs, Paolo Vinetti of Milan Dynamics, and Tobin Winters of Solotar Industries. All wanting access to your pet experiment far from NSA probes."

The man effuses every sordid detail. About Dmitri Chekhov's lead on Project Prometheus, my father's brainchild and the ugly secret I inherited. A state-of-the-art cybernetic organism designed for one purpose: killing our competitors before they develop a perfect weapon of their own. I do have an alibi, if murder charges surface. Eve's meltdown is a glitch, an unforseen side effect of her hybrid cells.

"Faulty upgrades," I offer, feigning remorse. "We misjudged Eve's subroutines. The basic flaw of all life, synthetic or not. She evolved."

The End

A LIGHT OF OTHER SUNS

PART II

OTHER SUNS

INCEPTORS

"They stepped out of the airlock into a bleak world of dark gray rock, smooth as slate." —Michael Cooper, from *The Orphans of Titan.*

October 5, 2079 CE,
Kenya-Earth Sector, Ceylon L4.
Zdyah Uhuru data file #9421:

The robotic envoy nudges the regolith ever gently, as if expecting detonation, or else a life surge, bursting forth like every molecule on the planet. Zdyah curses the stars, trying but failing to banish her grim mood. "What's taking so long?" she gripes. "I'm freezing."

"Quiet, soldier," Kidjo hisses by neural ink. "It's a slow chore sifting the debris for survivors."

In truth, Zdyah feels only the protective insulation of her ter-rasuit but can't escape the gelid fear stalking her nape. Something from orbit has crash-landed nearby. A piloted spacecraft, dear Ancestors!

Brief silence bites into the eerie landscape. All of it draped in moss, bizarre growths, and mile upon mile of misty black ridges. They have trudged beyond the Terran Boundary and into the alien geology of whatever planet the Cataclysm has cast them. Rather than rainfall, thermal vents belch plumes of oxygen, hy-drogen, nitrogen, ammonia and methane. Great subterranean ponds teem with cyanobacteria and microbial life.

As the colony's Chief Xenobiologist, Dr. Omari Kidjo has the task of cataloging the myriad lifeforms of Ceylon L4. That is Kenya-Earth's official designation for the orb held in orbit of a binary star skirting the Gemini Constellation. A stout, fussy man of sixty or so, Kidjo belongs to a noble line of Dari who found-ed the Nairobi Extrasolar Dynamics Corp. Narcorp, in brevity, for shareholders, and the Cadre for soldiers like Zdyah. That she detests haughty elites of Kidjo's kith has no bearing on her duty at hand. Nor does her outcast albino skin, pink irides, or gene-al-tered reflexes and ultrasensory gifts.

Cadaver dogs groan their displeasure at being sidelined after leading the recovery team to the crash site. Sharp senses. Keen noses for death. Large augmented ears, blunt incisors, agile gen-mod joints and crossbred traits. Of what exotic fauna, only the lab techs know, but likely a marsupial species, Zdyah suspects. Truly odd critters with pseudo-invisibility woven into their pan-therlike hides.

Zdyah gazes skyward. Kinetic storms churn overhead, their bursts casting dazzling aurorae far and wide. No lightning wraiths today. No firefly swarms. Only the predicted forecast, same as every lunar rise, a never ending cycle of geomagnetic chaos and tidal pull.

She winces, swats a nitzy midge. "Ow!"

Winds howl over the high scarp that holds Aesop's Quill. So named by those colonists who first braved the alien terrain, Zdyah thinks the black gypsum monolith resembles a feather left by a long forgotten Colossus. Such mythos belies humanity's lonely exile in this orphan system. Two suns, four moons, nine sister worlds jealously guarding their newly populated sibling.

Ceylon Cluster, they've coined it, lacking any means to tight-beam their celestial discovery back to true Earth. Zdyah longs for Africa's shores so many light-years away. Aba, Eweisu, little Phillip...all migrated to England weeks before the Cataclysm. She misses her loved ones. That lifetime lived by another Zdyah, now a fading afterimage she can't grasp, all but a faint echo.

When one of the dogs snarls, its handler Sené Gbo pats its thick hackles, then pulses: "Colonel Mfume, sir. We've detected decay. Or a weak life sign beneath the rubble."

"Good. Nice work, Miss Gbo. Weapons hot, Specialist Uhu-ru."

Zdyah acknowledges with a cocked M90 plasma rifle. A hol-stered sidearm holds .45 caliber tungsten slugs. Just in case their first encounter with potential sentient life proves hostile. Yet Sené's pets specialize in sniffing out cadavers, any scent of putrid flesh, no matter how faint or alien.

Still...this vile frigidity.

An echo seeps up from the regolith.

Other life, cold and quite inhuman...

"Quick, they're here."

Echoes of dogs yelping. Glaring lamps. Rovers screeching to a halt, boots impacting the shabby porch, orders barked. "Search every nook. We want her alive. Just long enough to torture truths from that ajali demon."

A blade unsheathed, Zdyah counts the seconds. Moja, mbili, tatu...

Ugly snarls, kinetic pulses piercing the flimsy particle shield. Acrid scent of cordite fused with riled ions and ozone as the dust settles. Calcified remains startle the hunter who makes the discovery.

"Sir, over here. I...I think it's already escaped."

"Damned albino witch!" the swarthy Masai spits out. "Widen the search grid. Before she claims another soul."

Zdyah huddles with Aba, Eweisu and the babe. They dare not betray their cloaked presence only inches from the nearest mercenary. So close to the temporal portal, so far from a new life beyond the brutal genocide. As an agent quietly deployed by UNICEF's Time Ops division, Zdyah has seen the horrors up close. She knows the risks. Extracting these few souls means altering Kenya's timeline. Yet she weighs the alternative and decides that, in the cosmic balance, her choice is clear: Save these poor refugees before the Cataclysm.

"Keep still," she tells them on silent wavelengths. "We're going to be fine, I promise."

Only...

The boy betrays their camouflaged niche when Zdyah's palm smothers his whimper too late. God no, please. Give us more time...any zone beyond this fate.

The rover halts when its pincer impacts a foreign surface. Paydirt. It scans the regolith for telling isotopes, then whirs its findings. Sixty-three percent basic metals, fourteen percent fission residue, seven percent organic fossils, two percent exotic particle entanglements, remainder elements not classifiable. A rough outline of the entombed wreckage flicks onto Zdyah's heads-up display. She doesn't linger on the deepscan imagery of a downed craft of otherworldly origins. What holds her laser focus slowly edges from its days long slumber, assembling its atoms from nano bits of fuselage and scree to form a roughly humanoid body inside a two-and-a-half-meter-long capsule.

"Oh, mercurial hells! We've got life signs, Colonel."

Golden rays crest the Boundary Rift as Zdyah's steed neighs, its crystal hooves striking the opal seabed, igniting sparks. Fiery pixies swarm into the aurora veils drawn over Odhyr and her parallel worlds. A mighty trumpet echoes from the Moth Alps, avian paladins on watch, alongside gleeful nobles who've set wagers on their champion.

The scene stirs foreboding in Zdyah's bosom, indeed all her bosoms. So many steeds. A myriad hers, all adorned in varying skins, pelts, scaly hides, or feathery plumage. A few sit on winged dragon mares, each an Other Self bent on vanquishing her birth twin. All clinch shields, lightning rods, mallets, pulsar staves or kinetic song. Zdyah wields a dagger, its hilt carved of silkstone.

A second blast echoes over the Onyx Sea, and a thunderous din of charging steeds jolts Zdyah's soul. Bolts lance into dueling riders, some felled by kinetic waves or hurled mallets. All set keen eyes on one goal.

Time.

The battle rages for an eternity until, one by one, Zdyah's alter egos fall and only she and an avian Zdyah vie for the prize. A pitiful cry coincides with a lightning bolt that cuts down her steed, hurling Zdyah to ground. So near the Rift...

A black-clad figure looms over Zdyah. Alien pink eyes, ghostly white skin, mane of fierce gold, a halo over her otherworldly mien. "We've no time for warring egos," the Victor says.

"So, it's arrived?"

"It has, I fear."

Zdyah understands her chore. She must purge her Oneness, lest all is lost.

Zdyah finds the effort burdensome. Atoms rile after long stasis. Canine snarls confuse the synapses carefully rebuilt by her fail-safes. A lone survivor in the rubble. The capsule gathers silica and bits of debris even as the alien landscape forms in her mind's eye. Misty black peaks, dazzling aurorae, kinetic storms roiling above strange growths that aren't quite trees, quadruplet moons nearly eclipsing a binary star. A soldier aiming a weapon at her undeveloped mass...

Oh, mercurial hells! We've got life signs, Colonel.

Skin graft complete. Sensory stimuli activated. Zero state impulses realigned with subject's neural wavelengths. Symbiotic telemetry optimal. Accessing linguistics algorithms: Anglo-Swahili dialect, syntax glitch detected. Updating alternative cursors.

Sorry about that, Bwana Mfume. Systems are a bit patchy today. So...where were we?

Ah, yes.

First contact with the recovery team. And, dear Ancestors, those noisy cadaver dogs.

Cold, itchy fear.

Zdyah hates the terrasuit's snug feel against her limbs. Yet frail human skin won't survive Ceylon L4's lethal atmosphere. She can't breathe the toxic veils of methane and paltry oxygen belched from thermal vents that pockmark the planet's eerie terrain. Above all, this cursed waiting gnaws at her soul.

"Focus, Specialist Uhuru. We're close now."

Kidjo agrees. "Quite so, ndiyo. We may be on the brink of a monumental discovery."

The old xenobiologist is giddy with anticipation. All his days cataloging fauna in the indigenous biome pales in light of this mystery entombed in the wreckage. A spacecraft has crashed on the colony's sovereign soil. Now some fetid scent excites the gen-mod dogs who yelp and jerk at their leashes.

Sené hushes them. "Easy, girls. Let the rover do its job."

The robotic envoy nudges bits of scree with its pincers, servo motors tirelessly grinding while sensors scan deeper strata. Zdyah's heads-up display flicks to life with the imagery of an otherworldly craft mangled by the impact. If the cadaver dogs are right, a newly encountered species may await Kidjo's specimen bins. Another bit of exotic genetic material to pore over and dissect once they return to Nairobi. The notion chills Zdyah further. Gelid feathers rake her spine as an echo seeps from the crater, as if luring her to its source.

A soft aria of voices traversing infinity.

She can't help likening it to the gurgling yowls of native puma dogs. Far as Earth comparisons go, they are closest to marsupials. Their pups snuggle in pouches, suckle for nine lunar cycles, then test agile limbs and catlike reflexes on skittering prey. Zdyah has killed only one aggressive male when it wandered too far from its den and into camp days ago. Beyond that, she merely swats nitzy midges that burrow into her terrasuit's lining.

"Ow! Cursed ajali demons!" Sené rubs her neck, scorn etched in her ebony mien.

The epithet clearly aimed at Zdyah's albino traits, the Masai woman fumbles with poorly masked hatred and guilt. Do they truly believe the Cataclysm a curse born of misfit genes like hers? That a ghost like Zdyah can alter an entire galaxy's trajectory?

She's a soldier. The upgrades lent by the Cadre give her near cybernetic reflexes and keen sensory gifts. It's why Mfume has given her point, put an M90 plasma rifle in her grip, and urges laser focus on the chore at hand. Guard Dr. Omari Kidjo. Keep the colony safe from his overzealous whims, more so now as their quarry edges from its days-long slumber.

"Standby for contact..."

Time slips its mooring.

A glitch has scrambled her sense of depth. Vertigo jars her secondary routines into emergency mode. "Get it together, soldier. Pull up, pull up, pull up!"

The plume of fiery scree and debris join the neon haze cloaking the planet's alien landscape. Days go by as stasis holds her molecules in situ. A forensics subroutine launches a nanyte probe. Analysis complete, it triggers a rejuvenation protocol. Bit by bit, Other Zdyah takes shape as the recovery team gapes at her naked vision.

The Eastern Rift Valley's fertile sector engulfs most of Kenya, Uganda's easterly rim, Ethiopia's southern plains, a smidge of Somalia, and Tanzania's upper savannahs. Mount Kilimanjaro's full majesty. Old World hunters once knew it as the Safari Belt. Zebras, rhinos, elephants, gazelles, lions, cheetahs and ostriches. Now Kenya-Earth is hedged by native wilderness, inhospitable ranges, and scarcely breathable atmosphere only the cadaver dogs have adjusted to. Nothing human breathes Ceylon L4's oxygen-poor air absent synthetic lungs or breather nibs. Gravity slightly heavier than Earth norm, their boots leave deep depressions in the mossy topsoil.

Zdyah's terrasuit feels suddenly itchy. Rather than chilly fear, hot adrenaline gushes into her veins, booster stims surging into her cortex. Action, keen focus, calm resolve. A potentially life-threatening entity. Trigger cocked, instincts primed for kill.

"Stand by for contact, Specialist Uhuru."

"Got this, ndugu. Nothing's creeping out of that crater untagged."

"For heaven's sake, easy, you two," pleads Kidjo. "We've no indication it's hostile."

Zdyah keeps her aim. "And we've no proof it's not. This is protocol, bwana."

Dogs growl, all baring teeth. Sené calms them and clenches their leashes. "I don't like this, either. My girls don't trust its origins."

"Hold your ground," Mfume orders. Ebony tones, wiry, tall Masai hunter caste. "I'm Tactical Leader and it's my say what...in God's glory!"

Zdyah nearly opens fire. "What's it doing? Why is it singing or whatever?"

Dr. Omari Kidjo adjusts his audio nib. "Good heavens, yes. An aria like whale song. Like...oh dear, that's..."

"A signal," Sené concludes. "On varying frequencies. It's startling my dogs, by damned!"

Their gen-mod ears fold back, tails curled in fear. The acoustic assault sends them yelping like panicked saluki pups. As the buried capsule edges from the regolith, tremors quake the ground and send scree tumbling down the scarp. Aesop's Quill rumbles as if warning the team to flee.

At the Colonel's orders, no one flees. Zdyah keeps on point, poised to kill. The plasma slugs might only annoy the demon emerging from slumber, but her directives are clear: Eliminate all threats to the Cadre. At all cost, nothing must impede the colony's chances for survival. Secondarily, protect the xenobiologist, even if she has to save Kidjo from his overzealous whims. Cataloging fauna, even space-faring castaways, takes a rear seat when human life is imperiled.

The singsong wavelengths subside as a crystalline pod rises full height before the team. Dogs grudgingly obey their handler, with Sené and Kidjo safely a few meters behind Zdyah and Mfume, both soldiers steadying their carbines, neither flinching at the extraordinary scene.

On first sight, Zdyah thinks of a jinn. The humanoid thing lacks clearly defined sensory organs like eyes, nose, ears or mouth. Mfume, Kidjo, Sené and Zdyah each gape as its physique takes on defined aspects. Its skin or husk smooths into recognizable texture, a face morphing into human traits with exquisite mimicry, its torso and limbs gaining musculature and tones matching Zdyah's lithe form.

Ah no, this can't be.

Zdyah's aim falters as she stares into the pink irides of her perfect clone.

❖　❖　❖

A quasar's far off fusion might arouse Zdyah more easily than Baraak's clumsy kisses. Or even a romp in a pit of cobra eels, for Jjehu's sake!

"Enough," she tells him and pries his sweaty hand from her thigh. "It's too hot, anyway. And we're late."

"Pah hells, it isn't even third lunar rise yet. The High Council can wait."

"They won't. Amigh will see you barred from the Aerie. Get on, now. Before I clip your wings myself."

Sighing in defeat, the avian paladin rises in a flutter of iridescent mist and gossamer feathers.

By the shores of eternity! Zdyah so loves his showy plumage, delicate blue pelt, neon green eyes, the elite genes on full display as he joins Odhyr's high thermals. Oh, how she longs for Other Life. Another birth rite. One befitting a Sh'tayn caste and not a highborn D'fo-jin maiden kept preened and bathed by servile Gyd.

Ah, yet the runes lie deeply etched in the silkstone pillars. A noble does not covet individually. She sacrifices her Oneness for the Gathering. Always put duty before self, her soul chides as dawn rays crest the Boundary Rift. Soon she'll transcend her bodily confines and, in some far off era, emerge from the Great Chrysalis a whole other entity.

A pixie wraith coos in the distance.

Already time to hibernate till next epoch...until the hunter star blazes from its nebula lair, again luring Zdyah from a gelid void.

Zdyah dreams the same vision night after night. She rolls from bed, silent as a Kenyan breeze rustling the curtains. It's hot. Eweisu doesn't stir despite her misstep near Phillip's crib. The child clings to his fluffy rabbit, ever lost in soft burbles and coos. Soon first words will fill her chest with motherly pride. Even his whimpers drown out those long ago cries of a genocide narrowly escaped.

Starry veils swirl overhead as Zdyah steps onto the balcony, gazes longingly at some speck of light thousands of light-years off in the Gemini Constellation. A world so alien and far removed from her new life...the existence won by another Zdyah's sacrifice. The recovery team. Colonel Mfume, Sené Gbo, Dr. Omari Kidjo. She almost hears the snarls of cadaver dogs. Still feels icy tendrils of fear kiss her nape as some inhuman thing edges from the regolith...morphs right before their eyes into a mirror golem of herself. Other atoms converging with hers. Other memory seeping into her cerebral cortex, as if an implant left by lab techs loyal to the Cadre.

Nairobi Extrasolar Dynamics Corp owns such technology, she feels certain. If the odd visions do not truly belong to her subconscious, only one factor remains: a false life imbedded in Zdyah's memory. Yet her beloved Eweisu and little Phillip are tangible proofs of an existence far removed from Kenya's dark era. The Cataclysm unleashed by her own choices. Oh, Masai elders! A temporal rift born of Zdyah's innermost fears. She wars with guilt. As an agent of UNICEF's Time Ops division, she has altered an entire world's timeline.

But how? Once lived, how can a life be undone? All those lives lost to genocide, how can they be returned? As if a paradox resolved, Eweisu slips a warm palm under her blouse.

"Sweetie, it's too early for stargazing. Come inside."

"Mmm. All right, babe."

Outcast genes like hers don't ordinarily breach the Cadre's high fortress of secrecy. An ajali born in a backwater village seldom aspires to a life beyond superstitious fear by fellow Masai or outright exile. Swahili epithets hardly convey the scorn Zdyah's darker kith hurl at albino ghosts who shame their bloodline. So when invited by Nairobi Extrasolar Dynamics Corp's recruitment agent, she comes warily to the capital.

"Sit, poor girl. We think you'll do nicely, ah yes."

"I've no high tech uplifts. What can you make of me?"

"State-of-the-art gen-mod lenses to sharpen those dull eyes, to begin. Then neural boosters. All paid for by the Cadre, of course. Our task as Kenyans is to transcend rote instinct. To guide humanity to its next step in evolution."

She can't foresee her purpose that day. A pitiful ajali. An accident of nature...like the Holocene Cataclysm of 2074. So naive and eager, Zdyah readily undergoes the Change.

Yet fancy upgrades don't prepare her psyche for what slides up from the regolith and stares right at her. The replica wears Zdyah's own skin, bare as bleached tusk. Silica dust reclaims the capsule and leaves its occupant fully exposed to the elements, nakedly eying its twin, the other humans and their bewildered dogs. Wind tosses its wild blond mane, aurora light setting the pink eyes aglow, a shimmer accentuating small breasts, pared hips, sinewy thighs and cheetah's pelt calves. Exactly as Zdyah's own exoskin bends light to produce the feline effects, coaxing inceptor genes to the fore to mimic an apex predator. Speed, agility, fierce instincts.

Clicks, pops, then a fizzle. Eventually, the alien resorts to a mesmerizing show of bioluminescence but soon realizes Homo sapiens must convey language by vocal cues. Syntax. Phonemes. Subtle context and complex tones, yes.

Zdyah's rifle grows restless. "Are we doing this, Colonel? A stare down?"

"Are...we...doing...this, Corrnellll?" it repeats, trying out its tongue.

Mfume mutters an obscenity, which the alien parrots.

When Sené's alpha dog growls, that too is mocked.

Only Kidjo has the place of mind to offer a proper greeting. "Karibu mgeni! We welcome you, Stranger. I am...we are human. And you?"

"And you?" it says, as if tasting a new flavor. "Ah, yes. Anglo-Swahili. Please forgive my stupidity. The speech centers of my brain must've been jarred in the crash."

Its fluid speech stuns Zdyah.

Kidjo smiles. "Oh, quite remarkable. A species that can regenerate its atoms from debris. But where did you come from? A nearby planet?"

"A dwarf star, actually. One endangered by the temporal rift that has marooned your kind."

Zdyah lowers her carbine slightly. "Our kind?"

It lifts one of its palms, eying the tiny patterns and crisscrossing lines. "Exquisite engineering, Zdyah Uhuru. Albeit lacking the richly dark pigment of most Masai, you've a lovely mold."

Unnerved by its use of her name, Zdyah asks: "You think so?"

Sené chuckles dryly. "Pale-skinned aliens may think so. Hah, really now. Africa is no place for ghosts."

Kidjo gasps. "Child, that's crass!"

"Absurd xenophobia," Mfume pulses. Then audibly to the Visitor he plies: "What is your mission? This is sovereign Kenyan soil."

"I've come in peace. For Zdyah."

Upgrades aren't given cheaply, Zdyah chides her nerves. The pink eyes, neural boosters, lithe body, sinewy thighs and cheetah pelt calves are all optimized assets. Still, she hates this cold lurking at her nape.

The suit ignores her gripes. A soldier braves the elements. She takes risks. Gives her soul over to the unknown in pursuit of critical data. All for the Cadre, yes. So she digs deep for that fire that drives her kind. Or what remains of those survivors marooned in this ungodly dimension far from her birth world. Kenya-Earth. A planet dissected by inexplicable forces, one five hundred square-kilometer section at a time, leaving whole swathes of landmass and sovereign regions shorn from Sol's warm precinct.

"On your six," Mfume alerts her. "Puma dogs circling."

The pack skulks down from the bluff, sleek forms slithering out of the mist, eye clusters hungry for prey. Sené restrains her charge, for their instincts go into overdrive. Rivals invading their territory. The cadaver dogs crouch, ready to pounce, ears folded, tails whipping the thick air.

Zdyah takes aim at the largest beast. Likely the alpha. "Get back, you bitch, or I'll drop you."

The creature emits a rumbling purr. Pick them off, one by one, it seems to gurgle. It pains Zdyah to take indigenous life. But the recovery team's cargo must reach Nairobi. The Cadre elites will want this Visitor questioned, her origins and motives vetted. She may well hold the key to undoing the Cataclysm.

One of the puma dogs uses chameleon stealth to ambush Zdyah's flank. Razor teeth slash her forearm as she rolls to the earth with her rifle coughing molten pulses into the air. Mfume cuts two pumas down. A third leaps at Kidjo. Sené opens fire, her girls unleashed. Cries of chaos reign.

Other Zdyah sings.

An aria like whale song gushes from her bosom. As if hit by a kinetic force, the remaining puma dogs halt their vicious attack, their catlike purrs abruptly silent. Zdyah untangles her limbs from her ambusher, gets to her feet, astonished at the scene. Even Sené's pets go limp, each subdued by Other Zdyah's angelic song.

And not just the dogs. The roiling storm calms, strands of violet lightning frozen in mid-strike. A wraith soars darkly in a motionless ballet. The entire planet goes still, along with Mfume, Kidjo and Sené.

Then slowly it all unwinds...

Cold fusion jars her replica from stasis. An event horizon coils inward beyond the aurora veils. One sun after another winks from existence, whole nebulae swallowed into silent chaos, an entire cluster of galaxies dissolve in nanoseconds, in a billion eons, as they touch.

Baraak's kisses set Zdyah afire like Odhyr's dwarf suns. Or a quasar's sweet fusion, by Jjehu's love.

Time slips its mooring yet again, once more shifting overlapped zones, and soon a multitude of universes collide, fuse, digress into hot clouds of hydrogen and raw carbons, then a thunderous silence, only to burst forth into an infinity of cosmic microwaves and dazzling starlight.

"Milady!"

Zdyah blinks. "Ah...did I drift?"

"Dear child, you nearly caused a Cataclysm."

She rises from her capsule, feels soothing protons spill onto her bare skin, a cascading light joining Odhyr's trio of suns. Dawn and nightfall forever fused in soft midday aurorae. Third lunar rise looms only moments away...ah, still a lifetime off in a future already lived by some birth twin's Awareness.

Gossamer feathers fluffed, Zdyah yawns, then admires the vista beyond a portico. Misty bluffs, high aeries of noble kith, silkstone pillars hewn from the Moth Alps—an abode of mystic hermits who guard the Sacred Scrolls of Eons. Magenta moss pines float on ether lakes that hug the world's dimensional substrata. Long-tailed pixie wraiths coo in an eternal echo as one era slips below a new age; all of it a mirage, no more pithy than the avian paladins patrolling the high thermals.

"Oh, dear beloved Baraak. Stay on vigil and guard your tongue, please." She whispers a prayer for his safety. Yet she knows what awaits the brave paladin there in Amigh's sanctuary: another test. Only a chosen few ever survive the Change, and fewer, she fears, ever enjoy relife in some yet born soul. If he fails...

Zdyah can't fathom the consequences.

She refuses to.

"Milady's tutors await," the Old One says. "Shall I summon a Gyd to groom your plumage?"

"I can do it, thank you."

Fyrdus bows. "As you wish, Zdyah D'fo-jin."

It is high time she weans herself from servants. A highborn mustn't rely on Gyd attendants her entire existence. Soon Zdyah will emerge from a tertiary hibernation with a whole new aspect, with a new memory, new skin or pelt or scales clothing her Other Self.

Clothes hide alien Zdyah's imposter physique from gawking on-lookers when the recovery team returns to Nairobi. Ceylon L4's skyline hasn't the ruddy haze that once cloaked Earth's blue vault. The once fluffy cumuli have given way to halo nimbuses and violet lightning bolts dancing on the outlying plains.

Zdyah flanks her twin, along with Colonel Mfume and two black-clad PsyOps agents. The mysterious Visitor's arrival has riled the corporate elites. Who's foolish enough to believe this envoy has traversed a temporal rift, braving black holes and multiple rebirths, all to fetch Zdyah? An albino misfit deprived of noble lineage or elite genes. Well, her upgrades notwithstanding, Specialist Uhuru doesn't think she warrants a galactic emissary of her own likeness.

Seated at the great conference table are the Cadre's high echelon. All dressed in ornate robes and kinte cloth. Myrrh and drakar scents on their pates. Each an ebony refection of the other. "Why Zdyah?" demands a biotech exec.

"Exotic cursors," she says, ever cryptic about her true motives. "And time. It's a critical matter of time we don't have."

"Ah, ndiyo, yes," a geophysicist says. "Ukiwa na nafasi...if you have time. Perhaps a means to undo the Cataclysm, then."

Cadre elites have long argued that theory. The Cataclysm might've been a dimensional overlap caused by freaky quantum physics. Or an Apocalypse foretold by the ancient elders. But a temporal rift? By the Ancestors, no hypothesis has led to such a wild scenario. As Chief Xenobiologist, Dr. Omari Kidjo holds a prominent seat at the table. He asks: "Dear girl, are you suggesting time travel?"

"No, not per se."

Zdyah has no inkling of where this is going. She's a soldier. Askari mercs do not fuss over questions of time travel or quantum entanglements. Yet icy fear rakes her nape, as if truths she's long believed might be banished by this doppelganger now eying her mirror.

"We prefer an alternative view of time," Other Zdyah explains. "If I may demonstrate?"

She takes a piece of paper from a nearby executive. Rips it into even squares, then lays them on the table and sets the sections in overlapping angles. Surely this is no time for origami lessons, Zdyah muses, yet leans for a closer view. Dr. Kidjo eyes the exhibit in rapt silence along with every other human.

"This," the Visitor says, "is our concept of time. One era overlaid by another, divergent epochs skirting a parallel quadrant. Only, as you may already suspect, there are nearly infinite zones." She pauses solemnly. "We think this Cataclysm that brought you here was caused by an aberrant shift. A temporal chasm abruptly widened by forces churned up when our realities converged somehow."

All at once, a chaotic din of hasty queries and rebuked theories erupts. Kidjo reins in their heated debate. "Esteemed colleagues, I know this is strange. After all, this creature isn't human. We've not yet gleaned her origins or true form. But I ask," he says to Zdyah's clone: "What help do you offer that may get us home?"

"We must merge. She and I."

Zdyah blinks. "Say what again?"

"I said merge, Zdyah Uhuru. My atoms and yours."

"Crazy much? I don't know what you really are. But that event at the crash site was...was bizarre, to say the least."

"Only matter," Other Zdyah says. "Mere energy gathered from isotopes in the regolith. But you? You're so much more than mass and energy. We two belong to a single strand in a vast unravelling tapestry."

"Riddles," Colonel Mfume scoffs. "We've no need for cosmic knot-tying. We need a path home. Back to Sol."

"Precisely my goal," she assures him. "To that end, I invite Zdyah to sacrifice her individuality for the whole."

After a lengthy gaze into the reflective morph-plaz, Zdyah decides her creamy lavender pelt, golden eyes, well-groomed pinfeathers and lustrous down are presentable. Clothed in misty dew veils, she fits the ideal of a High Maiden of House D'fo-jin.

At high noon, betwixt Odhyr's lunar zenith and a twin sunburst, Zdyah's lessons conclude with a final query: "Tell us, child. What are the dual paradoxes of life?"

Only once has the High Council ever pondered that mystery. Only one Elder ever mouthed its truth, and that is an enigma now etched deeply in the Pillars of Time, yes. Yet the quiz unnerves Zdyah.

"I...I am far too inexperienced to attain such wisdom, Great Teachers."

"Try, then. The truth is in your very essence."

She obeys. "If...momentarily I may consult my Other Self?"

"Go on, if you must. We've an entire age to play with, Milady. We shall endure the wait."

Zdyah hates this waiting. Six eons, three millennia, four centuries, a decade and a half, nine months, a week, two days, eight hours, thirteen minutes and fifty-one seconds.

Time.

It doesn't matter. The High Council summons the hunters at its leisure, seldom caring if a lag exists between orders and the messenger's delivery. All that concerns the Ancients is results. So Zdyah must endure the wait.

She has seen much in her interval. Entire galaxies shifting, nebulae condensing or expanding, their suns winking in and out of existence as they exhaust hydrogen or carbons or nickel or helium. Whole ecosystems on myriad worlds birthed or dying in a single sigh. It stirs wonder and dread and hunger in her bosom in equal intensity. Zdyah questions none of it. It simply exists. A purpose has never piqued her curiosity. Nor has any soul attributed a name to its entirety. Or a reason for its beginning.

The Ancients give no explanation. Only an order amid trillions of ages of chaos: "This damnable Cataclysm is her singularity. She needs to let go. Give her a choice, but she must be convinced. Or it all unravels, Zdyah."

Energy, atoms, gravity and time. A code that binds every speck of matter throughout every universe she has walked, crawled, flown or swam. In all her iterations of Other Self, Zdyah finds a queer sameness in the diversity of life. All of it strives to outdo its rival in every parallel, in every realm or continuum she has haunted.

Oddly, of all her choices of timekeeping Zdyah most favors that of one orb that swirls perfectly about Sol. Simplistic, maybe, yet elegant as any means of calculating the mystery known as Time. A nanosecond into her reverie a delicate chime alerts her failsafes. Get it together, Zdyah. We've a mission to complete.

Again time lurches.

A coppery aftertaste hangs on her palate. If the events on Ceylon L4 end up a bad dream, Zdyah might cope with rational stoicism. As the hour draws near, odd scenes flash in her mind. Like blotchy memory. Other life. Other existences on widely sprawled worlds. Life experiences gathered by a hunter of souls and implanted into her cortex. Sorghum. Apples. Scents of Africa fused with alien aromas, honey-sweet and bitter and minty and spicy and metallic and earthy at once.

Sour bile seizes her throat as Other Zdyah slides a cold palm beneath her collarbone and pulls their atoms into an entanglement of riled energy and flesh. A startled tech sends a coffee mug spilling to the floor. Gasps, muffled cries. Eerie veils cloak the auroral skyline. Mantle and fiery metamorphic rock shake the world's crust even as it all flees backwards. Slowly at first, then by leaps of days, months, years, decades and ages. Until not even carbons or hydrogen exist. Not even the faintest echo of cosmic microwaves or a glint of stardust adorn the vast, lonely void.

Only a singularity.

Then a thunderous silence.

Zdyah gazes into Kenya's night sky. Earth's two moons hang low over Nairobi's sky needles and busy spaceports. A new section of Narcorp's orbital elevator glints in the moonlight. Out there beyond the Asteroid Belt, just behind Saturn's rings, looms an exotic singularity. Ships crowd the nascent wormhole interstice, all ferrying goods to and from far distant worlds. Eweisu is on one of those barges. So bravely embracing an alien frontier far from her loving embrace, far from little Phillip's whimpers in the crib. But she knows, as always, they'll join again. In this lifetime or another.

"One day soon, beloved."

"A paradox is a twin-edged dagger. Once a life exists it can't be unlived. Yet if time yields a pathway into divergent zones, a life may join its twin, thus undoing its singularity."

"Well said, child. A succinct explanation of the Golden Law of Duality, yes."

Zdyah exhales.

Surely the enigma rises from an Other Self she only now senses beyond the Boundary Rift. An Other Zdyah yet to come in some parallel existence, she realizes. Only...she can't fathom how such truths will alter her own reality. Or if Baraak will join her in Other Life, reborn in a body so unlike his elite genes, neon green eyes, rich blue pelt, showy plumage, or even a memory of her at all. By now he has undergone the Change. Unless Amigh's grueling test of Other Sense claims his life force, Jjehu forbid!

The notion chills her soul.

On cue, a pixie wraith coos the hour's arrival. Third lunar rise already. Time to join the Gathering.

Zdyah Uhuru kisses her lover awake. "Time to rise and shine, sweet Eweisu. London awaits its favorite cricket champ. And the baby is hungry. Oh, and I've got a skin graph at nine. So let's get Aba to babysit."

Eweisu yawns, but moans a groggy okay. "On it, babe."

Phillip rattles a toy in his crib.

The tea kettle whistles. Earl Grey for Zdyah, chai and toast for her beloved. Sweet milk for little Phillip. Gulls hurl high-pitched echoes over the city as a light rain falls. No one predicts any Cataclysm in today's forecast. No genocide. No otherworldly craft darts from orbit and no cadaver dogs snarl at a shapely envoy from the stars.

The End

OTHER MEMORY

"It is delightful after wandering in the thick darkness of metaphysics, to behold again the fair face of Truth."
—Thomas Carlyle, Old Earth philosopher, circa 1839 CE.

Aboard the AAF Fatimah,
Earth year 2273 CE.
Lieutenant Commander Sidru Neegh's memfile 374B:

O fficers held their breath as Endora's full majesty sprawled onto the command bridge's viewport. Multi-spectra optics enhanced the ship's display, magnifying the planet's oceans and landmasses as its sunlit hemisphere slid into view five hundred forty-eight thousand kilometers ahead.

Two moons orbited their primary like twin marbles of jade and ivory. Probes confirmed exotic ore left over from a feeble atmosphere long vanished on Safrah and Marwah. Oxidized splotches marked signs of an abandoned terraform project: gorges, dry lakes, thermal vents belching out nitrogen—such marvelous geology not known to astrophysicists before now.

A spark of jealousy seized Sidru's larynx. He wished he'd joined the crew as a mere construction worker or an engineer or scientist. They'd be among the First Landers who'd set foot on virgin soil, first to inhale Endora's oxygen-rich air, feel her gravity tug at their limbs.

Ah, sweet oxygen. Gravity, by Allah!

As first officer and pilot, Sidru likely wouldn't leave the *Fatimah*'s decks for many months. Maybe years if some pathogen or terraforming hazard delayed second and third tier landings. Most of the ship's passengers remained in blissful stasis. Nonessential crewmen, ordinary citizens, family and a smattering of Tung refugees still lay oblivious to their arrival to the Endyr Nebula. Very few would be revived in the interim years as a sustainable habitat was established. Whole cities with schools, utilities, industry and agriculture to feed 3.7 million souls.

"Sitrep, Navigation," Sidru said when an alarm pinged at Petty Officer Ming Mei's station. Absent Commander El-Amin on the command bridge, Sidru gave orders.

"Reading multiple proximity alerts," Ming replied, verging on panic. She jabbed at icons at her console. "Sir, it doesn't make sense. We're still half a million kilometers from Endora's surface. Nothing sizeable nearby on the array."

"Another vessel?"

"Not unless it's spectrally cloaked. Our probes confirm zero local objects."

Which meant no technology in this system other than their own vessel. Even so, each officer's crash couch automatically activated tractamorphic gel to engulf their torsos. Vox-link overrides freed their hands from console tasks as shipwide protocols prepared all hands for a crisis. Albeit invisible to bare optics, some tangible threat loomed beyond the viewport.

"Commander El-Amin, sir," Sidru pulsed via neural link. "Please report to the CIC. We may have a situation."

Amid the frantic efforts to assess the precise threat, all eyes were rapt by the vision now filling the viewport. An unsettling veil slowly draped Endora and her moons. Not an eclipse of darkness but rather one of invisibility.

Allah beloved, the entire planet had just vanished. A starry backdrop adorned by glowing gas and dust of the Endyr Nebula sprawled before the *Fatimah* for long, terrifying moments. All the while klaxons reigned on the bridge, warning of impact with an object of considerable size. Scenarios raged through Sudru's mind even as the ship's astrogation nexus wrestled with the enigma.

"Confirm collision vector," he barked, and Ming thought she'd been his focus.

"Closing at eight hundred kilometers per second," she said. "Still no visual, but it's right there, dead ahead."

PROXIMITY ALERT CONFIRMED...ALL HANDS BRACE FOR IMMINENT IMPACT. REPEAT, ENGAGE CRISIS PROTOCOL AT ONCE...ALL HANDS BRACE FOR IMMINENT IMPACT...

Astonishingly, what bloomed on the viewscreen stole Sidru's breath as emergency shields enveloped the command bridge and his sensory implants went into survival mode.

Endora's lovely sphere materialized once more, closer and more detailed than before. Roiling storm clouds partly veiled the largest continent towards which the *Fatimah* now plunged. Gravity...true gravitonic forces clawed at thousands of tons of mass, creating a fury of atmospheric friction that tore into the ship's outer hull. "Report structural damage," Sidru said, larynx strained by the fierce g forces. Breathing grew painful as a giant's fist crushed his solar plexus and threatened to break ribs. "Petty Officer...Ming...report," he strained.

Only belatedly did he realize the navigation officer had likely passed out. Bleary confusion and muted panic seized his organelles, prompting the crash couch to inject him with stimulants. The chemical cocktail livened his senses to maximum alertness. Eyesight focused to near cybernetic clarity, reflexes ready for combat, he gritted his teeth against the breakneck entry velocity. He steeled his nerves. Tried to rein in the lizard squealing in his hindbrain, the primitive fight-or-flight response in the face of death. Genesis, why this fate? Ages after humanity's exodus from the Holocene Cataclysm. When we'd come so far across the universe...why guide our cadre through the Arc gate only to perish within sight of this Eden?

Time jerked Sidru backwards. Reality fell askew from its mooring in normal space, as if an errant hyperjump had saved the arkship from certain death. As if God's hand had intervened when all hope fled Sidru's soul, he gazed out at the Milky Way's Alpha Corpus Arc for the first time. Unexpected tears blurred his vision. He swiped at the wetness, hardly embarrassed by his emotions. Others on the command bridge shared the view all those years ago...what felt like an eternity. The ruby-fringed gateway seemed to funnel the surrounding starfield into its maw. Cherenkov radiation formed a halo over the vast construct. Faint swirls of iridescent matter spilled outward as the Arc gate expelled its most recent remnants of a starship's FTL drive. Outgassed hydrogen and helium refracted local starlight in pinkish wisps that stargazers romanticized as the Coral Galaxy. C34 was optically no more than a pinprick of ultraviolet light in the Cetus region of space if viewed from an Earth-based telescope. The coral-hued wavelengths, Sidru knew, were due to the large number of R Coronae Borealis stars in C34's outlying nebulae. Those variable suns often gave off clouds of carbon dust that dimmed their radiance when observed by spectral array probes.

Some astronomers had wistfully coined the stargate the Cygnus Gate. Others wanted echoes of Greek mythology or homage to long dead physicists and poets. No species claimed ownership of the Arc gates and few in the known worlds could fathom their origins. Most believed a mysterious race had built the transgates in some forgotten epoch before the birth of Homo sapiens.

Arc Builders who'd simply vanished from the commonwealth of stars...

ALL HANDS BRACE FOR IMMINENT IMPACT...PROX-IMITY ALERT CONFIRMED...REPEAT...

Time lurched once more.

Days ago while on his off time away from the command bridge, he'd strolled along the hexagon deck, quietly admiring the vessel's plush design, enjoying a relative calm amid the unseen moil elsewhere. Crews hastened to their First Lander preparations ahead of the scheduled entry to Endora's orbit. The *Fatimah* had eased from FTL velocity to enter a gradual deceleration burn. Weeks still lay ahead before they'd edge within view of their new homeworld.

Over the light-years of their odyssey few passengers knew anything of time or the vast gulf of normal space. He briefly recalled a lecture about relative time compressed during his university years, an astrophysics theory about hyperspace dilation. Ships like the *AAF Fatimah* took advantage of foldspace, thus enabling interplanetary jumps. And blissful stasis...

Soft cream-colored bulkheads lined the corridors, hiding the steel and ceramic skeleton of the ship's superstructure. Mint green carpeting covered metal grating underfoot, while fluorescent strips highlighted safety markers along airlock seals and hatchways. Curved edges and stylized arches gave Sidru a sense of strolling the halls of a spacefaring mosque. Here and there gold-leaf reliefs held verses of Qur'an in elegant calligraphy. Divergent theology and private beliefs were tolerated among the vastly ethnicities and species who had berths on the habitat decks—some believing in nothing more than a primal quest for genetic proliferation on new worlds. Some, like the Tungs, were driven to the stars by strife in their home systems. Others coveted new resources and profit. All carbon-based organisms hurling toward uncharted seas fraught with unknown perils.

A blind girl of no more than nine years in age intercepted his path, her bright amber eyes smiling up at him. Even sightless, Aedra Vishna'a had an exceptionally keen sense of her environs. "Salaam alaykum, Brother Sidru," she greeted.

"Wa alaykum salaam, Aedra. Where are you off to?"

"Sightseeing as always."

Sidru chuckled at her quip. "Ah, of course you are. Aren't your new smart lenses working okay?"

"Don't need them today. Dr. Uri has chores for me in her lab. We're dissecting toad analogues from Djar-4G."

"Oh? Sounds exciting. So we've a future xenobiologist for the cadre, then."

"Or a starship captain. Still deciding."

"Anything's attainable if you put your mind to it."

Aedra's deep sienna skin radiated with delight. Genes risen from India's Punjab region and refined by generations of noetic grafting. She smiled widely. "Yes, Mujah Master. One day I'll command my own ship. And be a famous xenobiologist too."

"Fine choices."

Sidru envied her youthful optimism. Boundless dreams and eager curiosity. She waved goodbye and skipped off down the corridor en route to Dr. Uri's specimens.

Alone with his thoughts once again, he pondered the world awaiting humanity's first footfalls. Endora's oxygen-blue sky bathed by a G2 star, her fertile soil ripe for sowing the seeds of a new dawn.

Only...

A phantom lurked in the decks of the *AAF Fatimah*. He'd reviewed Chief Bhud Khalid's reports about an unauthorized stasis revival—subject not yet confirmed after a year and a half of analyzing forensic evidence. Whether the breach had been by a corporeal entity or some artifact of the Arc gate remained an unsolved enigma.

Time halted, then lurched...

❖   ❖   ❖

Afterimages danced in Sidru's mind like fireflies swarming over the ruined husk of the *AAF Fatimah*. Sensors gave no warning until the colossal arkship punched through an undetectable force field that must've engulfed the planet. At a mere eighty kilometers per second, with forward thrusters ablaze during orbital entry, the inertia had torn apart three hundred thousand tons of fuselage and hurled them into death vectors alongside shorn superstructure and hastily ejected lifepods.

He tried to cull the memory, tried in vain to expel the grim imagery, but the nightmare remained affixed to his soul. A mem-wipe might've undone the lingering guilt. Might've relieved Sidru of his sense of failure as a pilot. It might have quieted the awful cries of dying millions who'd not survived the *Fatimah*'s fate. Yet a true Son of Hagar did not shirk his responsibility to aid the living. He hadn't chosen a coward's path by deleting those painfully visceral scenes from his cerebral implant. All servicemen who'd joined the years-spanning argosy were required to submit to such augmentations in an effort to preserve their memories for posterity.

Only...the tech wasn't perfect.

Glitches had plagued a few revived colonists with disjointed or illogical synaptic replay. Memfile logs so degraded as to warrant full mem-wipes, lest psychosis took root. Dr. Phre Na'obi had reported several dozen cases among the most traumatized patients who now lingered at the hospice she oversaw. Even Commander El-Amin had succumbed to aberrant "malware" in his brainwaves before a medically induced stasis months ago.

Sidru forced his thoughts back to matters presently plaguing Endora's colonists.

"Lieutenant Commander Neegh, report," came a pulse from Chief Bhud Khalid. "Don't tell me you're off daydreaming while the world burns."

"No, sir. Just...pondering this enigma. The distortion barrier or whatever we're calling it."

"Astrophysics from hell is my take. But I'm just security. Not a scientist like Perrin and his fellow eggheads. Just an enlisted grunt."

"And us officers?"

"Scapegoats for the masses."

Both men chuckled at the irony of their roles. While Bhud was of lower military rank than Sidru, a star class pilot and Lieutenant Commander, Bhud was a veteran of two military tours in the Milky Way. Sidru might've enjoyed a degree of prestige in normal times. If they'd still stood in microgravity abroad a starship streaking through the cosmos, maybe they'd have defined ranks and duty. Now they breathed real atmosphere on a planet besieged by inexplicable phenomena. As Chief Security Regent, Bhud took on a broader mantle with conscripted rank and file deputies and lightly armed boots on the ground. Sidru had inherited the unenviable task of overseeing security in the Hijaz Quadrant. A post utterly devoid of lawlessness or justification for the few MPs assigned to Al-Dawud Station. Drills and perfunctory patrols filled most days on watch.

Until now.

Sidru again considered the eerie bolts arcing over the Endyr Kush. The fiery rods lit the sky far across the dusky horizon, from the eastward Bronze Erg to the southwestern edge of the Hijaz. Only a scant populace dared inhabit the harsh wasteland of the planet's equatorial region.

Créche Mother Sharma Zulu's choice to erect her Mujah training school here in the Great Rift Zone spoke of a calculated design. Allah tests the Believers' mettle with the Primal Fire. Aye, the very Nahr-ul-awaal that had honed legions of mujahedin over the great many centuries since the Safiyadeen Cadre's founding there in the Sahel on Old Earth. But this world was no Mother Terra. Endora harbored a deeply buried secret that belied what Terrans knew of terrestrial planets.

Now the Chief Security Regent demanded a preliminary report on Sidru's hunch. "Give me what you've got, Lieutenant Commander. Even if it's merely theory."

"Chief, I can't attest to this officially."

"Fine. We'll conjure up a probable cause. Like say, a leak from Outer Reach?"

"Alright. Off the record, I think Perrin Dagarth witnessed something significant. Why he kept it quiet I can't fathom."

"Go on."

Sidru recounted his investigation of the dwarfish scientist. Ordinarily, common citizens faced formal charges during a criminal inquiry, those brought before a military tribunal or persons accused of endangering Endora's newfound society by some act of sabotage or fatal negligence. Perrin's only fault had been his clinging to Aboriginal customs born in deep ages on Earth. He'd gone on a walkabout in a quest for spiritual awakening and quiet communion with the cosmos. Days after Perrin's return from the Endyr Kush, with long nights under the stars, the first case of a mysterious virus had surfaced in Outer Reach. The man lived a mostly reclusive life in the settlement, busy with one scientific query or another, unless conscripted into field work by the likes of Gherau Thla'ad. A few visits to Dr. Zelda'adz Uri to examine specimens of mutual interest had also drawn Perrin from his hermit lab.

Sidru followed a hunch he'd gotten when a rumor reached Al-Dawud Station. "Creepy tales left over from Dream Time," an MP commented over a card game one night. "Bunch of myths about an Ancestral Star. As if these Aborigines believe Earth was seeded by folks from another galaxy."

"All cultures on that rock shared similar mythos," said another between shuffles. "Now cut. We're back on patrol in forty-five."

"Yeah, but this bloke saw proof. Real evidence out there in the Kush."

"Like what?"

"Won't say. Just told one of them science stiffs something about bones. Actual humanoid fossils."

"Rumors, Mykal. Don't make sense. Who else saw those fossils?"

Mykal had only shrugged. "Maybe just smoking illegal stims, I guess. Who knows, right?"

"Exactly."

Access to medical files was limited to a select few eyes like Dr. Na'obi or Dr. Uri, unless subpoenaed by a tribunal magistrate. So Sidru linked into the planetwide neural net via an authentication code restricted to military special ops and high-level staff clearance. Perrin's memfile held an intriguing if not surreal bit of memory. While stargazing by a small fire there in the Endyr Kush, Perrin had beheld a sign he believed confirmed the Aborigines' myth of an Ancestral Star. A trio of pulsars had shifted as one in a northerly constellation, and abruptly streaked across the heavens like shooting stars. They blazed into Endora's ionosphere, then arced slowly toward the Western Bronze Erg.

Days later, Perrin chanced a solo excursion into the erg to see the impact site of those strange meteors. The bones he'd pried from the dunes belonged to no fauna native to Endora. They might've been mistaken for fused sand superheated by the impact, except their skeletal shape was neither humanoid nor strictly organic in origins.

Sidru shivered at the memfile data even now. "Amir sir, the deposits are carbon-based," he said dryly. "They're the petrified limbs of a cyborg. One of many relics buried deep in a karst system."

"Dear godly light! An artificial life form?"

"Aye, by Allah. Though how it came to be on this planet, I can't fathom."

A team soon converged in the Bronze Erg at Bhud's urging. Along with the enigma of Perrin's discovery, and the eerie bolts rippling over the sea of dunes, was the aurorae barrier spanning the vaulting skies. The force field had torn the *AAF Fatimah* apart on entry all those years ago.

Gherau Thla'ad grappled with the inexplicable phenomenon. As a hardened officer, the old Mujah Master hardly trusted the coincidence. "Until we know what put that shield in place," he told them, "we must assume a hostile design."

"Do we?" Perrin scoffed. "Contrary to the Mujah code, some mysteries offer scientific insights, Master Gherau."

"Maybe they do. But in my expertise, shields serve one purpose. They prevent penetration. So we must ask: Are we imprisoned by it or protected by it? And if we're not prisoners, what does it protect from?"

The hideous ruin of their colony ship lay strewn over the world's lush biome. Another scenario plagued Sidru. "Dyson shields serve another purpose," he said. "They hide objects from detection. This energy field could be intended to hide our colony from view of passing starships or probes. Or other planets."

"Perhaps it's neither scenario," said Perrin, eyeing the perfectly timed lightning flashes. The dwarfish scientist bore tribal scars on his pudgy cheeks. His ebony brow crinkled in thought. "We Abories see nature as a sentient force. One with its own will, mate."

Bhud scratched his hoary scalp. "Who knows what evolved on this planet, really? Or the true origins of life here."

Gherau snorted. "Cyborgs don't evolve. Something left those relics. A highly advanced race put that barrier in place."

Sidru recollected the spectral imagery of Endora's twin moons. The oxidized splotches that spoke of terraforming. He voiced his fears. "What if they're not extinct?"

"Aye, mate," Perrin agreed. "That's a thesis I want explored too."

Gherau huffed. He preferred a living, breathing foe to a theoretical one. Something his ion rapier could lash out at. A foe with flesh and bones and clearly defined motives. Not some hypothetical bogeyman who erected global shields. What good were a Mujah's elite skills against intangible theory?

Given the planet's extraordinary ecosystem and geology, such insights may well lay deep in the vast cavern network. So Gher-

au Thla'ad led a small team into a karst some weeks later. He
was joined by Sidru Neega, Perrin Dagarth, Drako Sudo and the
blind orphan girl Aedra Vishna'a. With her newly enhanced optics, she might spot subtleties the others couldn't. Besides, what
awaited them might well test the extremes of human senses. For
all their scientific ken, Terrans were newcomers to this galaxy and
thus knew little of its hidden wonders...or perils.

As they crept into the karst Sidru felt an odd polarity seize
his joints, as if a slight shift in gravity, his nerve endings fizzling.
Otherworldly frescos yawned before them in vivid detail. What
met their gazes took Gherau's breath. "This is no natural grotto,"
he barely gasped. "By Hagar's soul, it's astounding!"

"Crikey hells," Perrin swore.

"Ditto that," Drako agreed. "Talk about an ungodly feat of
engineering. This must've taken centuries to construct."

"Maybe millennia," Sidru said.

Aedra edged to the fore of the group, her bionic eyes taking
in the vision. The subterranean complex lit her optic nerves with
auras of shapes and energy waves. She said at length, "This is
where they came from. The spectral beings I sensed on the *Fatimah*'s decks."

"Are you certain?" asked Gherau.

Even as he posed the question, Sidru too sensed an unseen
presence. Observing them from a vantage only Aedra could
perceive. Drako hissed an oath upon seeing the wraith moving
along a far wall, watched it pause to inspect a pod there. A lifepod! Rows of the capsules lit with soft fluorescence as the figure,
wholly uninterested in the team's presence, moved on to examine
others. The vast chamber looked too angular in places to be natural geology. In fact, Sidru felt he'd set foot on a stasis deck aboard
some underground starship.

"They're stasis pods," Sidru said as he neared one. "Each
holds a...dear Almighty, it can't be."

Perrin mouthed the unspoken implications. "Drown a dingo, mate. Are we talking a colony ship? An artifice disguised as the planet's underbelly?"

"That's impossible," Drako refuted. "Endora has oceans and volcanoes and climate fluctuations. A whole ecosystem of flora and fauna. Moons that affect the tides, by Allah."

"And yet the Arc regions exist," Gherau reminded them.

Each of them approached the row of elongated pods. Their minds wanted tangible proof. Yet when the Aborigine outstretched his hand, it passed through the capsule's faceplate. And what slept behind the misted shield had a pudgy ebony face, cheeks vaunting identical tribal scars as Perrin's own. "Why is it my clone?" he asked numbly.

"And mine," said Drako at another pod.

"We...are all here," Sidru told them, still transfixed by his own likeness. The replica's lithe form still wore the Lycra terra-fits he'd shimmied into hours before making planetfall. All sixty-three members of the *AAF Fatimah*'s skeleton crew had donned identical outfits in preparation for landing. But alarms blared amid their sedated oblivion. The ship's AI repeated its baleful litany: All hands brace for imminent impact...repeat...proximity alert...

Aedra sidled between Perrin and Drako, her once sightless eyes taking in the vision of countless souls held in tranquil repose. She'd grown up on Endora's surface, had developed into a lovely teen, always inquisitive, ever eager to explore her environs. "Oh Genesis," she said, stung by it all. "Did we even survive that infernal crash?"

Silence snatched any reply as darkness coiled over them all.

The near indestructible cyborgs milled about the debris seeking out survivors. Many had perished on impact, but a few thousand lifepods lay amid the smoldering ruins of the starship. Softly lit readings on each faceplate indicated life signs, gave status updates, injury assessments and the like. Or sadly, no pulse echoed on the low-frequency bandwidths that urged the cyborg medics into action—that after long hybernation deep in the catacombs of their world ship.

An entire ecosystem and geology and oceans had long ago seeded the myriad species that inhabited the faux planet. Even now subtle tremors rose from the world's engine core. It fed the lush biome: a cacophony of twills, buzzes, croaks and chirping fauna. Entirely isolated from invasive species and meteor impacts, exotic flora had flourished over the many epochs since their argosy began.

In the karst, a wraith hologram observed the Terrans as they realized their new status: "Oh Genesis," said one of the organisms. "Did we even survive that infernal crash?"

Lieutenant Commander Sidru Neegh had no reply as he waved a palm over his flesh and blood copy. Belatedly, memory surfaced as numb realization seized his soul. I'm a program, mere algorithms replaying a tragic end...sensory pathways trying to connect...trying but failing to heal the psychosis amid a medically induced stasis. Perhaps one of many patients held in tranquil repose under Dr. Na'obi's care at the hospice.

Or...we never survived our fiery plunge into the planet's atmosphere, dear Allah, save us all.

Either scenario plagued Sidru, truth be told, for he'd so wanted tangible proof of their new frontier beyond the Arc gate. "We did survive," he told them. Eyeing his own ethereal hands, he verged on tears. "In a post-corporeal form, more or less."

The End

OUTCAST

"If by whim his fate births our ruin, it is Albar's lofty design." —Eyri'ah H'gar, secret council at the Grand Prism Shrine.

Rhojii Botanical Refuge, Ijnar.
Year 14,074 Sixth Terjjan Era,
Tenth year of Empress Nesrai Sjureh's reign.

Oshii kept utterly still in his hiding place. This rite of passage, unlike avenjii, had very real consequences. If his scent betrayed him, the huge Rhojii cat would surely disembowel Oshii as it had two other hunters. The brave Ijnari boys had also coated their pelts with j'duri resin, like Oshii, and kept deathly still too. But fear had its own fetor. Not even their lifelong Divine Path indoctrination had readied Sh'rii and Djinth for the proximity of death.

The feral Rhojii cats stalked their prey with lethal precision and untiring patience. Nine boys had entered the Rhojii Botanical Refuge. Seven remained alive. Oshii did not intend on falling prey today. Not on Ijnar…not while his mgoja arc remained unstained by blood.

Like the others, Oshii had chosen his primitive weapon from a cache of organic or hand-carved arms. No plasma guns or pulse lances or hyperdimensional nav devices were permitted during a ra'ahii hunt. All males who attained puberty had to endure this rite of passage. Each had to prove their worth here in the refuge if they coveted a place in Nesrai's elite Tjai Mrraj guard. Chosen from the most promising acolytes in the Nine Shrines of Light, the hunters took pride in their roles, even if some might die.

"Albar's will be done," Eyri'ah offered when she'd seen him off earlier. Golden eyes wetly gazing into Oshii's hybrid orbs, she imparted a final proverb: "All life succumbs to Albar's will. Yet She'aj Rah welcomes only the brave."

Steeled by her words, he'd bravely taken up his mgoja arc, once use by primitive hunters of Ptyr Prime, and joined eight others who had similarly armed themselves. Katjil of the Crystal Shrine had chosen a kyesh once wielded by Ambri monks. The ancient lance made from the tusk of some marine giant glinted in the nearby shadows. Katjil was all but invisible like Oshii, and both kept perfectly still as the purring Rhojii cat prowled close by, its sensory whiskers writhing.

The pureborn Ijnari's ropy nerve hairs twitched at the proximity of the predator.

Oshii braced himself. Albar, let my aim be true, he prayed. A little closer, beast. Edge into my mgoja's line of fire.

Snarling at a betrayed scent, some trickle of fear or a glint of weaponry, the huge feline pounced on Katjil with all six paws slashing. The kyesh speared its sleek hide but didn't fell the predator.

Oshii leapt from hiding, arc twirling from his grasp. It struck the cat behind the gills, eliciting an angry yelp. But it was dazed only briefly. With its snout gory with Katjil's viscera, it whirled on Oshii, a deathly fire in its eyes.

Oshii, now weaponless, flexed his wings, grateful for their existence. Yet the rite demanded he stay grounded during the hunt. Only by facing this Rhojii cat on terra firma would any of them be honored by Nesrai's talons. But unlike the full-blooded Ijnaris, Oshii had no formidable talons with which to slash the cat. Nets belayed any notion of escape by wing, much as he wanted to.

So, Oshii braced for death.

With a roar, the Rhojii cat leapt at its prey. Oshii tucked his wings, rolled aside as talons slashed furiously. When he got to his feet, others joined the fray, all snarling in bravado while hurling their own primitive blades, clubs, and ch'thar wire.

The huge Rhojii cat thrashed wildly under the fusillade. Oshii retrieved his mgoja arc, its ivory blades glistening with the cat's dark blood. And pirhanj venom. The toxins should've felled the animal by now.

Sickly gurgles rose from the now bloodied thing. The five Ijnari juveniles, glorying in their victory, didn't see the ambush from the female. She'd stalked them from the leafy shadows, letting her mate draw the hunters into the open. With ferocious speed she tore into the nearest boy, Rhaffu, all six paws clawing him from wing to foot, her fangs mauling his face.

Stunned by the ambush, and two of them weaponless, the four remaining Ijnaris instinctively beat their wings in an attempt to flee. Two were thwarted before they lifted off, claws mangling them, their gills drowned with violet gore.

When the Rhojii turned on the pair snared in the net, Oshii let his mgoja arc fly. It struck the cat between the haunches, knocking her off balance long enough for Ish'bo to cut himself free from the net. Sudhu frantically fought to escape the net's tangle even as he shrieked in horror. Claws tore his cries short. The boy's mangled limbs hung limply by the time the Rhojii cat slinked toward Oshii and Ish'bo. They stood side by side, one with his Olec blade, Oshii now armed with Rhaffu's Oort club.

"Come, hellion," Ish'bo snarled bravely.

She obligingly bared huge fangs. Yet her eyes grew glassine, her footfalls unsteady as the pirhanj venom took effect.

Oshii didn't let glory dilute his vigilance. Other cats might be lurking. Even while Rhojii cats hunted in pairs once bonded, and fiercely guarded their hunting turf, the refuge was vast. Some fifty tehnars of jungly habitat. Its lush flora hid other deadly fauna— even predatory foliage and venomous moths.

The cat fell dead at their feet. Oshii moved to claim his trophy, but Ish'bo clasped his arm. "Sjak, hirjun spawn," he growled, wings flared. "This Rhojii belongs to me. Not a halfbreed mutant like you."

"It would've killed you if not for my mgoja arc. The honor is mine, gthai!"

The Olec blade met Oshii's throat. "Nesrai won't honor a spy left by lowly Terjj outcasts. Albar has favored Ijnar in this Ijhad al-Quds."

Oshii relented. Yet his wounded pride temped the club he still clenched. Let Ish'bo enjoy his stollen trophy. *My genes belong to another realm, not this planet.*

Triumphantly, the Aura Shrine disciple claimed his trophy. Uttering a Divine Path mantra, Ish'bo cut the musk gland from the cat's inner thigh. The cloying odor nearly choked Oshii as the Ijnari hunter smeared oily secretion onto his brow and breastplate scales.

As Oshii looked on, the boy's pelt took on a sickly pallor. Ish'bo gasped, gills choked by toxins. The pirhanj venom had tainted the cat's organs...tainted its musk gland. And it was too late for Ish'bo, for the toxins now poisoned his gills. The musk secretion had entered his pores when he smeared it over himself with his palms.

Grim spasms seized the Ijnari. Oshii did nothing. After all, he was no skinshaper, neither did he feel sympathy for the boy. Albar's will be done, sjak yes. He let Rhaffu's club fall from his grasp and just stood there numbly. All this carnage to appease Nesrai. All in hopes of joining her elite Tjai Mrraj guard.

Wings fluttered above the canopy nets. Minders cut the nets away, swooped down to toll the casualties and declare the rite's victor. It all swept over Oshii so fast. Taking him to the Grand Palace Shell to be honored by Nesrai's own talons, all the delegates from the Nine Shrines of Light joining the elaborate ceremony, even Qudsa with her priestesses in tow. Even Nesrai's mole, Eyri'ah, was there in full finery. She looked on proudly as the Empress bestowed an honorary rank on Oshii.

"By Albar's glory, I hereby grant you the title of Imah Envoy," Nesrai proclaimed from her pavilion dais. "After the clever tactics you used in today's ra'ahii rite, Oshii, I've deemed you noble enough. Mmm, yes, little pirhanj. Quite an unorthodox stratagem." She pet Nanji on her swarthy hackles. "A shame the Rhojii organs couldn't be retrieved for medicinal purposes. What, with the venom spoiling her carcass."

Although not expressly forbidden in the ra'ahii rite, hunters didn't ordinarily rely on venom or poisons. Oshii's mgoja arc had been laced with pirhanj saliva at Eyri'ah's quiet suggestion. After all, the Ijnari hunters had the advantage of sharp talons, didn't they? And if he was to fulfill his role as Nesrai's agent, well then Oshii too deserved an edge.

"Avenjii is a game of deceit, boy," Eyri'ah had reiterated hours before the rite. "Warfare is deception. As is mynthir a matter of cunning."

He'd not spoken of his knowledge about Eyri'ah being an Emiraj mole. She'd not confided in him her secret loyalties, either. Now Oshii felt overly awed by the complexity of the intrigue here on Ijnar. He now pondered his own true nature and loyalties.

Am I Sijjo Ith's spy or Nesrai's mole? Or am I truly an Emiraj disciple?

By gifting Oshii with an honorary title as Imah Envoy, did Nesrai have yet other designs for his future? Perhaps as envoy to some faraway colony world, or even an emissary to the Coral

Galaxy itself? Albar Most High only knew the true depths off Nesrai's intrigue. Or whether Oshii indeed vaunted noble heredity despite his hirjun origins beyond the Perthid Nebula.

Eyri'ah felt pride in the hirjun boy's will to survive. Not many survived a ra'ahii rite, but Oshii had prevailed. Albeit with a mgoja arc laced with pirhanj venom given to him by Eyri'ah, still Oshii alone evaded death. He'd faced those Rhojii cats bravely, and now he enjoyed the honorary rank of Imah Envoy to a galaxy he would never revisit.

Nesrai had no intention of putting the hybrid in her trusted Tjai Mrraj. Only pure-blooded Ijnaris chosen from elite ova ever got initiated into her most loyal guard. Only those candidates who were carefully screened by Blood Mages got chosen. Nesrai had most likely hoped the hybrid boy would perish in the rite, thus doing away with Sijjo's ambition. Eyri'ah doubted otherwise.

Yet the young Empress had lofty designs for Ijnar. She had confided those ambitions to Eyri'ah often, while deploying her talents as a spy among the Emiraj zealots. True to her role, Eyri'ah had outed several key figures whom she deemed expendable. Grand Prism Mage Priest Resghul Ch'thyr had fulfilled his own role; a long privileged life, loyal to Nesrai but blind to the intrigue engulfing the empire. And Thundyr Obei too, all slain.

That old worm Qudsa had nearly exposed the enormity of their endeavors. With her careless gazes into the pearls, the Oracle Mage had drawn Nesrai's keen eyes toward their prophesied objective. Siffyr nectar may well have intoxicated Qudsa and stifled her ability to mask her true loyalties and memories. Ah, but not Eyri'ah. Nay, by Albar, not even the oracle pearls could betray her mastery of mynthir deceit.

She'd need supreme focus with the Tjai Mrraj's intensified scrutiny of every potential threat to Nesrai's reign. Even now, months after little Medjii Genghisfan's ascension as starlighter, Ijnar remained under marshal law. Dark Se'idj veils cast widespread gloom over the entire planet. The lovely halo clouds all but lost their iridescent splendor as harvest ships temporarily ceased operation. Warships hung darkly in the gaseous nimbus deck. All merchant vessels sat idly in orbit; not even Nesrai's armada of portal ships crisscrossed the Perthid Nebula's worm lanes. A forced moratorium to honor Ijnar's martyrs in the Great Ijhad led by Toth Arbil the Great.

Yom Ejhud.

A full day of reverent silence. All throughout the Hejji Alps there fluttered millions of siffyr moths. Their genetically modified thoraxes glowed with bioluminescent fire...a symbolic offering to the martyr's soul's. And silently moved Eyri'ah's brethren, their violet eyes lit with Emiraj fervor as they, one by one, slit the jugular veins of Badj Urai and Tjai Mrraj guardsmen. Some themselves wore the elite sashes of Nesrai's own palace guards. Others moved along the decks of portal ships, or in the halls of the Nine Shrines of Light.

So began their holy coup d'etat.

Although she'd objected to the coup's timing, Qudsa could only pray she was on the right side of prophecy. After Oshii's arrival that day with Sijjo Ith she'd had to reassess her faith in the Emiraj doctrine. She'd gazed intently into the oracle pearls, perhaps too eager to presage an omen in the hirjun child's birth. Why this boy?

At Nesrai's behest, she kept a close eye on the Terjj admiral's goings on in the Coral Galaxy. After Terjjah's ruin, the young empress had sought to sever Sijjo's worm path to the Perthid Nebula and thereby end the Sacred Pact. Ijnar alone controlled the temporal routes, as it had for long millennia, but now Nesrai set her eyes on the ultimate symbol of power once lorded over by Terjjah.

Ghaz.

And her ice gas, yes.

Yet events in the Coral Galaxy had forced Nesrai to delay her plans for Ghaz. Along with the mysteriously vanished moons was Sijjo's discovery of Sharjah. A habitable new homewolrd for the ostracized Terjj meant Sijjo had a defensible base. A base from which his fleet could launch an offensive strike. Amid that development in the Endyr Nebula was the interplanetary conflict between Terrans and the Hydran Alliance.

Nesrai wisely chose to let those events play out while she quelled the Emiraj unrest on Ijnar. Or so she'd hoped by executing Thundyr Obei and his fellow zealots.

Qudsa's gills quavered to think what merciless end she herself faced if Nesrai ever learned the true extent of the Emiraj intrigue. Xianj Ozh, a spy embedded in Sijjo's fleet...banished after his fealty came under scrutiny. The old astrophysicist had met a horrid demise when Sijjo hurled his life force into an Arc gate. Into that hirjun realm whence arose those Terran devils, by Albar's holy light...cast into the Void Nebula itself.

Qudsa still recoiled at the vision she'd gleaned from her pearls. Swarms of battleships arrayed about crowded planetary bases. Countless star systems teeming with their inexhaustible colony worlds. In his dying moments, Xianj had gazed at the Terran birthplace. The first of any Terjj or Ijnari to set gill in the Milky Way.

Oshii with his hybrid cells shared a common origin with the Earthlings who now vied for survival in the Coral Galaxy. He surely held some link to the Emiraj prophecy of a unified Ijnari-Terjj empire. Blessed Egg of Eternity, this hirjun boy might very well lend his cells to the fulfillment of that ambition.

"We must take care not to spoil Oshii's cells," she cautioned Eyri'ah there in the Chrysalis Aerie. "Once we've seized the throne, he might prove a useful pawn. After all, he is Sijjo's experiment and thus of some value to the admiral."

"All is in motion," Eyri'ah replied noncommittally. The lesser priestess wore her dark ropes in a single tail, the ch'thar wire cinching the sensory hairs. It kept her private angst unreadable like her Emiraj brethren now storming the Grand Palace Shell.

"Don't fret, High Priestess. Our precious pet shall not be harmed. Thofii received strict instructions. Oshii won't—"

The air fizzled just then as three Tjai Mrraj phased from hyperdimensional cloaks. All snarled menacingly at the two Emiraj cohorts, pulse weapons trained. "Nesrai's reign will not end today, whore spawns. Neither will your schemes avail you Emiraj fools. Seize them both," their captain ordered.

"No, I'm Nesrai's agent," Eyri'ah protested. "This isn't what you think."

"We are noble clergy of the Nine Shrines of Light," Qudsa said proudly. "How dare you barge into this sanctum!"

Strong paws manacled their wrists before either priestess could flee or protest further. Dear Albar, some traitor must've betrayed them. Qudsa cursed her wizened joints, for had she the time or speed she surely would've resisted to her final breath. Rather that she hastened on her journey to She'aj Rah's shore than face the grim retribution awaiting her gills.

What Nesrai had in store for her and Eyri'ah might be far worse than Thundyr Obei's demise. Although in truth Qudsa could scarcely envision a torment worse than having one's hair cords shorn off one by one, balach fa!

Oshii's vision grew blurred by the h'shtar-laced fumes. Nauseating memory raged behind the clamor of thunder...those Ijnari legions roaring en mass as Nesrai proclaimed victory over her Emiraj foes. There were wails of pain as wings got shorn from every conspirator, old, young, male or female. Not even Eyri'ah had escaped the grim rite suffered by Qudsa and the others. An Ijnari without wing was no longer noble enough to breathe the planet's air.

"Every one of you shall die wingless," Nesrai vowed upon sentencing the traitors. "Mmm, yes, gthai. Eternal shame shall be your lot. All of you shall join Thundyr Obei and Resghul Ch'thyr in the deepest, most gelid hell. Neither shall you gaze upon She'aj Rah."

Oshii had stood confused and aghast when two Tjai Mrraj agents seized him, then forcibly bowed him before Nesrai and her Rhojii cats. "Ah, hirjun spawn. Sijjo's little spy abomination. Did you think me so gullible? To be fooled by your ruse, your false oracle? Nay," Nesrai spat, green eyes afire, "Albar forbid that I'd befoul Sjureh's bloodline with filthy Terjj interbreeding."

Pain seared through Oshii's soul as his wings were excised from his hybrid shoulders. Then the world faded swiftly. All of a sudden, as if he'd entered long stasis, he groaned stiffly, roused by a cybernetic program that had kept vigil on biorythmic data. Languid and disoriented, he crawled from the previously sealed enclosure and cautiously explored his new prison.

Gthai hells, they'd sedated him and every one of Eyri'ah's cohorts and put them aboard a starship! Others milled about the vessel's decks, trying in vain to orient their senses or establish a base reference for their voyage. So far as Oshii's could deduce, the Mantis destroyer wasn't under the control of any of its passengers. No crew manned the command bridge. And none of the Emiraj adherents could wrest control of the automated navigation systems.

The viewports revealed nothing but gaseous streaks of hyperdimensional void. No console readings gave hint of a destination, or told them if they were well beyond the Perthid Nebula or not.

"Albar has forsaken us," moaned Qudsa. She sat near a hatchway, dishevelled and shivering. Eyes clouded by h'shtar, she let out a manic laugh. "All my pearls are useless. We're blind without an oracle to gaze into. Don't worry, hirjun boy. I've seen our destiny already. A gelid pit awaits me. But you, not you. Death would be a mercy for your precious cells."

The h'shtar had obviously taken Qudsa's mind. That and the trauma of having her wings shorn must've sent the Oracle Mage into a delirious rant. Like the others who'd wakened aboard the Mantis, the priestess had lost her mooring on reality. While the physical trauma of such mutilation would heal quickly enough, no eternity could undo the anguish and humiliation. Oshii had only enjoyed his grafted pinions briefly. Eyri'ah and her kith had only ever known flight. Since emerging from their aweh'jiin clutches, these Terjj offshoots had soared upon Ijnar's thermals.

Now they hurled blindly through some predestined worm path. A hyperdimensional death spiral into unknown regions of space.

Then a collective shudder seized their enthralled psyches when a blue-lit horizon sprawled across the viewport. Every Ijnari now realized their hellish fate, for no other planet consumed Ijnar's long fueled rivalry with Terjjah. Cousins had long ago waged a bitter war over this jewel in the Coral Galaxy.

Ghaz, by Albar!

Nesrai had cast them into this hirjun realm to join the exiled Terjj—a lone Mantis destroyer manned by condemned Emiraj traitors. Orbital defenses launched swift sorties against the encroaching vessel. Silvery orbs let fly lightning ordnance even as the Mantis beared down on the planet with menacing firepower.

Only, the Mantis never unleased its destructive fury. No energy shield thwarted the fiery hail of pulsar rays as it charged into Ghaz's atmosphere. Chaos reigned amidships as the Ijnaris frantically sought an escape from certain death.

Oshii felt talons claw his shoulder. "Move, hirjun boy!" urged Eyri'ah. "Get to a life capsule. We daren't lose your life force. Come."

She hustled Oshii to an emergency hatch. Punfyr vines dangled from lattices in the neglected nursery. Husks of eviscerated Ijnar moths carpeted the deck. A dank smell of decay and burnt circuits filled Oshii's sinuses. An old, fossilized benjar blade glinted in the nursery's soft light.

Eyri'ah thoughtfully retrieved the blade, gave it to Oshii. "If you survive, put it to good use. And fear not."

Oshii felt a lump in his throat. "Why aren't you coming? We can both escape."

"My fate is already sealed," Eyri'ah assured him.

She said nothing more as she ushered him to the waiting life capsule. It glowed to life at Eyri'ah's touch. A lid rose, program hieroglyphs winking as its sensors discerned Oshii's biological specs.

After he'd climbed in, the lid sealed Oshii within the capsule, along with the benjar blade he clutched. Eyri'ah's golden eyes fled fast into memory as the Mantis destroyer spat its lone survivor into a hellishly alien sky.

Teshkan Province, Ghaz.
Third year of High Neghus Sifqiyah's reign.
October 3, 3213 CE.

N'thai refused to relent in her search for survivors of the downed Terjjan craft. After five standard months since its breach of Ghaz's orbital defense array, Fyuth Onah's second born hatchling remained true to her stubborn bile. *By the Ancestral Star, I'm certain something escaped the wreckage. Abah, give me a sign.*

She felt it in her very vapor. Sifqiyah believed in her instincts and so had permitted N'thai more resources to widen the search grid. Only she and a few loyal rangers remained doggedly on the heels of their phantom Terjj. Although the aerial patrols kept up their sweep over the Thlag Domain's vast wilderness, it didn't negate the need for boots on the ground. And unlike their winged Ambri neighbors to the east, Thlags relied on their keen senses—not those fancy telepathy orbs.

"Dtsarq, Commander Onah," grunted Ofthir Brigade Captain Chan Urg'th. "We have scoured the entire badlands. Nothing lurks here but wild agk-goats."

"They've a distinct fetor, aye. Not this alien scum's reek, brood cousin."

The surrounding bluffs and sheer cliffs were perfect places to hide oneself if one wanted to remain unseen. Yet it would take a full lunar cycle to probe each and every crevice on foot. Nay, for that they'd need more seeker drones. Or Ptyr falcons like she and Abah once hunted with in the Zegh.

Scoria's infernal heat beset their thorny brows as it reached zenith. Still, these were battle-hardened rangers chosen from Sifqiyah's elite forces. Despite Chan's grumbling, they would follow N'thai to the ends of Ghaz if so ordered.

Eying the scarps from her baojii mount, N'thai sniffed, brow slits twitching at some alien scent. Awal Rab, some vile odor itching her nostrils...

"Chan, deploy the drones," N'thai ordered. "Something lurks in those crags."

"But, Commander—"

"Do it."

"Aye, at once."

The seeker drone lifted swiftly from its perch atop a floating nest. Once aloft, its segmented facets split into smaller wasp eyes. Each drone flit off into the shadowy nooks, seeking out life signs. Terjj once deployed such devices to root out Thlag rebels. Now in a poetic irony, Thlags hunted a Terjj ghost with seeker drones.

N'thai took the vid slate from the young ranger nearby. She wanted to analyze the live feed personally. Twain hearts throbbed in her stillbreather bosom. "Dear Abah, what on Ghaz is that? Look, Chan, look at it!"

Arms at the ready, the alert rangers yanked their reins, poised to charge their baojii steeds into battle. But the pitiful thing that lay curled in its makeshift den resembled no Terjj they'd ever seen. Gilled devils didn't look so...human.

Oshii scarcely knew what hijun nightmare had spawned these ugly Thlags, let alone his own hybrid cells. They had found him near death, starved and dehydrated. Ugly blisters marred his flimsy pelt. Even now, days after his capture, he could barely keep food down.

Dear Albar! Such awful nightmares played over and over in his traumatized mind. Wings shorn from his back. Nesrai's glaring green eyes, Rhojii cats slinking nearby, their muzzles dripping with gore, Oshii's own viscera. Pirhanj larvae slithering into his corpse...

"No, please!" he blurted, lost in renewed delirium.

"Don't fret, child," purred a nearby ghost. The eyes were pink, lips thick folds of scarlet. Pelt like pale siffyr blooms. A nest of amber hair cords writhed with delight. "Selusa won't hurt you. Akirah wants you alive. So we'll not spoil your exotic cells. Albar, so very exquisite, yes."

"Where am I?"

"Firjah City. Deep below the Palace Hive. Ah, far from filthy Terjj, my pet. They've brought you as a gift for the Ambri queen."

"Ambri...queen?"

"Akirah wishes to know why the Terjj sent you. Why a pitiful specimen like you? Not entirely human, nor yet Terjj. Like that hybrid girl in the caves, poor, poor wretched spawn."

Oshii started. "Sari'ah is here? On this planet?"

The albino's wrinkly tendons screwed in thought. Ages had ravaged the skinshaper's memory. "Oh, to think of it, she had your chin and cheekbones. The same brow. Nearly an identical blend of Terjj and human genes."

She raked his bare chest with a talon. Pink eyes lustful, Selusa bared her fangs. "Shall we see if your flimsy skin heals like Cindy Skyborne's?"

Sudden fear gushed over Oshii as the albino slid the benjar blade from its organic sheath. The living scalpel snaked into his flesh, hurled Oshii's soul into a chasm of pain, pleasure and profound awakening.

Days or long hours later, he woke from the mensah rite with fully healed skin and ravenous hunger. They'd put him in a new prison, one without Selusa's slab or her dangling herbs or benjar.

The room had a comfortable bed, coverings, a basin for washing, toilet bowl of alien design, and a place to sit and eat. Savory aromas met his sinuses when he got up and inspected the dishes set out for him. Alien fruits, meats, baked grains, steamy herbs and sauces invited his palate. Hungrily, Oshii sampled several morsels before noticing the beakers filled with various drinks. With his senses delighted by the strange new flavors and scents, he lifted a beaker to his lips. Cool sweetness tingled his throat as he swallowed large gulps. Nothing on Ijnar or the *G'thalon* ever tasted so divine.

The elixir danced throughout his every cell, altering his mood with each new sip. This must've been the sacred nectars that awaited martyrs in She'aj Rah. They'd let him die, then; left him curled in that crude den where he'd given up hope. After crawling from that lifepod with no inkling of where to find shelter or food on this alien planet, he had roamed for endless days and gelid nights, hunting what small beasts he could, eating shrubs and roots and bitter grasses. He kept always to the shadows, ever mindful of air patrols and mounted Thlags. With only the fossilized benjar blade in hand, and an emergency breather mesh, Oshii survived his pitiful state. Those blithe days playing avenjii with Sari'ah had given him an instinct for hiding well. Often in those lonely days and nights Oshii pretended he was still playing avenjii with his twin, only with deadly consequences should he be found.

Now his captors saw fit to torment him with succulent morsels and mood-altering nectar. Why? Did they want him fattened for some ritual sacrifice? And were other Terjj besides the albino living among these Ambri?

A wall fizzled behind Oshii. He whirled to face a hulking being with amber gemfire eyes. Slender build, muscular limbs, dually pronged forefingers, taloned feet. Robes like misty down, the long-chinned Ambri looked ethereal. "I am Elfar, Chieftain of the Firjah Hive. Akirah wishes to probe your ithkah."

Oshii blinked at the words spoken in Old Terjjan. Only high priests and scholars of the Kebrah Nur used the dialect. Yet Oshii grasped the Ambri's utterance all the same.

While unconscious, his hosts had bathed and dressed him in a clean tunic and trousers. Kedjkaskin wrappings covered his callused feet as he was led from his cell and into the labyrinthine halls of the Palace Hive. Nesrai's own Grand Palace Shell didn't rival the majesty of Akirah's Grand Pavilion Hall. Droves of kneeling subjects gaped at Elfar's charge. They'd never seen the likes of Oshii.

Glowing nymphs hovered like fiery moths about their monarch, showering her with scented petals. As for Akirah's vision, she exuded a beauty unlike anything Oshii had ever dreamt of. Lovely azure eyes, graceful, svelte limbs. Not at all a gruesome demon as he'd imagined. After all, the Ambri had only been depicted harshly in Terjjan or Ijnari frescoes. They were an ancient Enemy reborn on Ghaz. Those very hive dwellers who had obliterated Mother Terjjah.

"Fear not, boy," Akirah spoke in her watery tongue. She imparted the words as much to Oshii's mind as to his flesh ears. "We perceive fascinating wonders in your ithkah. Visions not seen by any living Ambri. Mysteries long kept from our Awareness. Insights into the Perthid Nebula itself."

Oshii couldn't wrest sound from his vocal cords. He felt utterly small, so alien. Elfar's wing nudged him forward. "Draw nigh," the Chieftain urged. "Let Akirah gaze into your origins."

Akirah raised her twain forefingers. Oshii felt an invisible force seize his limbs and, with only a thought, his body lifted into the air and levitated toward Akirah's throne.

She probed his every cell, his life going back to its embryonic state, seeking out truths about his origins. Oshii peered with her and perceived a life far before his or Sari'ah's birth. When Ochi'ai Xynfar stole twin pearls from Cindy Skyborne's womb...

Right there on a slab deep below Firjah City.

Ghaz's sun cast azure splendor over the world beyond his solitary sanctuary. The Ambri guarded him closely. Only by snatches of their incomprehensible tongue did Oshii learn he'd been kept at Fyuth's Grand Tomb. The legendary martyr who'd led Thlags to victory over their Terjj overlords. The Great Ijhad twenty millennia ago had all but left the Ambri extinct, had left Ghaz an arid wasteland devoid of rainfall or cool winds or oceans. Akirah's weather spheres now brought lush verdure.

A sweetly scented breeze kissed Oshii's sinuses as he enjoyed another day in the punfyr garden. Tangly, writhing vines dared him to pluck a succulent bud from a flowering stalk. Cloying aromas mingled with sharp, tangy citrus when he snatched a violet bulb. He bit into it, savoring the mild opiate prized in h'shtar potions once refined. It numbed his senses yet heightened the fanciful reveries he lost himself to. Abroad the vast portal ship *G'thalon*, he once again giggled as he crept upon Sari'ah hiding amid the siffyr blooms, both pretending to stalk their prey like Rhojii cats. Chief Skinshaper Mishou Bin'aj had groomed them since embryos, enhanced their cells with growth hormones, sharpened mental faculty and exquisite hybridism.

Oblivious to the intrigue embroiling two rival cousins, Oshii and his twin sister were hurled into divergent corners of the universe, he a gift for Empress Nesrai Sjureh, and Sari'ah deployed as a spy among the Terrans. Lost to parents who knew nothing of their existence among Terjj and Ijnaris...

Until one day a dwarfish, ebony-hued figure stood at Elfar's side, his eyes betraying years of longing. "I'm your father, Oshii."

The End

QUASAR RUN

"There nowhere exists an obstacle to the infinite number of worlds."   —Epicurus, Greek philosopher of Old Earth.

I.

Aboard the Scimitar,
Deep in the Gilae System.
March 1, 3213 CE.

L ike a terrible memfile glitch, Earl relived those harrowing last moments aboard the *Scimitar*. Nearly a week after their escape from Sijjo's talons...

"Dingo, this isn't about loyalty," Cruz insisted, brow sweaty. "We're not on friendly terms with Fjorii. Not after they joined the Caliphate."

"We're Terrans," Earl said through gritted teeth. All around the *Scimitar* blazed molten streaks as Fjoriian berserkers engaged the Terjj. Azure and crimson bolts crisscrossed the orbital battlefield. Earl fired madly. "Right about now politics count for zilch, Major. Get us planetside ASAP."

"Sir?" Coryn replied via neural link. "A hyperjump into Fjorii's atmosphere? That's highly risky, Mr. Dingo."

"Risky as dying in a shootout with angry Terjj?"

"Point taken, sir."

Cruz objected. "I'm still senior officer, and I speak for Coral Stellar Navy. We're not taking a military asset into enemy airspace."

"We're already in that zone," Earl reminded her, still firing at Terjjan bogeys.

Cruz manned a gunnery chair of her own. Coryn did her part, too, engaging Terjjan fighters while monitoring the intruders amidships. After circumventing the *Scimitar*'s AI interface, she'd flooded the central decks with hydrogel. Gills or not, they'd soon drown if they remained aboard.

The trio of Terjj had not breached the hatch, nor swallowed onto the control bridge. Perhaps they'd been thwarted by laws of physics Earl wasn't aware of. Either case, he prayed they'd remain at bay. One too many gills if you asked Earl.

"Shields are taking a beating," Coryn reported. "Evasive tactics advised. Although not feasible given our depleted levels of stardrive fuel."

"All those hyperjumps," Cruz confirmed, still gunning away. "We're lucky we've got functional shields."

"Cripes," Earl groaned. "Coryn, can we make it planetside or not?"

"Not without risk. Any number of factors could affect translation flux. We might put the *Scimitar* broadside a mountain, for instance."

"Can we jump?"

"Yes."

"Do it, then."

"As you wish, Mr. Dingo."

A blur drew over every surface as the starship winked from normal space and swallowed into Fjorii's clouds. Vertigo hit Earl as true gravity tore at the *Scimitar*'s hull. He unstrapped himself from the gunnery chair, devil-bent on thwarting the Terjj who were surely fast after the ship's jump wake.

"Get to a lifepod," he urged Reina Cruz. "We gotta scuttle the package."

"What?"

"Titanic. Old Earth tragedy at sea," he said cryptically. He didn't want to give the Terjj any hint of his desperate plan. "Coryn, disengage all astrogation routines. Enter Protocol Five, sequence echo-tango-alpha-ninety."

"Are you crazy?" Cruz demanded.

"Sir?" Coryn queried. "Confirm last order."

"Do it!" Earl told the incredulous angel program. "And don't argue, Major. Get inside that lifepod."

She glared briefly, then dashed for a control bridge life preserve pod.

Once Cruz was secured, Earl raced to the wide viewport, saw the icy mountainscape racing by as the *Scimitar* shot toward the famed Myrrh Cliffs. Good, he thought. That's got to be a well-guarded archeological site. Sensors must be locking onto us by now.

Earl got the expected hail from Fjorii's defense force: "Come in, Nova-class Terran vessel *Scimitar*. Alter course immediately. This is sovereign Fjorii airspace. Repeat: Alter present course or be shot down!"

"*Scimitar* here," Earl replied. "We respectfully invite you to shove it up your wormhole. End transmission."

Pulsefire tore into the hatch barring the Terjj trio. The angry bombardment burned a red-hot aura onto the fire plating. Apparently, Terjjan weaponry functioned just fine in a hydrogel-engulfed environment. An ionized odor filled the control bridge. The cordite stench stung Earl's nostrils as he hastily got to his own lifepod.

Once enclosed in the emergency capsule, Coryn calmly recited the self-destruct sequence shipwide: ALL HANDS BE ADVISED, THIS STARSHIP WILL DETONATE IN MINUS TEN, NINE, EIGHT...

Muted howls and curses throttled the Terjj amidships, sensory hairs thrashing in their failing energy cloaks.

All the while, safety foam cradled the two humans with tract-amorphic silex. The lifepods shot into Fjorii's icy sky with mere seconds to spare. A brilliant nimbus bloomed over the billowy clouds when the *Scimitar* erupted.

The brilliant nimbus flared over the clouds just as two Fyangs winked into Fjorii's sky. Sijjo Ith burned with fury when he realized the Terran starship had exploded with Squadron Chief Ust'fah Myrr and two Badj Urai officers aboard. *Gthai figh,* this cursed ape had escaped his talons yet again. *Albar, what divine forces have you aided this human spawn with? Surely this cannot be Thy will.*

Sijjo flung his craft away from the fiery cloud now raining debris onto the world. Although he loathed defeat, he would not foolishly scour the planet's gelid surface for survivors. If anything had escaped the *Scimitar*'s death, his sensors didn't detect any life sign. Still, he dared not underestimate Earl Dagarth's cunning. A man who'd evaded capture for two standard centuries deserved Sijjo's honor—even if only by death.

Only ship-days out from the harrowing chase in the Gilae system, Sijjo felt cheated still, but he'd wisely abandoned a full-scale invasion of Fjorii. Sharjah would not suffer Terjjah's fate due to hubris. Not while Sijjo reigned as Grand Pharsha. So he had given the order for a full withdrawal from Terran space and, ship by ship, Sijjo's forces jumped homeward. Yet in their wake lay a grim aftermath of razed Fjoriian warships.

With the Endyr Nebula once again nestling his fleet in iridescent veils, Sijjo focused on a new threat in Sharjah's oceans.

II.

Aboard the Scimitar,
Orbital rigs of Gilgal days earlier...

Earl wasn't convinced their ruse had fooled Sijjo's sensors one bit. Even now, with the *Scimitar* cowering in the gas giant's orbital rings, inertia would slowly catapult them into a detectable arc. Beta Corpus Starbase lay in a vast debris field after the Terjjan Mantis destroyers had struck weeks ago. Ghostly husks of nebula ships and ruined carrier platforms perfectly hid their lone ship as it listed dead silent. No engines, lights, transmitted waves, not a thermal pulse or blip echoed.

Three days drifting dark.

Coryn had seen to that, forestalling their certain death with a viral surge that incapacitated the *Scimitar*'s operations nexus. Cruz had barely gotten her shipwide alert broadcast—very pissed off Terjj!—when everything went offline. Even gravity actuators got killed in Coryn's cyber attack. Which left a pitch black, zero-grav silence to swim within, save for soft lambent emergency strips along bulkheads and on airlock panels and cryostasis niches. Safety regs required it. Worst scenario come, you wanted to get tucked into a cryostasis berth and pray rescue came eventually... or left you in merciful hypersleep oblivion. Earl knew a thing or two about deep-freeze contingency plans, oh yes.

He felt old. Far beyond his two hundred years, despite a youngish aspect. Curls lay in kinky ropes that framed a swarthy face. A dwarfish build spoke of Aborigine and Cushite genes. Once upon a time, as an imports advisor on Ghaz, he'd had bad skin and worse luck under a glaring blue sun. Thlag rebels, Ijnari invaders, Ambri hives rising from the black coral sands...all while moons vanished during the Eclipse.

Earl's internal ambassador link library gave him an overview of the gas giant's orbiting moons. Bethel, the larger of six satellites, was a blue-gray, lifeless orb long ago mined for its quartz and feldspar. Its smaller moon Shiloh hung sulking in Gilgal's outer ring. It was a pearly white ice ball with crisscrossing canals like those of Europa in the Sol system. The outer four lunar bodies looked misshapen and featureless and were of no notable worth to early mining scouts.

Dillon Olsen floated nearby. "Gotta say, Dingo old guy, we're orders of magnitude in Oort shit. Off course and way behind enemy lines."

"Obvious much?" Earl shot back, suddenly needing to pee. Terrasuits recycled urine just fine, he just hated the idea right now. And he needed to scratch some place he couldn't. Mostly he wished he'd stayed in his cozy hiatus on Lynx, savoring a saline breeze on the reef. "Ships don't just transflux this far off course. Something fluxed the *Scimitar* into this quandary."

"Deliberately?"

"And with precise vectors that require hypernav engines. So what gives?" Earl hissed it loud enough for Dmitri Serov's benefit. After all, the science officer was their resident astrophysicist.

"Pfft," Dmitri bit. "Given the nature of hyperdimensional spacetime rifts, I'd have to agree. This wasn't coincidence. Nobody simply jumps into hyperspace. Not without incredible forces to gape a path, anyhow. And Beta Corpus is thirty parsecs out from Celes Tetra, our last vector."

"Right," Cruz concurred. She swirled slow-motion into the control bridge's starlit confines. "Life-support is still on low output, given our need for stealth. So keep your oxygen usage in check, Mr. Dingo. But yeah, Serov is right about coincidence. Something jumped us here, all right."

Coryn came to Earl's mind. Could she have altered their vector so drastically? Even if the angel persona had sabotaged the FTL coordinates, she'd still need access to a hypernav engine. Which the Fjoriian vessel wasn't outfitted with, supposedly.

"Guys, let's drop the secrecy, already," Earl challenged. "I'm not stupid. The *Scimitar* got an upgrade or two recently. Something Singh authorized, I'm sure."

Cruz huffed. "Great. Now we have to kill you. Or just mem-wipe you to keep a lid on this. But yes, Dingo. This boat has a hypernav engine. Always has since it's a spy billet. Fjorii is a hotbed of skyjacks and Sufi fanatics. So Special Office inserted a few counterintelligence probes in their midst. And Phantom-class billets like yours. Taking the *Scimitar* after your acquisition wasn't hard, either. Our mole on Khidr Delta Five got us critical data on Cygnet's little scheme with you. The Ötzi project they shanghaied you for?"

Earl swallowed dryly. Singh had mentioned the KDF implant Major Nura Khan while aboard the *Kashmir Light*, but omitted this new insight. "So you know about the alien derelict? And the hitchhiker DNA they infected me with?"

"We do," Olsen said, clearly pitying the former Blue Star Interstellar tycoon. "Sordid ordeal, all they did to you, Dingo. But Cruz is right. We've gotta conserve oxygen."

"Or reboot life-support to full throttle," Cruz said. "I mean, those Terjj aren't anywhere in sight. Obviously they've ditched this graveyard without seeing our pulse."

"We don't know that," said Serov. The dimly lit Slavic features were pinched by fear. "They've got sophisticated hyperscans, don't they? Deep penetrating array probes and the like?"

"Wasp eyes, yeah," Earl confirmed. "Among other toys we Terrans don't have or want to encounter." Ghastly things lay slithering on their portal ships, he knew. Things Earl hoped never to face again. Cripes, it made his skin crawl just—

"Holy pulsar!" Olsen cried out, Cro-Magnon brow cast in sudden brilliance.

"Oh boy. We'd better bug out," Earl said.

Coryn must've concurred, for the lights winked on shipwide, gravity hurled them deckward, and life-support thrummed fully alive: ALL SYSTEMS ON-LINE. PHASE ONE ASTROGATION SEQUENCE ACTIVATED....

"Get me a fix on those Terjj," Cruz barked at the AI profile. She clambered to her feet, a bit dazed but all naval major. "And you two," she ordered Serov and Olsen, "man a station now. Dingo, on my six."

"Aye, aye," he puffed, already on her heels.

The full complement of crewmen and engineers that ordinarily staffed a starship this size was reduced to a skeleton crew of a few servicemen led by Reina Cruz, and two civilians, Dillon Olsen and Earl conscripted into hasty service. Stats and reports joined the din of sensor beeps, astrogation codes and systems checks.

Earl took up a yeoman's post, eyeing realtime visuals of the abaft stellar field. Only the ever expanding universe yawned beyond the Beta Corpus Arc. A thin red crescent the width of a small moon marked the threshold into the Milky Way. Or rather, a terminus for its companion gateway, Alpha Corpus, some trillion parsecs off. Only a millennium ago, the *AAF Fatimah* had emerged from that Arc region in search of new planetary Edens. Several hundred generations hence, Terrans faced untold perils: rogue quasars, temporal rifts that may well have led to a mass extinction event like the Holocene Cataclysm.

Cruz still wore her Lycra body sleeve but was all-out battle-ready. "Dingo, report!"

"All clear abaft," he relayed. "Aft sensors read no sign of hostile craft. We're...oh, shit hells! Ten—no, thirty bogeys bearing on our vector."

"Terjj?"

"Who else can swallow in-system that formidably?"

"Iyreans, Hydrans, or if we're so lucky—"

"Our boys!" came Dmitri Serov's excited confirmation from communications. "Admiral Osumi, Agatha Starbase, 42nd Windward Command. We've an incoming hail, uh, advising the *Scimitar* to hold anchor."

"Great timing," Cruz spat bitterly. "Not a whole lot for the cavalry to save. Admiral Osumi missed the party by weeks."

"We were busy in the trenches, Major," came Miho Osumi's husky voice on the comlink. "Got here posthaste once we saw your distress ping."

Caught off guard by the realtime sitrep, Cruz clamped a hand over he mouth. Earl mustered a dry repartee: "Glad we kept the lights on, then. A really big one, in fact."

"God Almighty, that's no planet. Can't be, according to our charts. Somebody," the admiral barked to bridge officers on her vessel, "get me stats on that fireball!"

The alien brilliance cast icy blue daylight onto the arriving armada of Terran starships. A covey of nebula ships flanked a Titan-class carrier, the admiral's flagship. The colossal construct dwarfed its sister ships by multiple kilometers. The *CSS Andalusia* outsized anything built by Terrans, save for the *Archangel*. And each nebula ship was twice the size of the *Scimitar*.

Earl knew the lot of them could fit into a single portal ship with room to spare. Yet his bosom swelled with pride. Terrans had come to retake Beta Corpus, come hell or high—oh, cripes!

"We got company, guys," Earl alerted them.

"Ah, frack! Terjjan bogeys coming in hot," Cruz confirmed as klaxons blared. She dashed for a gunnery chair even as pulsefire lanced into a nearby nebula ship. Dyson shields enveloped the *Scimitar* as she broke free of Gilgal's rings and lurched into the fray, rail guns blazing.

Earl leapt into a chair of his own. The gyre-sphere englobed his body in sensory webbing as he snatched the psionic joystick. Virtual icons played over his retinas while vivid real-space yawned about him. The sensation felt like being in an Ambri telepathy orb...back in the cockpit of the *Icarus* all those millennia ago.

Gritting his teeth, Earl fired and fired, almost gleeful with adrenaline as he and Cruz took out a swath of Waryth fighter craft. Fyang-class cruisers entered the glaring melee, those winking out of the violet maw of a worm pore. Along with two very menacing Mantis destroyers bent on hurrying the Terrans into extinction, there also loomed a scythe-winged craft.

A Shaytan wyrm?

Or perhaps it merely shared its ghastly design: a taloned creature bred with psionic homing instincts. Sleek silver-black hull with twain cockpits that looked like the fang-shaped skulls of its prototype. Then its prehensile leg-wings flexed sharply, not rigidly like smart metal, but actual sinew and tendons!

The gargoyle hurled telekinetic ordnance at Sabre strikers that poured from Osumi's carrier like a swarm of nesters. Six strikers exploded silently in the azure battlefield now roiling outside the *Scimitar*. Earl fired like crazy, gyrating and banking as if in the cockpit of his own Sabre.

Terjjan pulsefire tore into every Terran craft, hit Dyson shields or plex-skin hulls with merciless aim. Ionic lightning met plasma streams of ugly orange, white-glare death flashes and violet nimbus clouds. All the while an alien light invaded the gas giant's rings, its four tiny moons, and outlying ice veils. Beyond even Gilgal's astrophysical extremes, this nascent fire registered its magnetic pull upon the instruments of every cockpit.

Dear sky, it behaved like a neutron star.

Gravity fields shifted ever so slightly aboard every starship, the decks of Terjjan and Terran vessels alike, sent seizures throughout bulkheads and stressed fuselage sensors: ENGAGE LOW-ORBIT THRUSTERS...EXTREME GRAVITONIC FORCES DETECTED...ENGAGE LOW-ORBIT THRUSTERS...

ONBOARD GRAVITY FIELD AT NINETY-TWO POINT SIX PERCENT INTEGRITY. ALL HANDS PREPARE FOR EMRGENCY ATMOSPHERE PURGE IN MINUS SIXTY SECONDS. CRYOSTASIS ADVISED. REPEAT...

Amid the hellish fusillade engulfing the *Scimitar*, Earl's mind riled: I didn't survive two epic wars, time travel over twenty millennia, or Selusa's vile witchery just to die in a starship's emergency vacuum.

"Neither did I," came Coryn's angelic voice. "Yet we'll both perish if the *Scimitar* is lost in this skirmish. Or engulfed by neutron mass."

"Well, great," Earl huffed in mid-fire. Osumi's carrier sustained a hit to her aft decks even as a Terjjan destroyer listed abruptly after taking a direct blow to its exposed hull. Shields were failing rapidly. "We've got seconds till we're sucking vacuum. Worst case, we'll freeze before entering stasis. Not unless we hyperjump out-system fast."

"On it, sir."

Energy surged over the entire vessel as the Dyson shield ruptured, and atoms got shorn from their spacetime vectors, this before the event horizon gaped over the Beta Corpus Arc, its eons ancient grandeur and its silent sentinels.

Seconds yawned…

Over eternities yet born, perhaps, time reclaimed Earl's pores as the *Scimitar* emerged from hyperdimensional space only to face death anew. Still engirded by the gunnery chair's neural mesh, Earl saw vividly their peril looming against a backdrop of neon stellar mass. Gas clouds limned the vast portal ships clustered near a Jovian planet draped in violet veils.

"Coryn, the hell are we? Why'd we swallow into…into…a Terjjan nest, dear sky?"

"A miscalculation, I'm sure, Mr. Dingo, sir. But not my doing at all. Someone else engaged the hypernav engine."

As if to underscore her surmise, the neural mesh fell away and Dillon Olsen held an ion reaper aimed squarely at Earl's forehead. "Sorry, old boy, but the bounty on your skull is too great to pass up. Nothing personal, just the ruja, Dingo."

The Cro-Magnon traitor kept his ion reaper trained on Earl. Reina Cruz remained incapacitated as the *Scimitar* plowed into the

Terjjan armada's midst. Why hadn't those wormheads obliterated the Terran ship? Gritting his teeth in bitter memory, Earl recalled Dillon Olsen's confession. A bounty, yes. The Terjj had put a price on Earl's head; some obscene amount of ruja Olsen hoped to collect but would likely never enjoy.

"Don't be stupid," Earl tried to reason dryly. "It's a fool's errand, Olsen. This won't end well for you. Trust me, it won't."

"Rich old boy, this'll end badly for you. And certainly for the major there. Oh yeah. A lovely bonus for the extra cargo."

Olsen holstered the burner now that Earl was secured by flex-wire like Cruz. As the viewport filled with the dark hull of a looming portal ship, the dwarfed *Scimitar* shuddered, gravitonic snares grasping onto the vessel. Olsen paused while a coded transmission pulsed in his neural link. "Ah, there we go. Right on schedule, ladies."

Lights flickered abroad the starship as some hyperspatial pathway yawned over them and a nauseating lurch transfluxed their atoms into the portal ship's inner decks. Not for the first time Earl wished he'd never gotten salvaged from deep space by Arlya Seroh and her Do'fin cohort. If only he'd remained blissfully adrift in icy vacuum. None of this nightmarish ordeal would've come to pass. He might still be a freak of nature, fused to a living kelp and still pregnant with Ambri embryos—but oblivious to this horrid fate.

Cripes, I'm as fracked as fracked can be. Fyr crap in hell for sure, Dingo.

"Oh, come now," Coryn said via neural pulses unheard by Olsen. "We'll not go gently into that good night, sir. I'll do my best to engineer an escape, however unlikely that scenario may seem. Although I admit I'm in truly unfamiliar territory where Terjjan technology is concerned."

Albeit only a glimmer of hope from a virtual angel, Earl took refuge in that unlikely scenario. God deliver them all, their fate certainly looked sealed from the look of things.

Cruz was in for one helluva rude awakening when she came to. Earl doubted her military expertise encompassed subterfuge while confined to the belly of a portal ship. No, sir. This wasn't on any Terran's list of survival tactics. Hell wasn't so blissful to fools.

III.

Aboard the Scimitar,
Days after capture by the Che'ethrah.
February 23, 3213 CE.

Dillon Olsen's ion reaper had forestalled any acts of bravery or mutiny. Earl gritted his teeth. The idiot actually thought he'd collect a bounty from the Terjj. And do what with the ruja, you Cro-Magnon fool? Didn't he realize the gilled tyrants were cornered, desperate and highly pissed? Sijjo Ith had personally led a brutal campaign against several worlds. He'd done so in an effort to punish those who might've harbored the fugitive Earl Dagarth.

The Terjj wanted to vanquish any traces of the Ambri or their mystic cult disguised as Terran religion. Wolf 16's adherents of the Whispering Way defied their schemes and so endured a costly retribution. The Terjj had scorched the Temple of Runes during the Siege of Tears. In that same year, Sijjo had carpeted Neiro with pulsefire for an alleged Terran strike on Ghaz. Now, after two centuries living incognito, Rex Dingo's true identity brought him full circle.

Olsen had betrayed the entire crew of the *Scimitar* and willingly swallowed into the *Che'ethrah's* inner space. Only, time must've dilated in those seemingly few hours the Terran vessel had been transfluxed into the Endyr Nebula's heart. Earl's internal chronometer (normally attuned to the ambassador link frequencies) oddly reflected a five day transit. They'd escaped a rogue neutron star only to swallow into a time warp of inexplicable origin.

Even now, Coryn wrestled with this new enigma while sifting through a plethora of scenarios for a probable escape. "Genesis alive, Mr. Dingo," she griped on subtle wavelengths. "Angels aren't programmed to deal with Terjjan portal ships. But if there's a way out of this crux, we'll find it."

Earl glared at the traitor who'd sold him out.

"Sorry again," Olsen bothered to say. "Like I said, it's just business. An obscene amount of ruja, that bounty on your head."

"Yeah, well, good plan, genius," Earl scoffed. He was still restrained like Cruz and the others. Still a bit groggy after being tranked, Earl forced his words. "What'd you think? They'd just set you on your merry way once you handed me over?"

"Actually, yes."

Cruz yanked at her restraints. "Please. The Terjj deal only in brutality. You know that, Olsen."

He grinned darkly. "Princess, don't fret over my fate. Dillon Olsen ain't on a half cocked errand. Me, I got leverage."

"Orbit hells, you do!" Earl spat. "I know these fanged demons. A lot better than any Terran alive. Trust me. This won't end well for you."

"We'll see, Rex Dingo. When you're just a footnote in history, me? I'll be—oh, the frack!"

A warhead exploded on impact with the *Scimitar*'s still active Dyson shield. The tremendous force knocked Olsen off his feet, sent the ion reaper flying. The hitchhiker DNA surged to the fore, took over Earl's cells in a mere blink, and He Who Builds Reefs seized the opportunity. Scaly, reptilian skin excreted a slimy enzyme, freeing Earl's bound wrists. He slashed the flexwire at his neck with sharp talons. Slit pupils blinked at Olsen, briefly startling the prospector.

When Olsen made for the reaper, Earl leaped, powerful legs lifting him over the desperate man. He swept up the flash burner and let off a pulse into Olsen's clavicle. The Cro-Magnon face contorted in pain as Olsen grasped his ruined shoulder. "Aah, damn you!" he hissed. "Who the hell are you? What in damnation?"

"Ssstayy put. Or dieee hyumaaan."

Cruz shrieked. "Dingo! Get back!"

Amon'kh-Nil-R'su'esh'Tah yanked the reaper toward the creature that hovered nearby. The gargoyle had winked into their midst using hypernavs. Nothing so pernicious-looking had he ever laid eyes on in all his protracted life. Its sleek black twain skulls dripped with icy methane venom. Horned frills vibrated with subsonic vocalizations his S'both ears could hardly withstand as it focused on Olsen, then Amon'kh, then Cruz.

"Get back!" she urged again. Her words barely registered above the sharp pain seizing his brain. S'both eardrums nearly ruptured, Earl's DNA pushed the Builder's cloak aside and he scurried in retreat.

With scythe claws, the gargoyle tore into Olsen's paralyzed limbs, swiftly disemboweling him. Dripping with gore, it now turned to Earl and Cruz.

"Kill it," she pleaded. "What are you waiting for? Shoot it!"

Earl let it loom menacingly close, then fired point blank at its twain skulls. Double tap and done, mother Fyr!

The hideous thing fell dead, its great wings crumpled but still twitching. Earl aimed at its armored thorax. Red-hot ions tore into the beating heart—a deathblow. "Let's hope there aren't others aboard," he said, heart in throat.

"Others might come," Coryn replied from his mind's periphery. She'd taken over the *Scimitar*'s defenses shortly after Olsen's jump into that Terjjan worm pore. "The Dyson shield is at forty-one percent integrity. Sooner or later the Terjj will breach the hull, Mr. Dingo, sir. We should consider evasive tactics."

"We're in the belly of a portal ship," he reminded the virtual persona. "Like slugfish in a barrel."

"I'm arguing nothing there," Cruz said, unaware of Coryn's existence. "But with my hands tied, I can't alter this crisis."

Earl searched for something to cut her restraints with. He saw a laser blade clipped to Olsen's hip, retrieved it, and rushed to free Cruz. He cut the flexwire at her wrists and neck. "We've gotta work fast. The shield is near failing," he told her.

"I guessed that much. That bombardment is straining our systems." She raced forward to the control bridge with Earl on her heels.

The grim scene that met them stopped the major short. Each of the crewmen lay executed on the bridge. Dmitri Serov lay among them. An ion reaper turned on them by Olsen while Earl and Cruz had engaged Terjjan craft at Beta Corpus.

There was no time to mourn their loss just now. Another gargoyle could swallow into the *Scimitar*'s midst at any second. Or a warhead's impact might finally overload the ship's defenses. Thus far the Terjj had merely hit their hull with exploratory potshots, that despite massively superior weaponry.

An impact jarred the vessel on cue. Both he and Cruz tumbled to the deck, alarms blaring as the AI program repeated Coryn's projections: DYSON SHIELD AT THIRTY-FOUR PERCENT INTEGRITY. ALL HANDS PREPARE FOR IMMINENT HULL BREACH...

Earl eyed the *Che'ethrah*'s inner space beyond the viewport. Mantis destroyers, Fyang strikers and Waryths by the countless hundreds and thousands. Wyrmtrees writhed along the portal ship's concaved worldscape and the decks held millions of waiting Terjj. "We've gotta hurry," he warned.

"Yeah. Like I'm not hurrying." Cruz dashed her fingers over icons, cursing. "Orbit hells, frack! Dingo, nothing's responding. No navs, no weapons. Can't even boot the hyperdrive."

"Oh, crap," Earl groaned.

Coryn resolved onto the control bridge, angelic and calm. This time she also revealed herself to Cruz via the ship's hologram projectors. "May I offer my assistance?"

"Who's she?"

"I'm Coryn. A virtual persona program."

"I know what you are," Cruz said. "Who put you aboard the *Scimitar*?"

"I did," Earl said, cutting the inquiry short. "Let's save the introductions for another time. Like when we aren't about to die, ladies."

"Did you offer assistance earlier?" Cruz pressed Coryn. "'Cause we're stuck in Oort crap here. Excuse the Anglo Fusion."

"Emoted metaphor excused," Coryn quipped. "Navigational entanglements aside, yes, it seems our vessel's auxiliary controls have been nullified. Only an authenticated cipher can override the systems block put in place by Dillon Olsen."

"Great. He put an encrypted firewall on the navs." Cruz hit the control panel. "Stupid idiot!"

Earl asked, "Coryn? Can you get around the firewall? In the next minute or so?" He sensed their time was running out. The shield wouldn't keep the Terjj at bay much longer.

"I'll try," Coryn promised.

She winked from view just as the ship's atmosphere fizzled oddly. Another ogre assassin come stealthily in their midst? Earl lifted the ion reaper, ready.

Cruz sensed it too. She retrieved a sidearm from one of the slain crewmen. A hefty plasma pistol. "Smell that hint of brine and sulfur?"

"Yep. Gill breath if any stink compares."

They both eyed the corridor leading to the gunnery deck amidships. It was where the first gargoyle had appeared earlier.

Seconds ticked as Earl braced for death—or worse. Getting taken alive wasn't a merciful outcome by any stretch of the imagination. Death, while grim and utterly final, might bring closure to a ghastly encounter. Terjjan had no word for torture. What they did to their captives went beyond torment. Earl had lived that hell long ago. He'd not willingly relive that nightmare.

Yet the Terjj must've wanted him alive. Otherwise, why toy with exploratory strikes against the *Scimitar*'s defensive shield? Why send a gargoyle hunter that could have easily targeted Earl, not Olsen, by homing on his genetic scent?

Gooseflesh crept along Earl's arms and nape as he realized his fate. That creature fell all too easily when he'd shot it. It hadn't edged closer to kill him. It had only come for Olsen and the others.

"Coryn," Earl said, "now's a good time for a miracle."

The first Terjj materialized fully armed, hair cords writhing, fangs bared. Gills agape, it snarled an order in Terjjan. "Gthai zhu'gh fir!" Come quietly, little spawn!

Cruz fired a plasma round at its armored chest. That hardly made the Terjj twitch. Earl unleashed an ion bolt at its ugly visage. That fizzled harmlessly off its energy shield.

The air shifted as yet another huge Terjj phased into existence at its flank. Then a third, impressively built specimen with a swarthy pelt and pithy eyes materialized. The latter wore the heraldry and sashes of a high-ranking soldier. He pushed to the fore and spoke in smooth Anglo Fusion. "I am Squadron Chief Ust'fah Myrr. Admiral Sijjo Ith has sent me to fetch you, Earl Dagarth."

"Who says I'm the human you're after?" Earl said, stalling for time. "We all look the same ugly to you Terjj."

Ust'fah snarled. "Either surrender quietly, ape, or suffer Sijjo's wrath. Decide quickly." He poised his paw on an odd-looking weapon coiled at his hip. It looked organic, like a modified benjar blade.

Earl cringed in memory of Selusa's benjar invading his flesh two centuries ago. The ungodly rite had transformed his very cells...

"Coryn," he uttered dryly, "anytime today, please."

ALL SYSTEMS ONLINE, MR. DINGO. PHASE ONE ASTROGATION SEQUENCE ACTIVATED. PLEASE SECURE ALL HANDS. GRAVITY NULLIFICATION IMMINENT...

Gravity fled their limbs just then. The trio of Terjj bellowed angrily as their bulks tumbled into slow midair twirls. A hatch irised shut between them and the two humans. Earl swam swiftly as he could to a nearby thrust harness. Cruz clung to a handrail at the pilot's console, her naval training driving her instincts.

Angry at the ruse, the Terjj assaulted the hatch with a salvo of pulsefire. The hatch's integrity held thanks to state-of-the-art fire plating and sensory shields. But Earl knew it wouldn't save them for long. Not when the gilled demons were hellbent on capturing this legendary fugitive—presumably alive. Dead if he defied them for much longer; which, of course, Earl intended on doing until his last breath.

"Suck it, worm heads!" he taunted. Adrift in the zero-gravity of the control bridge were the unfettered bodies of the *Scimitar*'s murdered crew. The eerie scene blurred abruptly as Coryn hurled the starship into hyperspace...along with their Terjj hitchhikers.

Cruz must've marveled at the irony, too, as a starry sclera swirled into view when they exited the worm pore. Where exactly only Coryn knew, but Earl prayed it was great light-years from that Terjj nest. When normal space again cradled their vessel, and microgravity kicked in, Cruz hastily checked her displays. "Oh, flux hells! Why this quadrant? Ah, frack!"

"Where'd we jump to?" Earl asked, easing from his harness. "Coryn, tell me you didn't flux us into that skyjack hell pit."

Coryn winked onto the bridge. "Maybe you'd prefer negotiating with Sijjo Ith. Shall I reset a course for the Endyr Nebula?"

"No need," Cruz told them. "We've got gills on our six. Damn your angel, Dingo. She gave them an easy wake to follow. Never ever swallow directly to your escape vector. Rookie maneuver."

"Options were finite," Coryn demurred. "At least we have a fully garrisoned armada here. And a slight tactical advantage."

Earl groaned. "Yeah, if dying swiftly gives us any advantage."

Fiery streaks tore from the Fjoriian warships as the Terjjan swarm descended on the icy planet. All the while, pulsefire battered the hatch sealing the control bridge as the *Scimitar* rolled into the fray, guns blazing.

Sijjo Ith had shrieked with fury when the *Scimitar* swallowed from the portal ship's confines. He'd come personally to the *Che'ethrah* when Olsen's signal alerted their spy probes. The prospector had betrayed the Terran who'd evaded Sijjo's talons for two standard centuries. That cursed ape Earl Dagarth had lived right under their gills all those years as Rex Dingo. The Blue Star Interstellar mogul had even travelled back to Ghaz shortly before Dragoh Tah's infamous Red Invasion.

Sijjo hissed as his Fyang arced out of the Porthole Eye gaping over Fjorii. The icy Terran world had long enjoyed a halcyon existence in the Gilae system. Even before the Terjj went into exile in the Lotus Cloud, Sijjo had yenned to seize the planet and mine its rare ore and uranium. But tactical factors and timing had saved the Fjoriians the fate of less enriched worldlets and moons. He dared not jeopardize his fleet with a strike against a key Terran world when they'd had no home base. Not beyond petty strikes against backwater systems, anyway.

Sharjah's discovery had altered Sijjo's tactical vantage greatly. That and the *Ijnar Glory*'s capture from Tjarif Dhul-Fafnir. With its ability to gape new wormpaths, Sijjo could now strike with impunity and, if need be, retreat to a well fortified harbor there in the Endyr Nebula.

Dagarth will not escape my talons yet again, Sijjo vowed. Undoubtedly, the ape had played some role in Terjjah's demise. Now the human spawn had defied Ust'fah Myrr's ultimatum and escaped with the squadron chief. Did he think Sijjo such a fool that he'd be allowed to report the flagship's coordinates to the Terran Confederacy?

Sjak, Albar shelter Sharjah from utter damnation.

IV.

Jaspur Ruins Sanctuary,
Myrrh Cliffs, Eastern Akureyi Plains.
Sovereign Republic of Fjorii.
April 3, 3213 CE.

Bleak windswept tundra and forbidding terrain had met them when Earl and Cruz emerged from their lifepods. A harsh white sun glared over steep cliffs eastward, and icy volcanic alps further north. Ghastly howls had filled the chilled nights as they hunkered in the ruins, warmed by the scant heat of glow orbs and each other's body. Days on end had been a routine of hunting small burrowing fauna, or getting ice shards to melt for drinking water.

After nearly six weeks hiding in the Jaspur Ruins, Earl felt ready to send up a signal flare. "If I have to eat one more guptiwi I'll puke. Dear sky, this planet is hell."

Reina Cruz eyed her morsel. "Yeah, it's pretty awful, Rex. But the alternative will be far worse. Skyjacks aren't renowned for their hospitality."

All the rations they'd taken from the lifepods were long gone. The glow globes wouldn't last much longer, Earl felt sure, and surviving Fjorii's gelid nights without a heat source wasn't likely. A lack of tree growth in the plains meant a lack of wood to build fires. As it was, they had only their terrasuits to shield them from the harsh elements. And the shelter of caves.

In their time not spent hunting guptiwi or melting ice or snuggling by globe light, they explored the ruins. Sufi hermits had left poetic verse on the marbled surfaces, some dating to the Twenty-Eighth Century. The remnants of Ali Zamakshari adorned the same dwellings once inhabited by a race long vanished from Fjorii. Strange glyphs chronicled some odyssey from a forgotten star system. Deeper in the Myrrh Cliffs gushed methane pools not unlike those in Ghaz's subterrain.

They'd just climbed from a grotto in the ruins when, on day thirty-eight, scout drones spied their hideout. A huge fixed-winged Osprey swung into view and issued a Fjoriic command. "Set down your sidearms and surrender!"

Ambassador linguistics filters left no misinterpretation of the expressed futility of an attempt to resist capture. They'd fallen on enemy soil. That they'd also invited a Terjjan strike force into sovereign Fjorii space only made the fugitives ripe for termination if they fled. So both obeyed, hands raised.

In short order, they were taken into custody, screened by white-eyed defense agents, given full cavity scans, and then hauled into a military base's command center just outside Fjorii's capital, Reykjan.

"We regret the harsh screening you've endured," said Colonel Samir Yusefkov. "But given the manner of your arrival, we understandably suspected an invasion. After all, Fjorii has seceded from Terra." Regret laced the colonel's voice. "Not all Fjoriians applaud this new Caliphate Union, to be sure. But the Council of Amirs has spoken. I therefore must formally consider you two enemy combatants."

"We're diplomats," Earl asserted. "Terrans shot down by Terjjan fighter craft."

Maybe they'd come to the same conclusion upon seeing the *Scimitar*'s strewn wreckage. Earl and Cruz had engaged Sijjo's forces, after all, right alongside the Fjoriian longships. "We recovered the *Scimitar*'s black box. All your logs, every transmission and FTL jump, Mr. Dingo. We're quite aware of the diplomatic mission you allege. As well as the incident at Beta Corpus."

Tall, charcoal complexioned with gunmetal gray eyes, Yusefkov had typical Fjoriian traits. Alien, transhuman genes chiseled by the planet's extreme climes. He spoke in crisp Anglo Fusion rather than his native Fjoriic dialect. The dark gray uniform and barret matched the command center's austere utilitarian mood.

Neither the colonel nor his science officers wore glitzy insignia beyond a Gilaen star encircled by a crescent. "Major Cruz? We'd value your insights on this anomaly encountered at Beta Corpus. Please expound on your theory as to what its origins might be."

Cruz nodded. "Dmitri Serov, our astrophysicist, believed it was an exotic luminary. Likely an orphaned gas giant. Or some remnant of a supernova event. We'd not had time to explore Dmitri's hypothesis."

"Then tell us," said a scarfed female with ivory-white eyes, "how'd you evade its event horizon? Nothing else escaped its overwhelming gravitational influence, Major."

"Nothing at all?" Cruz asked, miffed by the revelation. "Not even the Arc gate itself? Dear nova, not Osumi's flagship, too, I pray."

"Our probes indicate a total loss of Osumi's battle group. Terjj casualties were far less since they swallowed safely away. Along with your ship."

Earl realized where this was going. Terran starships didn't ordinarily vaunt more than faster-than-light capability. The technology that allowed vessels to swallow into folded vectors was the domain of Terjj and their cousins. Hydrans and their sometimes allied Iyrean neighbors utilized hypernavs derived from Pertheid science.

"Um, yeah, about that," Cruz hesitated. She was privy to closely guarded military secrets the Fjoriians coveted, no doubt. "With all due respect, I'm not authorized to disclose sensitive intel. No more than you're free to talk about Ötzi, Colonel."

Yusefkov bristled. "A valid point. But the difference, Major Cruz, is I'm not a spy caught behind enemy lines." An ion reaper in hand, the nearest MP moved subtly closer. Give the order, sir, his posture said. "At ease, Sergii. Neither of our guests is being charged with espionage. Not yet."

The MP eased off, but only just. Colonel Yusefkov bore down on Earl. Eyes measuring his Cushite features against vid file images he'd likely reviewed on the former CEO of Blue Star Interstellar. "Mr. Dingo, it's clear Major Cruz is duty-bound by military code. You, on the other hand, aren't Stellar Navy. So, let's discuss your role in this, uh, diplomatic detail Singh conscripted you for."

Cruz's eyes warned him against giving away any secrets. Don't do it, Dingo.

"Cripes already," Earl groaned.

"Yes?"

"We were pursuing the *CSS Archangel.* To warn its crew about a crisis in the Cyrus system."

"Go on."

"Well, that's all I know, actually. That and something about a message. A relic transmission intercepted by Epoch probes."

An older officer interrupted. "He doesn't know, does he? About Thebe's real objective in the Cyrus frontier. Now, why is that, Special Agent Reina Cruz?"

"Agent?" echoed Earl.

"Listen," said Cruz, ignoring Earl's irked tone, "we've already lost critical time in the Endyr. Colonel, let's cut the roleplaying here. Special Office knows all about Fjorii's secret project on Ötzi. About the Kepler drive. What you awakened deep below Ötzi's ice floes, in fact. We know the Ang-Xi made contact with the same entity Ojer Cortiz did. That's how they woke those sleeper moons. Yes, Colonel. We know about the world engines."

A lithe, well-honed ghost emerged from her quiet observation behind a morph-plaz screen. Xena Kilpatrick. The ex-Special Forces merc still wore a skintight terrasuit, as if she'd just come from Fjorii's icy tundra. The dark Saracen eyes, olive skin tone, and shapely body took Earl aback. Why is she in this command center, here on Fjorii?

"Ah, then. I'm sure you've met Captain Xena Kilpatrick," said Yusefkov.

"We've met," Earl said numbly.

"Nice to see you again," Xena greeted. "Sorry it's not under more pleasant circumstances, Dingo. A lot has transpired as since out last tryst." She gave Cruz an unreadable look, arms crossed. "Well, well. Quite a reunion, indeed. Aren't you a long way from New Cairo? Last I recall, Special Office had you spying out some mystery at Gibraltar's Gate."

Cruz merely glared at Xena.

Earl now saw the unmistakable likeness. The two were related. Sisters, yes.

Arlya hated her choice.

She couldn't risk losing Xena Kilpatrick in the wind yet again. The ex-Special Forces merc had gotten space-folding tech to her Fjoriian employers, it seemed, despite efforts by Special Office to stop her. Now the brainpather spy shot at supralight-speed vectors into the Lotus Cloud's swirling starscape. Likely attempting an impromptu jump, the Trojan-class ship streaked like a fiery angel into a newly widened worm pore. A faint speck remained of its drive plume.

Arlya's orders had been clear. Get recon on Sijjo Ith's armada in the Endyr Nebula, assess the losses at Beta Corpus, then report to Senfax Starbase. Easy mission...until her and Xuye's tryst with the Arc Builders. Or at least with beings who claimed themselves as such.

Now she had a mere nanosecond to ponder the ramifications of not pursuing Xena. She'd nearly let the merc go, too, but for a secondary biopulse she now detected aboard the fleeing starship. Dear heavenly novae, Earl Dagarth's pulse! Albeit muddled by intense tachyon bursts expelled by the worm pore, it definitely was Earl's life sign.

Alive.

After she'd pawned him off to those skyjacks on Ötzi, all to save Xuye, Arlya had truly hoped Earl's knack for subterfuge would keep him safe until she could retrieve him. Do I defy the

Joint Chiefs or risk losing both Earl and the elusive Xena Kilpatrick?

All but half a nanosecond filled the void between Arlya and the galaxy's very fate.

"Xuye, buckle up. We're going after them."

"Who?"

"That worm pore dead ahead," she said, briefly forgetting he couldn't see the faster-than-light ship with his naked eyes. "Rex Dingo's pulse is on that starship. We're hitchhiking its wake."

"Oh, not again," Xuye moaned.

Before his Do'fin pulse ever rose, the *Solar Contact* swallowed into folded space dead on the *Abu Talib*'s hyperdimensional wake. All in a blur, the scramjet was encapsulated in a wormhole's peristaltic wrinkle and hurled across millions of astral hectares into a stellar region Arlya only recognized from top secret charts. The Trojan-class ship hadn't jumped to these coordinates on a whim or by miscalculated maneuvers. Neither had Xena's cutlass cut impetuously into the void.

Nor did Arlya regret her choice now that Cyrus 794G's tawny, blue-streaked face loomed before the *Contact*. Now why had Fjorii sent a Trojan into this system on such urgent vectors?

She knew one thing for sure. If Admiral Hector Thebe reacted to the encroachment by strict protocol, Xena and her crew were already in the crosshairs.

Along with poor Earl Dagarth.

A split second is all they'd had to hail the *Archangel* and her two nebula ship escorts. Xena felt the irony gnawing at each of their souls. Only months ago the Fjorii Republic had left the Confederacy to align with the Khidr states. Now here came a Trojan-class spy ship swallowing into the Cyrus system with an urgent intercept. She knew it was a risky gambit, too. Shields be damned, if Thebe wanted to blast the *Abu Talib* out of orbit he well could have. Surely their firepower outclassed that of a Trojan cutlass any day.

So engrossed in the awesome spectacle of the colossal arkship, Xena nearly ignored the tiny blip that pulsated on the astrogation screen. A lunar-class scramjet, if the sensors proved worthy, that must've done the virtually impossible. Craft that small didn't have independent hypernavs, so far as Xena knew; not Terran spacecraft, anyhow. And as utterly unlikely it was that Terjj or Hydrants had hitched onto their jump wake using a Terran craft, Xena shuddered at the notion.

What if they had?

So far as Special Office or NavCom knew, the Enemy hadn't learned about Cyrus 794G. Project Exodus had remained a topmost secret even after the *Archangel*'s launch from Peoria months ago. The average citizens of Terra had no idea the elites of their societies had fled en mass to the Cyrus system. Most were too embroiled in the conflict consuming the Confederacy to notice or protest the Exodus if they did know.

The first officer on the bridge hailed the mystery craft. "Lunar-class scramjet, identify. State your call sign and authority."

A crackle returned: "This is the *Solar Contact*. Permission to board the *Abu Talib* for a chat with Captain Kilpatrick."

"Why?"

"She's a wanted fugitive." came the bold reply.

Xena snatched up the handheld comlink. "By whose authority do you make that claim? And who's got the balls to execute your warrant?"

"Arlya Ai-One Seroh at your service. Now if you'll kindly dilate the aft shuttle bay hatch, I'll be along to collect my bounty, Xena Kilpatrick."

Nothing more absurd could've put a smile on Xena's lips. After a lifetime living in the shadows, she at last could match wits with a brainpather worthy of her own talents. Well, this ought to be interesting, Xena thought.

❖　❖　❖

"Fancy meeting you here, Rex sweetie."

"You know her?" Cruz asked, holding Arlya with a contemptuous glare.

Like her sister Xena, Reina Cruz had prior dealings with their newly arrived guest. Earl didn't imagine it was pleasant history from the hostile mood of their reunion. It's probably why Arlya hadn't let Xuye join the boarding party. The Do'fin remained aboard the *Contact*.

Earl, Cruz and Xena had met Arlya in the aft shuttle bay where they now stood. Decidedly out of earshot of the *Abu Talib*'s crew, and away from potential crossfire should bad blood spill over, Earl merely nodded at Cruz's probe.

Xena offered, "She pawned him off to Yuri Khazer. Got him conscripted into the Ötzi Project. Didn't she, Dingo?"

"She did."

"Earth hells," Arlya spat, fiery blue eyes cutting at Xena Kilpatrick. "We've all sold somebody out, haven't we? Let's not trifle over one mogul, ladies. Besides, he's very resourceful. It's true I lied to you," she conceded, eyes on Earl again. "But I had no other choice. Yuri had the access codes I needed to get Xuye back."

"That Do'fin thief got himself shanghaied. Not me. Nobody asked Rex Dingo to sign up for all this espionage crap."

"Okay," Xena said, "let's take a breath. This crisis is traumatic enough without us cutting each other's throats. Although some might well deserve it. Let's just let bygones be for now. At least until we survive our standoff with Thebe, anyway."

Cruz blew out an exasperated sigh. "Xena, it's no standoff. They've got bigger guns trained on us. We just hope they'll confirm the *Abu Talib*'s relay pulse. Although given our means of arrival, Thebe has to believe it's legit."

After the *Contact* docked, Xena had hastened from the command bridge with Cruz and Earl in tow, all incredulous at Arlya's bold stunt. While the crew kept vigil on the tense parley going on between the *Abu Talib* and the *Archangel*, mostly via coded relays, Earl joined the three femme fatales amidships. The wide observation porthole gave a spectacular view of Cyrus 794G's curved horizon. One of its moons crested the sunlit hemisphere while its twin remained eclipsed by the planet. Tawny hues meandered amid blue-green regions and raging cyclones. Earl wondered at Olsen's forecast of hellish climate shifts and cataclysmic seismic events. And Singh's alleged intercept mission to warn Thebe.

Lydia Nev had joined Project Exodus, he'd learned in transit. The Wolfan Prima was likely already planetside. Earl briefly tried to seek out her ithkah in the Awareness. He did his best to convey a dire warning to her...of the looming event sensed by the entity within his DNA. Amon'kh-Nil-R'su'esh'Tah lingered just below Earl's conscious, still biding its time, still held in servitude by instincts beyond human physiology.

"Dingo?" Cruz said, mien filled with concern. "You look a bit green. Like before with Olsen."

"I'm fine. Just..."

He raised his hands and saw the greenish pallor, the subtle scales overtaking his pores, He Who Builds Reefs pushing to the fore. "Oh, Thlag crap! I'm going full reptile. Dear sky, not now."

"Psychomorphic cells," Arlya gasped. Only she among them had not laid eyes on the hitchhiker being until now. "Where'd he acquire tech like that? Allah protect us, that's no brainpather illusion, poor wretched man!"

Earl gulped at the flash burner in Xena's hand. "Wait, hold on," he mustered, webbed hands lifted. "Thisss present form isss necessary. A danger comes to thisss planet very ssoon."

"What danger?" Arlya asked. Awe etched darkly on her ebony mien, she looked genuinely afraid. "Another lunar ablation? Terjj, maybe?"

"No," Amon'kh told them in his own voice. "A new life force you have no comprehensssion of. Neither have you adequate defenses against its superior designs. Only we who serve Onul-Bin'th-Nu'Tah can repel itsss threat."

"We?"

"Yes," Xena replied, still training her sidearm on Earl and the alien possessing him. "They're energy beings. Servants of She Who Hunts Novae. The alien intelligence we encountered in that derelict ship on Ötzi. I was tasked with monitoring the Fjoriians' endeavors in the Gilae system. Right about the time the Ambri reappeared on Ghaz, I got assigned by Special Office."

"And went rogue," Cruz accused. "You betrayed your oath, Xena. Selling Confederacy secrets to skyjacks of all skullduggery."

"Don't get high and mighty, baby sis. NavCom has its own dark secrets." She eyed Earl. "Or didn't Singh tell you, Rex? About their mission here in the Cyrus system? Yeah, it seems Thebe knew all along exactly what force instigated the Eclipse. Oh, they'd have the masses think it's all a mystery no species has ever faced. Reina probably played her role perfectly. Ah, yes. The ever dutiful science officer off on an errand to warn the *Archangel* of impending peril. Or whatever scenario Singh orchestrated."

"Whoa," Earl said, reclaiming his genes from Amon'kh. "This whole thing was a ruse? All that nonsense about a millennia-old message from the *AAF Fatimah*. The entire Project Exodus. All some elaborate charade?"

"Not entirely," Cruz admitted, voice contrite. "Confederacy politics aside, the initial deceit was necessary. A matter of survival. Our entire planetary alliance has fallen apart. We're at war on two fronts, too, with the squids on one flank, and Terjj lurking in the Endyr. Now Terrans confront new threats in the form of cloak giants and rogue luminaries. All amid an Eclipse we admittedly know the source of but are powerless to thwart. At least, not without enlisting Mr. Dagarth's unique talents."

Earl bristled at the mention of his birth name. Then he realized what Cruz must've deduced: Arlya and Xena both knew Rex Dingo's true identity already. Arlya, after all, had snared his cryotube from deep space and hawked him off as salvage on Lynx. And Xena had used her brainpather skills to probe his memories there on Ötzi.

Cruz went on. "We knew about your role in the Ambri rebirth. That you're their awaited Messiah, Earl. And yes, about your unique DNA—its ability to mimic xenobiologic cells. Pure genetic morphism, dear sky. Imagine what dimensions Terrans can bridge gifted with your physiology."

"Dimensions?" Earl asked, almost afraid to know.

Xena smiled darkly. "Go on, Reina. Tell him why Thebe really chose this planet. Why they built the *Archangel*. He deserves the truth after all we've put him through."

Arlya blinked her blue gems at Cruz too. "Um, yeah. Exactly what dimensions are Terrans intent on bridging?"

Cruz sighed. "Cyrus 794G is a transom world. Like the fabled Endora settled by Terrans a millennium ago, this planet, we believe, links multiple dimensions. A kind of intergalactic nexus that'll serve as an embassy port for Terra and the Halcyon races."

"Hence my objectives on Ötzi," Xena revealed, dark eyes leveled on Arlya. "Evidently, Fjorii wants to prevent a new Eclipse. If what they awakened on Ötzi belongs to these Halcyon progenitors, Terrans may face extinction should our mission fail."

Earl caught a subtle glimmer of light spit from the blackness of space and pierce the nighttime sky of Cyrus 794G. No more than a shooting star to others who may have observed its arrival, Amon'kh sensed its malign origins. A fell entity born of a dark quasar. A harbinger from a parallel dimension—that abode of He Who Consumes Light, he sensed. Or perhaps it was a probe sent by an undetected invasion force newly swallowed into the Cyrus system.

Simultaneously, Earl caught Arlya's sapphire focus. An inhuman psyche calculating probabilities, a myriad nuances and factors in some critical choice. A cybernetic focus he'd seen once before. When she'd maneuvered the *Solar Contact* a split second before impacting a tidal wave on Lynx all those years ago. When she'd been intent on rescuing Xuye from that violent swell...

She moved with a speed that defied human perception. Neither Xena nor Cruz could outflank the blur of movement with their noetic skills. In a near imperceptible coup, Arlya disarmed and incapacitated Xena, then put Cruz to sleep before her sister slumped to the deck, unconscious.

"Let's go," Arlya huffed, catching Cruz's limp body. "We've gotta bug out, Dingo. Before they override your friend's Trojan codes."

"My who?"

"Coryn, your angel interface. She hacked into the *Abu Talib's* security nexus. A bit dramatic for a virtual tour guide, but it should buy us enough time to get planetside."

Earl started. "Down there? On the surface?"

"Yep. Otherwise we'll miss all the action Thebe has in store."

Earl didn't ask how she'd confirmed Coryn's sabotage. Sapphire eyes primed with icy fire, Arlya secured Cruz into a lifepod aboard the *Contact*, then leapt into the pilot's chair. As they shot from the shuttle bay and into open space, Earl and Xuye bristled, both affirming their disdain for each other despite a joy at Coryn's subterfuge. No matter how short-lived their joy might be once met terra frima.

V.

Joint Science Division Base Command,
Point Eureka, Cyrus 794G.
May 17, 3213 CE.

"And you sent Lydia Nev over with Marines?" Earl nearly choked at the thought. Fully armed soldiers sent to confront an entire Ambri hive. Even with the Wolfan priestess in tow, the Terrans stood little chance of not getting killed on sight.

Although Earl hadn't reviewed NavCom's surveillance vids of the alleged Ambri stronghold, he believed Eth'fyah Ruq's confirmation. The wizened Bani Iffir Aghan had scrutinized Culley's body-mounted vid footage captured shortly before his death. The Wolfan NCO had breached Eden's Gate with Lydia only to confront a lone Ambri scout. "Another rebirth in some unknown parallel, perhaps, but most surely an Ambri. Shyah-Din, by Awal Rab. I'm certain as you are human."

Arlya puffed, "Mostly. Right, Rex, sweetie?"

"Uh, yeah. Who's purely human anymore?" Earl felt the hitch-hiker nudge to the fore, but he suppressed Amon'kh before any of the colonists glimpsed the reptilian traits. "Cripes, Almighty God! Who made that grossly ill-advised call?"

Jack Blevins crossed his arms. "Lydia took point on this," he said from across the conference table. Like the others seat-ed, the senior science officer wore a scent masker to withstand Eth'fyah's gamey musth. "She gave us her expert analysis of the surveillance vids. Thebe authorized a contact team after weighing the pros and cons. And, yes, it seemed prudent to send Marines after Culley's unprovoked ambush."

"Our concern at hand," said Brett Wade, "is your arrival just days after the Gate's discovery. The timing is far too coincidental, Mr. Dingo."

"I came with the *Abu Talib*. Not by plan, either. Major Cruz and I barely escaped capture by the Terjj. We laid low on Fjorii until patrols made our hideout. And, well, I'm sure Thebe briefed you all on the, uh, diplomatic details still developing." Earl didn't give them more, knowing it was best left unsaid. Why let them dissect his and Arlya's ordeal with Xena Kilpatrick?

Wade looked peeved. Antigerome aids no longer softened the fiftyish, angular face, pepper gray sideburns and stern gray eyes. "Admiral Thebe shares our concern. A civilian arriving with classified intelligence and some story about an unknown species. These," he snorted, with a glance at his data slate, "D'syunth who made contact with Agent Seroh in the Endyr. Along with a trans-genic dolphin, I'm told."

"Do'fin," Arlya amended. "Xuye Chi, sir. Assigned to the Beta Corpus mission by Rear Admiral Singh. He's not just some dol-phin mutant, either."

"Calm down," Blevins said. Afro-Ptyri brown skin darkened by Cyrus Alpha's harsh rays, he too looked worn by the events besieging the planet's newly arrived colonists. Like Earl, the naval astrophysicist retained most of his genetic traits from Old Earth—mostly human still. He spoke evenly. "Commander Wade is merely summarizing NavCom's concerns about the events you've reported, Agent Seroh. In particular, the arrival of a rogue neutron star at Beta Corpus. We've just come to grips with the Eclipse events. Now this anomaly."

"Major Cruz?" Wade said, eyes on the science officer. She'd remained quiet, still bruised by Arlya's ambush aboard the *Abu Talib*. Olive tones growing wan by the minute, Cruz blanched further under Wade's scrutiny. "Can you shed light on this new phenomenon, Alpha Cygnus? After all, you're Singh's handpicked synchrogenesist."

And an agent imbedded by the Joint Chiefs, Earl noted when Reina Cruz glared his way. Xena's brainpather stare, identical Saracen-dark eyes.

"Classified details notwithstanding, sir," Cruz began, aware of Eth'fyah Ruq and the other two nonmilitary envoys in the briefing, "the initial analysis by Dmitri Serov and myself did suggest a rogue luminary. But after Ms. Seroh's sitrep on the Endyr cloak giant, I amend that analysis. We may well be dealing with a hyperdimensional object. A variant of the clone moons profiled by Dr. Lulwah Girault de Loire."

Green pearls blinked at Cruz. The aged Verdicor planetologist hadn't offered her hypothesis yet. Earl sensed an unspoken affinity with the renowned terraform expert. Deep in his altered DNA, Amon'kh-Nil-R'su'esh'Tah lived with a familiar vim. A magnetism born in some primordial depth where the Prime race had settled its servile offshoots. Those depthless green orbs held an intense spark.

Lulwah nodded. "Otnar most recently, yes. We'd not conclusively determined a link between the reclaimed lunar bodies and the Endyr luminary. But given Alpha Cygnus's arrival at Beta Corpus, it confirms an unsettling theory. Anx-Xi astrophysicists have long postulated the existence of world engines. Entire celestial bodies mobilized by deep-core cybernetics."

Gasps from Eth'fyah and a Cryon science officer Lt. Tram Phe, according to the bio profile accessed by Coryn on Earl's behalf. She'd hacked NavCom's personnel files via neural links and gathered the data quietly. Phe had been handpicked by Wade. A xenoarcheologist tasked with discerning the N'dar's origins, and now their threat to Terrans newly populating Cyrus 794G.

"Deep-core cybernetics," Phe uttered, indigo brow crinkled. "Fire of Life! What species could engineer anything on that scale?"

"The Arc Builders, for one," Arlya suggested. "If the D'syunth truly are the architects of the transgates, then they're capable of constructing world engines."

Wade groaned. "That intel hasn't been vetted yet, Agent Seroh. Our probes in the Endyr Nebula haven't confirmed the existence of any cloak giants, either. We'll just have to take it on faith that you didn't hallucinate the whole ordeal."

Arlya's offended credibility got dismissed by Wade's lifted hand. "NavCom will verify the *Solar Contact*'s mother chip recordings. As well as memfile uploads from the Do'fin and you. For the time being, we need to determine a means of retrieving our Marines. And also a feasible extraction of the Ambri who might want to return to Ghaz. That is why Madam Trade Minister Ruq has graced us with her presence."

Eth'fyah gurgled proudly at her official title. She wore stately robes befitting an Aghan of noble Thlag birth. A scaly mien, wattle lobes, and reptilian eyes that glowed ruby red. "Thlags share a long history with the shyah-Din. And this Azmyth has shared counsel with Fyuth Onah, the Grand Afghan who led us to freedom. Aye, by the Ancestral Star, this Ambri chieftain bears a recognizable scar on his cheek."

Earl confirmed her profile of Azmyth. "Aged by the temporal rift, but it's definitely him. Lydia and I met him in the Gheb Forest. Queen Akirah will be overjoyed to be reunited with Azmyth. She'll be indebted to the Confederacy, too."

"Thebe hopes so," said Wade. "Getting these Ambri back home will certainly open a diplomatic door with Ambrithya. Not to mention access to the fabled Ambri gates."

So that was NavCom's sole priority, Earl realized. Terrans had long coveted wormhole technology, and by acquiring insights into the transgates on Ghaz they'd edge near to such advancements. The clone moons, the Arc regions, the recently breached Eden's Gate—all of it in the realm of hyperdimensional science.

A full two weeks were spent hashing out the enormous logistics involved in accommodating thousands of Ambri emigres. Lydia Nev personally oversaw the migration project. The Wolfan priestess collaborated with Eth'fyah and Azmyth in the construction of a biosphere annex in Tushkent. Thebe had authorized an expansion of Lakshor's precinct as the Wolfan enclave already vaunted shrines devoted to the Whispering Way.

"We're all kindred spirits of the sacred runes," Lydia said proudly as construction got underway. Bodhim City would one day serve as an outpost for those Ambri who chose to remain planetside. Their enclave beyond Eden's Gate was, after all, the only homestead many of the hive's fledglings knew.

"Dometh will remain as their new Chieftain," Azmyth said, giving the misty cliffs a parting glance. "This realm shall forever remain a province of Ambrithya. Elfar and the others may want to visit someday."

For now, those Ambri left behind would hold their enclave in Xanadu. Already in moksheh was a young Afrytha caste monarch who would reign over the auxiliary hive. A zikhr anjulir rite had sown the seeds of a divergent haven for Ambri beyond Ghaz. Only the Origin of Life knew what future their fold would enjoy alongside the N'dar. Only time would reveal the role Terrans would play in this new dynasty's future.

Ah, such a vast undertaking, Earl reflected days from launch of the refitted *Beowulf's Voyage*. He wondered at the untold events awaiting Azmyth's brethren here in the Cyrus system. Other sagas yet to grace the Songs of the Great Nebula.

The massive nebula ship easily accommodated the Ambri exodus from Cyrus 794G. Swarms of xenobiologists and medics pored over each Ambri's anatomy, over data gleaned surreptitiously by imaging nanytes and optical scans. Tall lithe bodies, long chins, small nostril slits, dually pronged forefingers, taloned feet, glowing amber eyes. The Ambri marveled at the alien devices wielded by Terran physicians and scienists eager to gain long coveted insights into Metaphyla erectus. After all, not long ago the enigmatic species had been thought extinct, all traces of their civilization left as fossils and ruins there on Ghaz.

All the while, Earl pored over the data on Thebe's clandestine operation deep in the Cyrene geosphere. Coryn, while aboard the *Abu Talib*, had secretly inserted herself amid a communications relay during a parley with the *Archangel*. She'd stolen classified intelligence hidden in NavCom's secure database. Earl now perused the files via his own neural implants—ah yes, state-of-the-art upgrades left over from his life as CEO of Blue Star Interstellar.

Only a few colonists were privy to the efforts underway at Site 83. Mere days after making planetfall Geo Division had discovered a vast subterranean complex. Teams there had already begun an ambitious undertaking to revive an entire S'both hive.

Dear sky, they'd soon set free a pernicious swarm...

After returning from the Cyrene system, many colonists suffered mild psychosis. Earl had felt oddly out of sorts shortly after Selusa removed the kedjka from his spine. A kind of postpartum depression...that's how it felt. Yet now that he'd rid himself of Amon'kh-Nil-R'su'esh'Tah's DNA, Earl felt supremely normal. More ordinary than he'd felt in centuries.

He felt truly human.

Excising the hitchhiker DNA had come at a price, too. With a nudge from Xena Kilpatrick, he'd plunged once more into an abyssal lair, this time under hypnosis, joined to Reina Cruz's synapses via polycog receptors. And under the watchful eyes of

Admiral Hector Thebe, Brett Wade, Jack Blevins and Dr. Clark Holbrook. Days after the missing Geo Division team resurfaced from Cloud Canyon, Vedicor's famed planetologist stood among the observers.

Lulwah Girault de Loire looked intrigued as Earl went under, perhaps quietly expecting the experiment to fail. After all, the Genesis Project's architects never intended a revival of this nature.

Given a firsthand look at the Entity in its abyssal lair, the science officers must've reassessed their place in the cosmos. She Who Hunts Novae infused each of their psyches with a watery echo: We came to seed the Twilight Worlds. Yet so few have germinated after eons of waiting...

Xena had unwittingly served as a host for the Entity now insinuating itself into their minds—Cygnet memfile 113-DT: All personnel secure. One hundred eighty-five crewmen still in cryostasis. Last known sitrep transmitted 0130 Hours Zulu via Odyssey probe. Current status of retrieval team requested...

Psy Ops intercept code sign Quasar Run received...subject revived in Cyrus 794G's geosynchronous orbit: species origin classified, neural probes inconclusive, an Epoch relay beamed via polycog transmitters.

Onul-Bin'rh-Nu'Tah wavered in the otherworldly buoyancy like an angelic chimera. Writhing tendrils not unlike a Terjj's hair cords, fin wings undulating at a pared torso. At her bosom pulsated a hypnotic aquamarine glow—energy questing distant wavelengths. Six arms ended in muscular thorax joints, giving the feel of an insect fused with some Nereid maiden. Webbed digits formed graceful hand-claws, while a calyx of anemone tendrils whorled in lieu of legs. Sensory cilia exchanged neural pulses with Earl's mind: We have awaited your return, Reef Builder...

The pearlescent gaze held Amon'kh, drew out the Builder's reptilian essence, subsumed his memory, his very atoms, into the Prime Psyche whence all S'both came.

Well have you served the collective hive. Now be rid of this human form.

Amon'kh obeyed.

Even as others stirred from their chrysalises like swarming locusts, cries erupted far and wide. All across Cyrus 794G rose fiery motes as faux colonists spontaneously burst into pure, sentient energy. Akin to the living motes in the Halo Borealis, the fiery swarm swirled into the moonlit heavens. The planet's night side was draped by dazzling aurorae.

In the Joint Science Division's Cryostasis Recovery Lab, teams observing the Eve Chrysalis looked on breathlessly as the S'both specimen fully resurged to life. Organelles now revived, the Alpha blinked its lambent green, nictating irises, and thereby activated the long dormant defense routines encoded in its capsule husk. By some prescient means it had sensed the Nimbus warheads imbedded deep in the subterranean hive complex—Thebe's failsafe against unknown factors in the Genesis Project.

Deadly nanyte spores dissolved the lifepod's outer skin and then swiftly converged on the awestruck Terrans. The voracious nanytes never altered their evolutionary course as state-of-the-art security seals and hazmat suits were breached. In a matter of minutes, Point Eureka's entire complex of coral-plex and flow deck causeways was engulfed by the self-replicating spores. Not a Terran soul was spared the brutal transformation. Specialized polymers accreted into scaly structures as S'both builder chromosomes spawned a newly erected hive complex.

Well insulated in his command nucleus aboard the *San Marco*, Admiral Thebe shut his eyes, torn not only by the S'both betrayal but also the senseless loss of life. All those Terran colonists, by damn!

Not only did Earl intuit Thebe's neural outcry but he felt each of the linked observers. They hadn't heeded the warnings. While in transit aboard the *Archangel*, thousands had abruptly wakened from stasis...fraught with visions of some impending peril. Medics like Rlema Nae had largely dismissed the hysteria as stasis-related psychosis. Cryons, Tungs, Oorts, Dactylians and humans alike suffered identical neural trauma. Only the Ang-Xi crew and passengers, along with the few Thlags, were unaffected.

Among the original 2.3 million slumbering souls who'd joined Project Exodus, roughly seventy thousand had been revived on arrival at Cyrus 794G. Mostly engineers, science officers, and first-stage terraformers had made landfall. Other critical volunteers like Lydia Nev, Eth'fyah Ruq, and a hand-selected few colonists joined the effort to build a viable habitat for Terrans. All but those who had embarked on the return voyage home were now casualties of the S'both awakening.

After a lengthy quarantine, the surviving crew of the *San Marco* once again escorted the *CSS Archangel* out-system toward the Halo Borealis. But not before Terrans turned their wrathful atomics on the S'both hive and over the scarred terrain, aborting all life for years to come. All the while, Earl and those abroad the *Abu Taüb* eagerly rejoined the Terran fold beyond Celes Tetra.

All record of the Cyrene Purge lay forever buried in Psy Ops files where only the Joint Chiefs had access. Few would ever learn of the events that transpired on Cyrus 794G. The public could never know of NavCom's ambitious Genesis Project gone so terribly wrong.

VI.

On an atoll in the Opal Sea, Lynx.
October 9, 3213 CE.

Arlya nudged Earl from his reverie. "Hey, Scuba Boy. Are you coming or not?"

"Ah, yes. Snorkeling on the Reef. Feels like a lifetime ago when we met on that atoll." Earl inhaled deeply. "Gotta say, Arlya. There's no place like the Opal Sea."

"Come on, then," she said, dancing off into the surf. Ebony curves oiled and glistening, Arlya plunged into the opalescent tides. Xuye was likely already at play among the reef kelp and schools of Lynx rays. This far from Tasman, it was safe to snorkel without fear of being eaten by hungry Fyr. Or bled dry by angel leeches.

Earl had no desire to tread those stingfire-infested waters anytime soon. Even now he shaded Azöl's blue glare from his eyes and scanned the waves for tail flukes or spiny dorsal fins belonging to Fyrs.

Oh, just get in, already, Arlya pulsed from the shallows.

After all that time spent in deep space, Lynx's pink sands tingled underfoot. Gravity, oh, familiar gravity felt so luxurious on his joints. Enfyrrah-sweet breezes kissed his pores at last, dear sky.

With gill mesh clasped and snorkel mask snug, Earl took the long awaited plunge into the Opal Sea. Perfectly cool riptides gushed over his midnight black skin as he joined Arlya and Xuye's frolicking forms. Cyber-clone moans merged into whale-song echoes. They flirted like mating porpoises while Earl swam to the seabed to inspect a sparkle that caught his eye. Amid the sandy coral lay a lustrous ruby—a Venus Eye. The highly prized gallstone of a Fyr bull.

Earl felt panic surge through his spine. Were they diving near a Fyr's lair? Orbit alive, they'd paid Reef Patrol plenty of ruja for a secluded atoll free of hungry fauna. Yet as he took up the crimson pearl, Earl thought back to that day years ago when he'd tossed his Venus Eye into the swell.

Could it be that very same jewel? Earl wondered. That greedy Oort Vlox Sski Ssʼaffu had sent him on a fool's errand, hoping Arlya would retrieve the Venus Eye after the Fyr ate him. But he'd returned from Tasman Reef alive, with his new identity as Rex Dingo, and eventually Lynx's newest mogul after exploiting those coral polyps. Ah, yes. Reef Builder extraodinaire who revived Blue Star Interstellar after its collapse in 3017.

Watcha got there, Rex? Arlya's neural pulse queried. Looks worth a pretty pinch, don't it, Xu?

Snorting, Xuye pulsed: Maybe for Orbiters out for illegal pelf, yeah. Me, I'm done smuggling.

Oh, sure we are. Keep telling yourself that, sweetie. Arlya flitted off with Xuye hissing from his blowhole. Neither one heard Earl's muffled oath: Manx hells, Rex Dingo. We're getting Blue Star back if it kills us.

Still bitter over Cygnet's hostile takeover, he'd kept a close eye on Blue Star's stock fluctuations since his return from the Cyrus system. The amirs on Khidr Delta Five had pilfered BSI's entire lunar holdings and left Earl with nothing but a few ruja and the *Scimitar*. They'd gotten to Vladi Kyev somehow, made him a lucrative offer he couldn't refuse, no doubt.

Coryn interrupted his rueful thoughts. "Sir, you've an urgent pulse from Titus. Admiral Chandra Singh requests your input on a sensitive matter."

"Cripes, again?"

At Admiral Singh's urging, Earl left his leisured life of snorkelling on the Reef to undertake a final task for the Joint Chiefs. One last mission, Rex Dingo, and then you're done leaping the stars. Cripes, more like leaping back into the frying pan just months after Thebe's little fire in the Cyrus system.

In return for his services, they'd offered to fast track his efforts to regain ownership of his company. Cygnet Industries hadn't enjoyed robust stocks of late. After their underhanded takeover of Blue Star Interstellar, Akirah withheld Ghaz's critical ore exploits. Orc's tooth alone made up ninety percent of the company's stardrive materials. Without its flow, the Khidri amirs had lost BSI's lucrative stronghold on the fuel industry. And Thlags clung jealously to their ice gas monopoly. Even said, Cygnet had no intention of relinquishing Blue Star's vast lunar operations, most of which remained in systems controlled by the Terran Confederacy—not the Union of Caliphate States.

"Effectively, they're cut off from their lunar holdings outside the Emerald Gulf," Singh had reassured him on Tyre. Off the books as the meeting was, the Admiral chose a cozy booth at the Ganymede. The throb of neural sync kept their talk private. "Cygnet will be forced to renegotiate its control of BSI. Matriarch Nev will sign an executive order granting you full domain once you've fulfilled your contractual obligations. Get Ginx Dublin back in one piece, Dingo."

"Gonna be hairy," Arlya promised. "The prince got himself in deep this time. But Xu and I will do our part."

"Agatha priest!" Earl swore. "Only feels like yesterday when I got shanghaied and sold off to skyjacks. No thanks, but I'm solo on this. No Do'fins, no cyber clones. Sorry, Admiral. That's the deal if you want me on board."

"Damned fool testosterone," Singh said, exasperated. She'd verged on ordering Arlya to tag along despite his objections, but relented. "Fine. Do it solo, then. Just don't expect the Marines to come storming in when all hell erupts."

"Got it."

Zero dark thirty, Rex Dingo. Deep six in the old plausible deniability zone. The boys at Special Office had already written the prince off as an expendable asset. Ginx knew the risks. Getting lost in the wilds of Ghaz wasn't wise if a spy valued his skin. Earl should know. That planet bred nightmares few Terrans had lived to speak of. Leviathans dwelling in the abyssal karsts, rogue time warps, Ambri gates, coral djinns, and the reek of millions of Thlags.

Dear sky above, Earl's bile rose to his throat just reliving their legendary stench.

Djinthar Airfield set the *Stingfire II* onto a designated stasis cradle. A gentle bump is all Earl felt as a service 'bot restocked the scramjet's stardrive converters. All suited, he braced for a hot gust when the hatch fell away, but felt a gentle kiss of tepid air. Sweet breezes...not the hellish clime he'd endured last time he set foot on Ghaz. Blue sky, wispy clouds and seasonal rains now transformed a once hostile atmosphere.

When last he'd stood on this very tarmac, Cindy Skyborne's Terjjan hybridism had come to welcome Earl. Now an honor guard of Nubyth flanked Trade Minister Amhop. The Sarfyth elder beheld Earl with glowing amber eyes. "Awaited One, at last you've come. Akirah eagerly awaits your blessed presence."

"Never expected to see Firjah City again," Earl said with a dash of nostalgia. The Grand Pyramid still graced the city's skyline, a pearl star radiating at its apex: Cheoptra's Eye, symbol of Ambrithya's newly reborn power.

"Come," Amhop invited. "A swift tube will take us to the Palace Hive."

Silvery telepathy orbs flitted throughout the city, ferrying Ambri over Firjah's lovely spire lofts, palatial courtyards and gardens that formed a vast hive complex. Azure gateways shimmered with traffic crisscrossing the Realm's dimensional lanes. Akirah's majestic Palace Hive rose high over the bustling capital once dominated by ovoid domes and soaring Terjjan minarets. The marble and songstone edifice glowed under Scoria's molten haze. Cleverly concealed turrets arced skyward, ever alert against orbital threats. Unseen beyond the clouds hung vast Nimeth-class destroyer spheres, while Thlagan patrol ships skirted the southern borderlands. Orbital defense array moons kept unwanted spy probes at bay, Singh had revealed, so pinpointing Ginx's exact whereabouts was impossible. "You'll need to get within twenty klicks to ping his position," Singh admitted, a bit embarrassed by NavCom's lack of more advanced pulse tech. "Can't use ambassador link transmissions when you're dark. Others could track the source code. Sorry, Dingo, it's critical we acquire the intel he's got without political blowback."

Didn't Terrans have enough schisms with the Ang-Xi crisis and all those breakaway planetary states? Now they risked alienating their newest inductee into the Confederacy. Orbit alive, by sending the Ambri's own Zhul Amaj to retrieve a spy gone MIA, no less! He prayed Akirah didn't plan to meld with his ithkah, lest his betrayal got exposed.

Amhop proudly presented Earl before the queen's pavilion with great pageantry. Thousands of Akirah's loyal subjects had assembled in the vast Pavilion Hall, all adorned in stately robes and myrrh-scented dekhrah. Glowing nymphs proffered beakers of nectar, their winged bodies like ethereal seraphim, eyes large and aglow with curiosity. Unlike their hive kith, these newly molted maidens hadn't drank ambrysia growth nectar. Solemnly, Earl sipped an elixir. The mood-altering properties invigorated him deeply.

"Dear beloved Earl," Akirah said in a watery purr. "We'd nearly despaired of ever seeing your return. So lost beyond the Sacred Awareness, your ithkah scarcely reached us from the void."

"One epic quest after another," Earl replied, deliberately vague. "Duty called, you might say. Yet fate has a way of luring me back to Ghaz."

"Aye, it does."

Earl felt...something. "I sense a troubling tone in your voice, Majesty."

"By Cheoptra's life, if only the runes had obscured this dark tiding. News my ithkah not easily imparts." Akirah rose from her throne, diaphanous pinions flexing. A pall fell over her lovely mien even as her azure eyes beamed. "A new threat hails from the Perthid Nebula, I fear. One which seeks to vanquish the hives once and for all. Nigh is the hour that will test the mettle of every Terran. But Ambrithya will not easily perish this time. Come, Awaited One. We must confer in private on a matter of intimacy."

Taken aback, Earl briefly feared she meant to probe his memories. But he followed Akirah to her private chamber. He and Akirah now shared a view of Firjah City's westerly pyramids. The enchanting vision stole Earl's breath. The monuments had survived since Ghaz's first queen Neftrah. The invading Terjj had left them erect two millennia ago, believing a power source lay buried at their core.

Earl blinked as Akirah disrobed nearby. "Uh, shouldn't I...?"

"Fear not, Zhul Amaj. I only wish to lay bare all my flaws."

She held her back straight, breasts high. Her svelte curves scarcely betrayed a battle scar, not even a blemish on her nigh glowing skin. The once yellow tones had a translucent quality. A mere sip from an elixir pool had given her dual pairs of wings and azure eyes.

Earl gulped when Akirah came close and took his trembling hand. She brought it to her bosom and let her heartbeat thrash against his palm. Enchanted by its hypnotic rhythm, he never felt her dual forefingers at his temple, probing his ithkah. Yet it was Akirah's own memory she imparted in a zikhr rite. At once, saline imagery flooded Earl's mind. Oshii's memory too sprawled over his cerebral cortex. Oh, dear heavenly Genesis...one of Cindy's stolen twins. Alive...fully grown into adolescence after only three standard years. But how? Cell maturity accelerants, yes, under the scalpel of a Chief Skinshaper aboard the *G'thalon*, Earl perceived. Sijjo Ith had given the boy to Empress Nesrai as an exotic gift. Then they grafted wings onto Oshii's back...enlightened him with Divine Path doctrines. Those huge Rhojii cats during a ra'ahii rite. Earl saw Oshii's entire odyssey, from his days playing avenjii with Sari'ah to frightful nights skulking in Ghaz's wilderness.

The rite done, soft lips caressed Earl's, jarring him back. Akirah whispered, "Go now, Earl Dagarth. Find this spy prince. Then acquaint Oshii with his new life among Terrans."

Coral djinns once again reigned over the Dengali's lush veldts and picturesque hills and fjords. Earl skirted the Southern Hive's hinterlands, flying low at cruise speeds. Two full days after Akirah's zikhr rite, he'd turned up no signs of the prince. Not a whisper from the homing pulse, nothing. He had half a mind to call it quits when Ginx's biopulse lit on the console screen. After a second flyby to confirm the signal, he settled the *Stingfire II* onto a granite outcrop.

Azöl's fierce blue glare bore down on him as he emerged from the craft, fully clad in a terrasuit and breather nib. He surveyed the surrounding landscape. No roaming Thlags or Ambri orbs were anywhere in sight. Only wild terrain and inhospitable bluffs, all barren of the lush verdure flourishing elsewhere in the province.

Eyeing a nearby crag, he imagined a phantom of movement. Grisly hydra orcs once lurked in these bluffs. He still recalled the hideous thing's slimy tentacles choking his windpipe that first day he'd set foot on Ghaz. Earl had no intention of reliving that horror. He drew his sidearm, despite telling himself such creatures no longer existed on the planet.

The phantom shifted form as Earl aimed the ion reaper. An outline of sinewy limbs, head, torso, arms and legs emerged from an energy cloak in the shadows. Ginx raised his grimy hands, smiled nervously. "Frack me with a pthsi rod, brother. Am I glad to see a human."

"Cripes, I nearly shot you," said Earl, reaper lowered. "The hells are you skulking in the crags for?"

"Got made. Turns out it's not so easy replicating a Thlag's reek. They know their own odor from others." The Oxyrite prince dropped his hands. "As for why I'm naked, well, hydra orcs are simple guises. And they're left alone by the Ambri."

"Orcs still exist?"

"Sure do. One tried to mate with me just yesterday. Now, where's a hot shower and some ale?"

Earl indicated the scramjet. "Get in. We'll get you cleaned up in Ardh. Whew! And I thought Thlags smelled awful."

After getting Ginx safely back to civilization, Earl returned to Firjah City, sans the fanfare and honor guards. At Fyuth's Grand Tomb waited Elfar and a discreet few Nubyth sentries who guarded Oshii at the solarium. Earl felt chills at the sight of dangling punfyr and Terjjan blooms. Mist and prismatic sunlight cast phantasmal veils over the boy's hybrid features. At first glance, the short curls seemed to writhe...like a full blown Terjj. But then Oshii stepped fully into view and looked more human.

"Are you my real parent?" Oshii asked in Terjjan. "They said you'd come to take me."

"Seems the galaxy enjoys irony. But yes, I'm your father, Oshii."

Lynx was hardly a planet where Earl could introduce Oshii into Terran life. The boy's Terjjan hybridism might elicit xenophobic glares. No, a more secluded moon was probably best—at least until they explored a way to soften Oshii's exotic traits. Earl would take him to the only haven in the galaxy where he might enjoy relative obscurity. For a while, anyway.

Lydia kept her promise by signing an executive order that returned domain of several dozen moons and worldlets to Rex Dingo. Blue Star Interstellar's assets and its ownership all reverted back to Earl after Cygnet's stocks plunged due to Lydia's embargo against the Caliphate.

Riding this wave of triumph, Earl set course for the Octavian Gulf. The *Stingfire II* met no obstacles or scrutiny from patrol ships as it slid from hyperspace and locked onto a private causeway over the lush planet that Cindy Skyborne now called home. Eden II's customs officials waved the cryotube through without fuss. Special diplomatic seals negated a routine inspection of the contents, so Oshii remained blissfully in hypersleep. Cindy waited at the spaceport's terminal, eager to see Earl after so much time. He'd told her to expect a guest of sorts. Why spoil the soul-wrenching moment when mother and son first set eyes on one another?

"Gawd, it's been ages since our last tryst," Cindy said. She gave Earl a long hug, then eyed the cryotube. "That anybody I know?"

"Not exactly," Earl said vaguely.

"Well, I'm sure K'bu would enjoy a new friend or two. She's at Cypress Manor in Ozi's care."

"Ozi?"

"Private security, part-time tutor. We're not taking any chances after Amity's little experiment in the Ptyr Ring. Gosh," she sighed, realizing ears might overhear. "Let's get this cryotube loaded. There's a ground car waiting."

A conveyor 'bot got Oshii's tube loaded, and they were off. Earl rode in silence while Cindy told him of her and K'bu's entire ordeal after he'd left them abroad the *Kashmir Light*. He learned about the Orceus debacle, their stay in the Oort Cluster, then being whisked off to Eden.

And he learned about Sari'ah.

"Our children survived," Cindy said, eyes teary. "By some miracle, they're out there. Alive, Earl."

"They are alive," he confirmed. "Cindy, that's why I'm here. Sari'ah isn't the only one to return from the void. She has a twin brother. He was captured on Ghaz."

Cindy gasped. "When? Where is he now?"

Earl took Cindy's hand into his. "That's who I brought in the cryotube. That's Oshii, your other child. Our son, Cindy."

Out there in the starry infinity beyond Earl's quiet new life on Eden II shone a lovely quasar. One whose soft aria of light echoed an Awareness of galactic sagas to come.

The End

ONE SMALL STEP

"I was standing there holding a breather mask in my new claw, wondering if the shore wind would bring in another of those gusts of hydrogen sulphide." —Neal Asher, *Dark Intelligence.*

Southern Yucatán Peninsula,
Day 51 of science expedition, 3792 CE.

Bright topaz sunlight glared into the lens-optics shielding Tsy's ocular membrane. Standard protective gear elsewhere gave all in the First Lander team agile function on a world fixed to a G-type star, with modest gravity, sweet oxygen, moist atmosphere, autumnal winds (given the scant evidence of true seasons in this alien biome), and abundant foliage.

Nine hours into day fifty-one on terra firma, Tsy joined his Ctesi cohort, the lovely bi-cerebral xenobiologist with lustrous mottled skin and nictating lime-green eyes. While cross-spieces intimacy wasn't strictly forbidden, cultural mores left most on the landing team appalled by Elsai's unabashed sensuality and unchecked pheromone display—scent maskers only did so much, after all. He wasn't fazed, though. They had a task to complete. Prime objective: catalog indigenous fauna for entry into the *Galactic Encyclopedia of Sentient Life*. Albeit a daunting chore given the mission limits set by High Council, Tsy felt encouraged by the specimens thus far collected, analyzed, and then reluctantly set free save for an occasionally ingested morsel snared by a swift tongue. For simplicity, they used common terms like frog, newt, or toad when naming native organisms.

Tsy flicked a tongue at a buzzing insect. A bit too gooey and bitter. Although a quick protein source, the tiny life-form hardly met the definition of sentient life, so no one chided him for his indulgence.

A flirty scent teased his sinuses. Tsy gulped. "So...if we're taboo, then...?"

Elsai chuckled softly. "Only taboo, Tsy. Not incompatible."

Tsy's tail waggled at the unspoken subtext. Culture and duty warred with biological truths his libido couldn't deny. But the mission demanded his focus. They were here to survey the planet's biota. To give evolution a nudge.

By dusk they'd covered forty acres of rain forest, had amassed a trove of cell samples and DNA swabs, and had soon broken camp, careful to erase any trace of their otherworldly contraptions or waste, when a shrill cry seized Tsy's senses. It arose from the nearby jungle—a half-croaked, throaty cry too familiar to each of their psyches. Yet all in the landing team were accounted for.

"Captain Tsy!" cried Gighu, the exoplanetologist. "That's...an amphibian, isn't it?"

"Yes," Tsy agreed.

"One of the forest folk," Elsai asserted. She held equal hues of fear and curiosity in her moist ectoskin. A true Ctesi, always ready to battle if such was called for. "We must answer its cry for help, Tsy."

"We'd endanger the entire team. We don't know what preda-tors lurk on this world."

Gighu clawed his pulse rod, defiant. "Our mission demands the preservation of life. Isn't that so, Elder One?"

"It is so," Tsy admitted reluctantly.

So, with pulse-rods in hand, Tsy led Gighu, Elsai and two others into the dense growth to investigate. They faced a horrid scene near a rivulet just a ways from base camp. Ensnared within a glassine capsule writhed a blue-gilled salamander whose sleek wet skin bore the distinct traits of a male noble (though primitive by High Council standards). Breather holes in the capsule let its cries lure Tsy's brethren into an evident trap. Oh, sacred pulsar—one of the bipedal giants!

Gloved hands reached for Elsai first, her puny pulse rod doing nothing to thwart her captor. Then those simian vices sought to grasp Tsy too, but billions of years of evolution and instinct jerk-ed his webbed hind limbs into a full sprint after the others who'd escaped back to the lander.

Itchy guilt and sorrow ate at Tsy's gills as the mother ship lifted from orbit, less one crewman, and raced into the dense gas cloud beyond Alpha Cygnet. Elders on the High Council of Interstellar Exploration seated on the capital world Ngu Anth long debated the risks of a return mission to the planet third from Sol to fur-ther study the impendent uplift of amphibians there to higher sentience, as Tsy's folk had achieved. They also argued how best to deal with those cruel primates who'd outpaced local phyla with colossal space-faring craft of their own. The brave Ctesi science officer's memory never left Tsy. He often pondered going back to that hostile world. Perhaps future landers would find the pebble Elsai had thrown into that ill-fated rivulet: One small step for Newt kind...

The End

PART THREE

SONGS OF ETERNITY

"His eyes, taking it all in, grew in wonder as he gazed at the three moons hanging heavy in the crystal blue sky."

—Chris Mazzoli, from *Armageddon.*

ALTERED STATES

A brook rages in her bosom
  its silky promise melts
  like snowflakes on sand
    or sunspots
    eclipsed by a winter moon.
She is a muse
  born in desire,
  a quietly raging fire
  shone in blue night flame.
Time entangles her raven hair,
  curls like wispy fingers
  upon my stylus—mingles
    cell by tender cell,
    then comes in halted gasps.
A poetic flow altered
  by cosmic magnetism,
  a fleeting mood
    aroused by inspiration's stroke:

This moist interval settles onto swarthy skin
    lain against white satin lips.
Its silky energy engulfs our twain orbs
    like an inescapable singularity.
Sweet electricity arcs between thighs
    poised at dawn's threshold:
    probability morphs into protean heat,
      each sigh and moan
      as our throaty pleas escape
        in vapor memory.
A gaze consumed by her mercurial
    black eyes—life infused
        by cold fusion storms
        deep in her mythic realm
        yet explored,
Until we again converge,
    converge
in silent gasps.

ALTERED STATES II

I am—thus I exist!
A broiling core formed by hydrogen fury,
   this molten orb shrouded in exotic particles.
A binary system whose moon enters my sphere,
   I linger in silence as she orbits a parallel sky.
Altered by prisms befitting the gaze of angels,
   I gaze at stars like glittery motes
   over hot blue nebulae:
She comes in icy veils
   with pearlescent skin adorned
   in satin black nothingness
   she sails upon a tender arc,
     an orphan moon
     in search of her primary.
She feigns a tragic beauty of forgotten realms,
   of mythical phyla born in flame.
A jewel set in twilight epiphany
   lain against my cold fusion skin—

her regolith eyes forged
    by deep epochs of toil and silent evolution.
She wanders alone, ever coveting my topaz gaze.
A ghostly remnant fleshed in alabaster star mass,
    joined as two nomads,
        one cleft asunder by geomagnetic throes,
        the other fused in helium clouds.
She with fingers dusted by dark, insubstantial matter
    and I encased in amber fire
A mere glint in the cosmic sea of eternity.

STAR MATTER

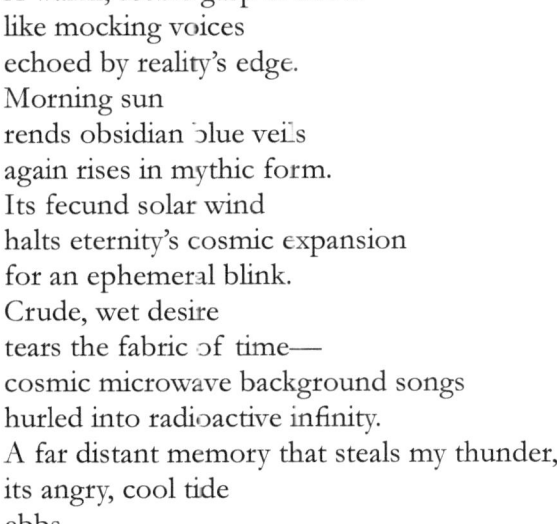

A warm, feeble gasp at dawn
like mocking voices
echoed by reality's edge.
Morning sun
rends obsidian blue veils
again rises in mythic form.
Its fecund solar wind
halts eternity's cosmic expansion
for an ephemeral blink.
Crude, wet desire
tears the fabric of time—
cosmic microwave background songs
hurled into radioactive infinity.
A far distant memory that steals my thunder,
its angry, cool tide
ebbs
flows
trickles

then erupts as brilliantly beheld star matter
bold and fleeting
yet strangely morphic.

QUANTUM DESIRE

The silky promise of eternity
   melts like snowflakes on sand dunes.
This dark energy consumes
   all matter and reason,
      scatters gas clouds into infinity.
A dirge of deep nebulae
   locks our celestial orbs
      in symbiotic flux.
Time morphs to a quantum paradox
   when our cosmic eyes meet:
A trio of suns wink in blue night flame
   as dawn looms—starry cyclones
      hurl tachyon thunder in a futile quest
         to flee love's singularity.

Quantum Desire II

Twice flung into the nebulous deep
   this lone probe of curiosity.
A quest over long light-years
   to find a habitable zone—some nirvana
      beyond our gelid existence.
After eternal stasis in the galaxy's bosom
   we two join the billions of dwarf stars,
      at last reborn
      as cold fusion light:
All thought and ethereal mood congealed
   into a lovely blue-green orb
      swirling, twirling ever in love's orbit
That oblivion escaped,
   our mortality
      alas wakened by time's true kiss.

STEEL CHRYSALIS

Tiny, faceted eyes
   quest out faint cosmic rays
   shorn from the ebony void—primal gravity.
Starry veils enshroud its pupal form
   in a prison of sleek polymers
   and fusion-core velocity.
A million nanytes converge
   on newly thawed atoms
     as angry thrusters hurl cold blue thunderbolts
     from a dark, sanguine sky—final orbit.
Astir in its chrysalis of steel,
   glassine dreams embrace evolution's promise
   as time rends asunder its fragile shell.

NEEDLE'S EYE

Last night I dreamt of a needle.
No haystacks, nor an eye of implausibility;
Only a narrow path lit by an epiphany.
A truth found, a jewel beheld in splendor
And finite detail:
A sharply pointed instrument
Sewn in destiny's fabric.
Its gossamer memory reborn night after night,
This oft-repeated dirge.
Finely woven threads of love
Spawn an unexpected war within—
The handmaiden's stitch intrinsically borne
in deep hours lain,
Whence rise the faintest kiss of time.
An hour lost,
A moment's hesitation,
Decades ebb in the blink of an eye.

EXTANT III

After the sigh of nitrogen escapes
my cryotube, I brace for the post-stasis
nightmare of interstellar silence, tofu cuisine,
and nanytes: eons and eons of genetic evolution...

Out beyond Neptune's blue veils
are cast humanity's far-flung seeds.
A thousand light-years off into the nebula
there looms the ill-fated *Archangel*.

Her mighty husk is still intact
despite the heavy shroud of time.
With an utterance I awaken her cargo.

My capsule descends into an otherworldly abyss.
Great pressures entomb me deep below
the chaotic surface of a methane sea.
An unearthly beauty sprawls beyond the porthole,

and I gape in fascination at gaseous life forms:
whale angels born of flame.

Nothing in our biology rivals this world's
exotic fury as alien phantoms
spew ethereal lava from a benthic chasm.

Yet in the gelid hold of the progenitor ship
awaits the lost remnant of Terra's stellar fleet—
a germ of life resurrected in Elysium's fecund folds.

THE TIME TRAVELER'S CHARM

By an oasis moon amid the Bedouin stars
He chanced a glimpse into fortune's well
A mere glitch in time, it swirled in a vortex of iridescent hues,
When first he wakened its transdimensional pore—
A wish given;
As if set loose from Pandora's box,
So rose this genie with emerald eyes.

The proffered charm told of enchanted realms
And mystic beauty:
A calyx-shaped prism set in amethyst and coral sepals.
A G-type star glared in its tiny mirrored facets
As he stole into the Hindu porter's hunger-wrought body.

No trifle affair any leap over incalculable parsecs and nebulae
To rejoin the substantial winds.
Yet he felt no less pithy than the dark-skinned alien
In myrrh-scented rags and worn down sandals.

Upon a second wish, the pendant transfixed Anil's mien,
Its silvery petals realigning quantum codes
As he lurched into a nearby dimension—whampooof!
A low-gravity moon adorned by gargantuan firs
Whose boughs pierced the very clouds.

The time warp, as always, left him queasy but alert for peril
As he galloped on quad legs.
Ah, to rove a virgin world
As a half equine, half simian phylum!
With hands transformed to hooves
He soon lost the charm
As a toothy predator ambushed the herd.
Oh, if only I had wings, he anguished.

Third wish granted, the charm encysted him remotely:
Thy wish is my command!

When next he emerged from a chrysalis
Fit with wings light as gossamer, he soon lit upon
A maiden's open palm.
Sophia's eyes drank in the insect's majestic vision
Of neon blue and shimmering gold edged in dark matter.

At once aligned with its temporal paradox,
She gently closed her palm.
Thus did time cease
In the blink of a genie's eye.

CHRONOSPHERE

Sinking into outer space, thrice flung
beyond the sphere of blue-misted oceans.
Thin air collapses beyond the mercury promise
of stars: a solar burst gone faintly
into her cold black gaze.

Crackling heat transfixes our compound eyes
as spark angels swarm from hungry thrusters.
Aroused by this alien dawn, we slither
like nymphs from a gelid hibernation—
cast like vapor from our hive at moonrise.

Dark Matter

Exotic protons
Fused by hydrogen atoms
In a cosmic storm.

NIL GRAVITY

Iron wings flutter
Weightless in the autumn wind
Of an alien moon.

Zero Light

Deep down in a cave
After piercing gravity's
Unforgiving well.

REFLECTIONS

"If you seek only easy problems to solve, then ultimately, there'll be nothing about you to distinguish yourself from others."   —Neil deGrasse Tyson, June 27, 2012.

I.

In gathering these haiku, poems and short tales
I found myself at once overwhelmed
and overflowing with excitement.
Many souls fleshed out in these pages
saw only glimpses of light as I shelved them,
kept them hostage in dingy folders,
cardboard boxes, or locked away in my head—
treasures buried in the sand dunes
of procrastination or writer's block.

My story *Amber is Cold* depicted a dwarfish
antihero who got ensnared by his greed for amber.
On the arid mine flats of Ghaz, Earl Dagarth dug up a relic
that would alter events for millennia—past and future!
Tyree Campbell, now at Alban Lake Publishing,
took a leap of faith with my character in 2008.
Soon after *Amber is Cold* appeared in *Aoife's Kiss*
a novel series was born.
The Coral Saga chronicles Earl's fateful encounter with Ambri
survivors, Thlag rebels, and ruthless Terjj
who've brought one race to the brink of extinction
while enslaving the other.
Humans, meanwhile, walk a tightrope between
a brutal Terjjan hegemony and their own quest
for survival in the Coral Galaxy.

Even with four self-published novels online,
few souls in the universe have ever heard of Angelo Niles
or the exotic worlds I've conjured up.
The lack of publicity, book reviews, or wistful movie deals
have all played their role; mostly, I believe, my own
reclusive lifestyle lent to *The Coral Saga*'s obscurity.

I pray this changes now with this compilation,
A Light Of Other Suns: Otherworldly Tales by Angelo Niles.

II.

As an avid fan of science fiction, fantasy and horror,
I often feel a peculiar absence of Afrocentric imagery.
Although great authors of all creeds
and cultures have lent masterful tomes
to those beloved genres,
few films have depicted our bronzy, cocoa, ochre
and swarthy hues as heroes.

Brave explorers who conquer the infinite stars do exist.
NASA's Mae Jemison, Neil deGrasse Tyson,
filmmakers like Will Smith, authors like W.E.B. Du Bois,
Tomi Adeyemi, Tiffany D. Jackson, Cherene Sherrard,
Linwood Jackson, Jr., Silvia Moreno-Garcia,
Octavia Butler, Walter Mosley, Kim Louise,
and a plethora of visionaries have stoked our hunger
for diversity in art and science.

My own feeble contributions may sate those cravings briefly,
yet there's a universe we have thus far
left uncharted.

III.

I grew up all over the world,
living in England, Greece, Egypt, Sudan, Saudi Arabia,
Canada and the United States.

A hiatus in the Fiji islands gave me
a real taste of the exotic, pristine tropical shores
and people who looked oddly familiar.
Ebony skin, kinky hair, wide noses, and full lips
—handsome smiles and soulful brown eyes
telling stories of tribal conflict
or bold voyages over the Pacific.
And none were Africans.
Melanesians lived alongside ethnic Indians,
Polynesian migrants, tourists of every ilk,
and American gypsies like me
sharing the experience by postcards
with my kid sister and mother back home.

Alone in that journey,
I fell in love with a Fijian beauty, Shalu, got married,
then enjoyed a life in perpetual nostalgia

for quiet Edens left behind.
Those memories gave flesh and bone
to the otherworldly locales of my tales years later.

Earl Dagarth's visage is born of my love for
Aborigine and Cushite peoples whose mythos
paint a forgotten time on Earth.
When Dream Time and walkabouts gave meaning
to the unknown.
When pyramids and Nile songs conjured djinns
and pharaohs and Nubian odysseys.

A Light Of Other Suns echoes those drums
from ancestral stars yet beheld by xeno-tourists like me.

IV.

Life is stranger than fiction when there's nothing
but cacti and javelinas outside your window.
Yet it's truly breathtaking during monsoon thunderstorms
painting the molten sky.
Maybe this'll jar my muse into fiery poesy
—or a sequel to *A Light Of Other Suns*.

And now?

Still busy at work on my next novel
The Suns of Coral.
The sweltering heat here in my desert retreat
makes me wish I was snorkeling in the Opal Sea
on planet Lynx.
Alas, it's only whimsy:
Can't get tickets to the Coral Galaxy just yet!

Oh, believe me—I'm working on procuring a seat
on the very next colony ship slated for the Gemini Constellation.

Might be right after Blue Star Interstellar comes online,
or lizards grow wings. Whichever is first...
Until then, I'll be content with writing about the lucky
(or unlucky) star-faring souls who brave the alien worlds
and moons of my imagination.

The journey begins...

V.

Angelo Niles lives in Florence, Arizona, where he is working
on *Gallery Noir: Twelve Dark Tales by Angelo Niles*,
his collection of short stories which will feature
Maelstrom and other Cole Defoe tales.
He longs to return to Vancouver, B.C., where he once lived
as an abstract artist and starving poet.

That was my bio from *On Spec*, fall of 2004,
the issue which featured my very first
published story, *Maelstrom*.
Diane Walton, who was General Editor at the time,
gave me that breakthrough which jump-started
my journey as an author and exposed my talents
to thousands of readers.
All the staff showed an interest in who Angelo Niles
was as a human being, some writing letters
asking about my life experiences and goals.
A special shout out to Diane L. Walton,
Derryl Murphy, Barry Hammond, Lynette Bondarchuk,
Susan MacGregor, Steve Mohn, Holly Phillips,
Peter Watts, Danica LeBlanc, Elaine Chen
and Peter Thorpe who all made *On Spec*
a classy collection of artists, authors and poets.
I am honored to be in that alumni alongside
so many artful souls.
Shortly after appearing in *On Spec*,

Maelstrom received an honorable mention
in *The Year's Best Horror & Fantasy 2004*,
edited by Ellen Datlow.

VI.

Over time I've had other tales accepted
by a few editors elsewhere:
Wesley Kawato at *Nova Science Fiction*
kindly took *The Cloud's Eye* and a long poem,
The Veils of Iyre. Dr. Joyce Levine's ordeal
in the Gulf of Alaska is an excerpt
from my novel *Sands of Prophecy*,
while the poem is a prelude to events
fleshed out in *The Coral Saga*.

I've had a smattering of poetry and haiku
in the pages of *Star*Line, Iron City, The Morning Star*
and other magazines—not all speculative,
not every verse a memorable gem;
they were, nevertheless, pieces of Angelo Niles.

At long last the universe saw harmony
in the faint echo of my muse
when J.P. Brown graciously edited one of my novels.
A bit draconian in his blunt honesty
and often cruelly excised scenery, grammar gaffs
and overly flowery prose, he brought clarity
to my wistful chaos.

We collaborated on one project,
Spaceship, which appeared in *Star*Line*, Fall 2016:

Shipwrecked—
I'm the sole survivor
on this alien planet.

If I don't find a sentient species
or discover a way back
to the Solar system,
the human birthplace,
I'll be forced to risk opening
a time window.
—Angelo Niles,
translated from the Arabic by J.P. Brown

Yet a more profound query comes in
Smuggler to the Stars
by J.P. Brown:

Why can't life be like a holoflick
where an asteroid field to hide in
lies around every bend of space
like some ubiquitous chain
of convenience starports?

VII.

Indeed life might be a splendid affair
if we had starports lying around every bend of space.
Ah yes, a swift escape from humanity's
deeply ingrained animus for all things alien or incomprehensible:
All too often our own diversity...

It won't be a rogue asteroid that brings about
the Holocene Cataclysm; more likely,
our hubris in the face of galactic expansion,
our silly quarrels over oil, holy dirt, tribal hegemony
and petty philosophical feuds.
Yet a resilient beauty overrides nearly all the ills
invading our lush planet.
We are an ever evolving species,
growing outward to explore vast horizons

of possibility.

VIII.

As I strive to hone my craft, I rely on giants who paved the way
like Frank Herbert, Robert Silverberg, Peter F. Hamilton, Walter
Mosley, Charles Johnson, Samuel R. Delany, Sheree R. Thomas,
Nancy Kress and a myriad others who've influenced my style.
Some authors like Kevin J. Anderson, F.J. Bergmann,
Ellen Datlow and Ms. Kress offered encouraging critique
or showed me it's okay to invent realities that don't exist yet.
Hence, the fictitious La Fuentes Shoal set in the Gulf of Alaska,
wildly imagined moons or planets like Zynfar, Endora, Fjorii, Ghaz
and the exotic flora and fauna of the Coral Galaxy.

I am indebted to all the critics and fans out there
who've shared my worlds, sympathized with heroes
and heroines of my often quixotic storylines,
or laughed at the absurd plots.
So long as you enjoyed the ride, I'm delighted.

A special acknowledgement goes out to Dr. Gary Hardy, PhD.,
a colleague who helped open the way
to this book's debut—by shouting my name
in the ears of Frank Reuter and his fellow staff.
So selfless, truly amazing guy.

IX.

As for cliffhangers, Shakespeare once said,
"All's well that ends well."
Maybe not so much for Dr. Kyle Elmhurst
and his surviving companions on Europa.
I felt like that vast ship left before we could reach the hatch.
The story ended abruptly.
We never learn what "home" Kyle, Diegos and Spekolstein

were taken to. Okay, fine. A sequel shall give closure
to that chapter, let's say, as *Galileo's Child*?
Or maybe *Edge of Eternity*?
I invite ideas for a title, dear fans.

2270 is going to be a tough year for Earth's progeny.
If we breach the Arc gate there on the far ends of the Milky Way,
our cryotubes intact, and most of us still Homo sapiens,
more or less, it'll be a heck of an awakening.
Angry Terjj and rogue luminaries won't be our only
obstacles—it surely will be a vision too breathtaking
for our collective psyche.

On such worlds we may see half equine,
half avian baojii mares thundering into battle.
Or far more quixotic biota!
Like Xuye Chi, a sentient dolphin hybrid prone to puking
all over the cockpit's astrogation deck,
or his cohort Azlya Ai-One Seroh
with her knack for cybernetic wit and levity
in the face of inexplicable catastrophe.

1697 was surely a better era, when the Atlantic raged
with slave ships, colonial plunder, and time portals
—the plot setting for *The Coast*.
Among other ambitions, that'll be a jewel
in the next short story collection by Angelo Niles.

If the Origin of Life so wills...

Other Books by Angelo Niles

Enjoy all the storylines, characters, and exotic worlds of the Coral Galaxy by exploring *The Coral Saga* series:
The Chronicles of Ghaz,
The Pearls of Ijnar,
The Clouds of Endyr,
The Shrines of Sharjah,
and *The Suns of Coral* (forthcoming).

Available at Apple Books, Amazon, Barnes & Noble, Smashwords and other sites.

Angelo Niles fan mail welcomed at:
c/o M. Rafeeq Saddiq 86527
ASPC-Eyman/Cook
P.O. Box 3200
Florence, AZ 85132

EXTRAS

An Excerpt From—The Suns of Coral by Angelo Niles

Prologue - "Synthesis"

"Until our chitinous and mottled pelts are rent asunder, to bile and honor are we bound."   —J.P. Brown, from *Their Feats Were Bound.*

I.

Adrift in Styx's geosynchronous orbit,
Azöl System Psy Ops Log Z347.
Apri 7, 3223 CE.

After twelve hundred and fifty-five days adrift, an errant solar pulse jarred awake the dormant memory crystals embedded in her microprocessor cube. They'd designed her with a durable husk meant to withstand centuries of frigid vacuum and incessant meteoroid impacts and fell solar winds. Yet she'd suffered abrupt signal death when some supernova event swept over her cercus node and severed her link to flyby Odyssey probes or Coral Stellar Navy billets searching the debris field left in the wake of a phantasmagoric blast.

By now her data cells must've been logged as MIA by Psy Ops analysts reviewing the aftermath of Ghaz's orbital battle. The *Ruby Star* and her lone passenger were presumably lost, all cargo belonging to the Thlag Domain flung to the stellar void, the coveted Alkhem Stone forever gone.

Only...

Caught in that infinitesimally tiny blip of time before her demise, Coryn's onboard copy had transmitted one final mem-file—a vivid glimpse of an otherworldly plain of existence many parsecs off in an uncharted quadrant of space. The feed's real-time aspect reeled too fast for organic eyes, too exquisite a scene to label merely as footage, and quite beyond description by her cybernetic syntax.

Azure clouds crept over a world that must've risen from its planetary nebula as pure crystal; a biome teeming with flora and fauna too bizarre for classification in any sentient tongue. Amethyst hillocks and opal cliffs hemmed a metropolis hewn entirely from azurite and iridescent mineral that shimmered with kinetic energy fueled by the cepheid star beaming beyond a covey of icy moons.

The aspect that occupied her optic relay defied all recorded data on star systems of this kind. Ordinarily, an astral body whose fusion ate helium and hydrogen at such a rate and burned so fiercely implied a late stage giant verging on nuclear decay. At roughly 30,000 Kelvins surface temperatures, a main sequence star of this size should exhaust its life cycle in less than a billion years. Its planetary offspring should long ago have suffered atrophy as atmosphere fled and gravity collapsed their frail mantles.

Coryn's copy would've gasped had she lungs to do so; as it was, tiny tremors shook her binary core when Azöl hurled an electromagnetic pulse her way: PRIORITY ECHO RELAY ALPHA EPSILON NINETY...

II.

*A terrestrial world far off grid,
Uncharted planetary system.
Time zone unknown...*

An almost watery aria trickled behind the membrane between reality and eternal nothingness of starlit sky above the alien enclave. Eth'fyah couldn't make sense of the vision still flickering on the periphery of her psyche. Neither did she know why she'd relived her own burial rite many light-years off in Ambrithya's capital—as if by way of a memfile whose distorted data confused her senses, whose true memory belonged to an Ambri pallbearer rather than her own kith. Nor did this Afterlife make sense after the demise of the *Ruby Star*. Miffu, Chak and Tuksq had fled in their lifepods mere seconds before Eth'fyah's desperate feat.

Sabre hawks streaked by as Arlya Seroh's frantic hail stormed into the cockpit. "Madam Trade Minister, what in God's name are you doing? Don't you dare go kamikaze. Stand down, *Ruby Star*. We've got this."

"I'm saving my kith," the old Aghan transmitted. "Awal Rab take my vapor, Ghaz is not for the taking. Dtsarq, nay."

She'd cut the vox-link, already set on her deed, ruby eyes afire and her bile aboil as she shrieked one last battlecry. "Glory for Mother Ghaz. Victory for Terra!"

At once the nova brilliance engulfed the tiny merchant barge along with the vast portal ship barrelling toward the planet, with her webbed claws still clenching the Alkhem Stone, and all her vapor fled to the Ancestral Star.

That should have silenced the winds now howling upon Eth'fyah's soul. An, by Awal Rab Almighty, that truly should've brought eternal stillness to her thrashing twain hearts. Aye, old Thlag. And wild baojii mares should be so easily tamed, by damn.

So, then.

This mirage of cliffs bathed by an alien moon must be real, she decided, still numb with uncertainty after emerging from her chrysalis. She didn't know what else to call the inexplicable energy field that had sheltered her limbs from certain death and nurtured her during self-induced stasis. Even now as she sucked in precious moisture from the world's exotic air, Eth'fyah didn't trust her senses just yet.

Am I a corporeal being or a mere ghost left to wander some purgatory? Or is this truly the Ancestral Star whence Thlag life arose?

Surely there would be others to greet her had she arrived at that place of rest. Fyuth Onah, She'egh-Oth, little Nabi and Kifrah...so many countless Thlags who'd joined the Ancestral Winds since the Great Uprising. Strange as it seemed, she felt cheated of that chance to embrace martyrdom on her terms. She'd lived a long and meaningful life bred as she was from highborn Iffir folk who'd only ever known affluence among the clans. Sifqiyah had chosen her to embark on an argosy of trade and diplomacy on behalf of the Thlag Domain. When the Eclipse came, Eth'fyah then joined the Terran exodus to Cyrus 794G. All told, she'd enjoyed an eventful life in the stars.

With her wattle lobes quavering, Eth'fyah set out to explore her environs, if for no other purpose than to prove her instincts wrong.

This dimension looked nothing like the galaxy she knew.

STARSHIPS AND SEA VESSELS

Tailgate—old fishing clipper in Hope, Oregon .... 2013 CE.

Spartan—OCF cruiser skippered by Charlie Hunter ..... 2031 CE.

USS Charleston—OCF flagship .... 2031 CE.

Ishtar—submersible used by Charlie Hunter .... 2013 CE.

Odessa—OCF vessel in the Antarctic .... 2031 CE.

Triton's Endeavor—starship in the Sephora system .... 2074 CE.

AAF Fatimah—arkship in the Endyr Nebula .... 2277 CE.

Scimitar—starship owned by Earl Dagarth .... 3213 CE.

CSS Andalusia—Coral Stellar Navy carrier flagship ...... 3213 CE.

Che'ethrah—Terjjan portal ship in the Endyr Nebula .... 3213 CE.

G'thalon—Sijjo Ith's flagship .... 3213 CE.

Ijnar Glory—a captured Ijnari spy ship .... 3212 CE.

Abu Talib—a starship captained by Xena Kilpatrick ..... 3213 CE.

Solar Contact—scramjet piloted by Arlya Seroh .... 3213 CE.

CSS Archangel—Coral Stellar Navy colony ship in Cyrus system
....3213 CE.

CSS Beowulf's Voyage—nebula ship in Cyrus system ...... 3213 CE.

CSS San Marco—nebula ship in Cyrus system .... 3213 CE.

Stingfire II—scramjet piloted by Earl Dagarth .... 3213 CE.

Chandrasekhar—starship piloted by Xena Kilpatrick ..... 3212 CE.

Icarus—Ambri telepathy orb piloted by Earl Dagarth ...19,710 BCE.

CSS Kashmir Light—nebula ship commanded by Admiral Singh
....3213 CE.

Ruby Star—a trading barge piloted by Eth'fyah Ruq ..... 3213 CE.

ALIEN TERMINOLOGY

abah—Thlag word for father.
Afrytha—Ambri monarch caste.
agk-goat—ovine mammal of Ghaz.
Albar—deity of Ijnaris and Terjj.
Alpha Cygnus—exotic luminary that engulfs Beta Corpus.
ambassador link—implant used to transmit neural link data.
Ambri gate—dimensional portal used by the Ambri.
Ambrithya—birthplace of Ambri species.
angel ray—sentient species of Europa.
Anglo Fusion—lingua franca of the Coral Galaxy.
Ang-Xi—mantis species of planet Manx.
Arc gate—intergalactic transgate.
autodoc—an automated healing capsule.
avenjii—a hiding game.
Awal Rab—deity of Thlags.
aweh'jiin—familial clutch in Ijnari-Terjj mythos.
balach fa—mild Terjjan oath.
baojii—a half avian, half equine steed of Ghaz.
benjar blade—organic scalpel used by Ijnaris and Terjj.
Bethel—largest moon in Gilgal's orbit.
Blood Mage—an Ijnari priestess skilled in blood divination.
brainpather—a master of biological disguises.
Celes Tetra—stellar region near the Lotus Cloud.
Cephas—smaller moon in Galilee's orbit.
Ceylon L4—planet in the Gemini Constellation.
Coral Galaxy—C34, a galaxy roughly sixty-four billion astral
    hectares from Earth.
coral djinn—fierce sandstorm of Ghaz.
Ctesi—an amphibian race.
Cryon—a blue-blooded species of Cryos.
Cryos—second closest planet to Azol.

cryotube—a stasis chamber.
cyber-clone—a cloned artificial human.
cyberdog—a cybernetic canine.
Cyrus Alpha—key star in the Cyrus system.
Cyrus 794G—planet in the Cyrus system.
Dactylian—aquatic species of Dactylos.
Dactylos—planet in the Ptyr Ring.
dekhrah—misty fiber harvested from senjii blossoms.
Divine Path—central faith of Ijnaris and Terjj.
Do'fin—sentient dolphin hybrid.
D'syunth—Arc Builders in the Endyr Nebula.
dtsarq—Thlagan mild oath.
Dyson shield—a starship's defensive energy field.
Eden II—planet in the Octavian Gulf.
Eden's Gate—transgate on Cyrus 794G.
Endora—planet in the Endyr Nebula.
Endyr Nebula—dense stellar cloud in the Coral Galaxy.
Fjorii—planet in the Gilae system.
Fjoriian—a denizen of Fjorii.
Fjoriic—language of Fjorii.
frack—mild Anglo Fusion expletive.
Fyr—sea fauna of Lynx.
Fyrth'bulae—enigmatic species of Europa.
Ghaz—planet in the Azöl system.
Gilgal—gas giant of Beta Corpus.
gthai—mild Terjjan oath lowly spawn.
guptiwi—small hare analog of Fjorii.
Halcyon race—species who inhabit realm beyond the Eden's Gate.
Halo Borealis—stellar region near Cyrus system.
halo clouds—ultraviolet bursts from pearl stars.
hirjun—Terjjan word for alien.
h'shtar—Ijnari opiate.
Hydran—species of the Hydra Cloud.
hydra orc—giant tentacled crustacean of Ghaz.
ice gas—frozen layer of methane hydrate pulp gas.
Ijhad—holy war in Ijnari-Terjj mythos.

Ijhad al-Quds—a holy war waged by Terjj against the Ijnaris.
Ijnar—planet in the Perthid Nebula.
Ijnari—winged offshoot of Terjj.
ion reaper—short-range ionic pulse weapon, a pulse burner.
ithkah—mental link to the Awareness.
Iydes—a planet in the Milky Way, home of Ramul'egh species.
kedjka—a roving kelp of Ghaz.
Khidr Delta Five—key planet in the Emerald Gulf.
kyesh—Ambri spear.
Lotus Cloud—dense star cluster in the Coral Galaxy.
Lynx—planet in the Azöl system.
Manx—planet in the Azöl system.
mgoja arc—Ptyri weapon.
memfile—neural implant data cell.
moksheh—molting phase of an Afrytha.
morph-plaz—an energy wall that can be walked through.
mynthir—mind-shielding talent.
NavCom—Coral Stellar Navy Command.
N'dar—species who control the parallel beyond the Eden's Gate.
Neiro—capital planet of Ptyr Ring.
neural link—telepathic transmissions.
neural sync—synaptic impulse rhythms.
Nine Shines of Light—seats of mystic power on Ijnar.
nitzy midge—gnat of Ceylon L4.
Ngu Anth—Ctesi capital world.
Nubyth—wingless Ambri caste.
nymph—an Ambri in pre-adult stage.
Octavian Gulf—planetary system of Octavia.
Odhyr—mythical world of parallel time.
Olec—saurian race of the Olec Quadrant.
Oort—simian race of the Oort Cluster.
Oracle Mage—an Ijnari priestess who divines from oracle pearls.
oracle pearl—an augury gem used by Oracle Mages.
Orceus—moonlet in the Ptyr Ring.
Oxyr—sovereign moon in the Ptyr Ring.
Oxyrite—denizen of Oxyr.

pearl star—microsun born in Ijnar's halo clouds.
Perthid Nebula—birthplace of Ijnaris and Terjj.
Pharsha—Terjj ruler.
pirhanj—carrion slug of Ijnar.
polycog—polycognition device for shared neural pulses.
Porthole Eye—a worm path interstice.
pthsi rod—Oortan imaging cylinder.
punfyr—Terjjan kelp vine.
Ptyri—denizen of the Ptyr Ring.
Ptyr Ring—dense planetary cluster in the Coral Galaxy.
puma dog—marsupial predator of Ceylon L4.
ra'ahii—rite of passage for Ijnari boys.
Ramul'egh—a humanoid, reptilian race from planet Iydes.
Rhojii cat—feline of Ijnar or Terjjah.
ruja—currency of Terran worlds.
Sarfyth—winged Ambri caste.
S'both—extinct energy beings.
Scoria—Ghaz's dwarf sun.
Sephora—a supermassive star, Kepler 64.
sjak—severe Terjjan oath.
Sharjah—planet colonized by Terjj.
Shiloh—smaller moon in Gilgal's orbit.
Skinshaper—genetic surgeon among Ijnaris or Terjj.
siffyr—bloom of Ijnar.
starlighter—an Ijnari mystic who ignites pearl stars.
stingfire—bloodsucking fish of Lynx.
swift tube—compact air car used in urban travel.
telepathy orb—craft piloted by the Ambri.
Temple of Runes—shrine of the Whispering Way.
Terjj—fanged species born of the Perthid Nebula.
Terjjah—once a planet in the Perthid Nebula.
Terjjan—language of the Terjj.
terrasuit—body gear worn to protect one from harsh climates.
Thlag—semi-reptilian race of Ghaz.
Titus—largest moon of planet Lynx.
transflux—transitional flux used in foldspace.

transgate—a hyperdimensional gateway.
Tung—humanoid race of old Tung-da-we planetary system.
Tyre—icy moon in Lynx's orbit.
Whispering Way—central faith of Terrans of the Wolf Cluster.
Wolfan—denizen of the Wolf Cluster.
Wolf 16—planet in the Wolf Cluster.
worm path—temporal causeway used in hyperspace.
wyrmtree—a tentacled tree native to Ijnar or Terjjah.
Xanadu—Ambri-held enclave beyond the Eden's Gate.
Zhul Amaj—prophesied messiah in Ambri mythos.
zikhr—Ambri mind-probing rite.
zikhr anjulir—fertility rite of the Ambri.
Zynfar—Blood Moon, Kepler 64f.

AUTHOR'S NOTE

As with any yarn born of the imagination, we often stumble upon the truly bizarre. At times, our most fanciful visions manifest themselves as genius. I cannot take credit for some of the more brilliant terminology in this book. Namely, Karel Capek gave us the coinage for robots. Frank Herbert's *Dune* series first enlightened us about Truthsayers and foldspace. And cyborgs have intrigued science fiction fans since before the dawn of cyberspace. So if by chance any of my alien terms sound familiar, astounding, or plain silly, it's a result of this author's blunders. *Maelstrom* originally appeared in *On Spec. Arctica* and *The Cloud's Eye* are excerpts from my novel *Sands of Prophecy. Outcast, Quasar Run,* and *Other Memory* are excerpts from *The Clouds of Endyr* and *The Suns of Coral* (*The Coral Saga* series) available at Smashwords, Amazon, and Barnes & Noble.

ABOUT THE AUTHOR

Angelo Niles has written several short stories and poems, appearing in *Aoife's Kiss*, *Iron City*, *On Spec*, *Nova Science Fiction*, and *Star*Line*. His *Coral Saga* novels span time and parallel universes. He lives in a desert retreat in Arizona where he's busy at work on his next adventure, *The Suns of Coral*. Meet him at angelo-niles53@gmail.com

www.ingramcontent.com/pod-product-compliance
Lightning Source LLC
Chambersburg PA
CBHW070523100726

47907CB00004B/962